THE HOUSE ON YEET STREET

THE HOUSE ON YEET STREET

PRESTON NORTON

union square kids

NEW YORK

**union
square
kids**

NEW YORK

UNION SQUARE KIDS and the distinctive Union Square Kids logo are trademarks of Union Square & Co., LLC.

Union Square & Co., LLC, is a subsidiary of Sterling Publishing Co., Inc.

Text © 2024 Preston Norton
Cover art © 2024 Union Square & Co., LLC

ISBN 978-1-4549-5040-0 (hardcover)
ISBN 978-1-4549-5041-7 (paperback)
ISBN 978-1-4549-5042-4 (e-book)

Library of Congress Cataloging-in-Publication Data

Names: Norton, Preston, 1985– author.
Title: The house on Yeet Street / by Preston Norton.
Description: New York, New York : Union Square Kids, 2024. |
    Audience: Ages 10 and up. | Summary: A quartet of thirteen-year-old
    boys' friendship is tested by ghosts, haunted houses, secret crushes, and
    a hundred-year-old curse.
Identifiers: LCCN 2023051846 (print) | LCCN 2023051847 (ebook) |
    ISBN 9781454950400 (hardcover) | ISBN 9781454950417 (paperback) |
    ISBN 9781454950424 (epub)
Subjects: CYAC: Friendship—Fiction. | Haunted houses—Fiction. |
    Ghosts—Fiction. | Crushes—Fiction. | Blessing and cursing |
    Humorous stories. | BISAC: JUVENILE FICTION / Humorous Stories |
    JUVENILE FICTION / Paranormal, Occult & Supernatural |
    LCGFT: Humorous fiction. | Paranormal fiction. | Novels.
Classification: LCC PZ7.N8253 Hp 2024 (print) | LCC PZ7.N8253 (ebook) |
    DDC [Fic]—dc23
LC record available at https://lccn.loc.gov/2023051846
LC ebook record available at https://lccn.loc.gov/2023051847

For information about custom editions, special sales, and premium purchases, please contact specialsales@unionsquareandco.com.

Printed in the United States of America

Lot #:

2 4 6 8 10 9 7 5 3 1

07/24

unionsquareandco.com

Cover art by Jensine Eckwall
Cover design by Melissa Farris
Interior design by Marcie Lawrence

To thirteen-year-old me:
Everything will be okay.
I love you.

THE
HOUSE
ON
YEET STREET

The Eye of the Witch

The Witch House of Yeet Street was a dilapidated, three-story Victorian monstrosity painted the color of bone—at least where paint remained, chipped and peeling. Its broken and shattered windows were like hungry mouths with glass teeth. Walls bulged and protruded in awkward places, going from square to triangular forty-five-degree slants, to hexagons and octagons, with a roof that simultaneously coned, slanted, and went flat wherever it pleased. The top floor ascended almost towerlike to a window that resembled an all-seeing eye, overlooking the small town of Curtain Falls.

In many ways, architecturally speaking, the Witch House reminded thirteen-year-old Aidan Cross of a Biblically accurate angel, which he knew all about from internet memes, not the Bible itself. The running joke on the internet was that these angels would say something like "ᗷƎ ᗡÖṬ Ä̊ꞘƦⱯᵻᗞ" while simultaneously being a cosmic terror made out of several burning wheels covered in eyes, wings, and appendages. At the end of the day, it showed how much we relied on someone to deliver the Bible to us through a filter because the *actual* Bible was kind of scary.

But Aidan had been told he had a hyperactive imagination.

△　△　▽　▽

Kai Pendragon was the most beautiful man in all of Aether. At least he *would have been* if he was 100 percent man. As it stood, he was only 50 percent man. The other 50 percent of him—from the waist down—was fish. Kai Pendragon was a merman of Meridia.

But mermen weren't just pretty boys for looking at. No sir. They were also powerful hydromancers—mages of the sea.

Kai Pendragon commanded the waters like he commanded Nadia Cross's heart.

And this was where things got complicated.

Nadia Cross was a Fyrian. She had long, red hair down to her waist. What she lacked in size, she made up for with a fiery tongue. She had what you would call "a real attitude problem."

Like all Fyrians, Nadia Cross was a pyromancer.

What this meant was that she was acquainted with fire manipulation and pyrokinesis. Fire was beautiful, hungry, dangerous. Easy to use but difficult to master. In Fyr (pronounced fear), fire was a weapon.

It also meant that she was a sworn enemy of Meridia. And vice versa. Practitioners of fire and water magic did not mix. And they *certainly* didn't fall in love with each other.

But if fingers were to be pointed, quite a few could be directed Kai Pendragon's way. In addition to having a charming personality, and a smile that made Nadia's insides feel all wobbly, Kai apparently did not believe in clothing. Sure, he was all fin and scale from the waist down, but tell that to the part of Nadia that couldn't stop staring at his naked *top half.*

Kai Pendragon's black hair was shorn to the skin on the sides, and long on the top, woven into warrior braids that dangled down his bare back. From the contours of his strong chest down to the hard plane of his stomach, ending just a little too prematurely when skin became scale, Kai Pendragon's body was

It was just

Hey, Aidan!

Aid, whatcha got there?

Aidan slammed his notebook shut.

The fictional world of Aether imploded into the dull palette of reality, and Aidan's consciousness was transported back to the embarrassingly dorky bedroom of one Aidan Cross.

Aidan was a matchstick of a thirteen-year-old—thin as a reed, freckled to heck and back, with hair like a brush fire. But that was the *only* part of him that resembled fire because he had a personality like wet socks. At least, that was Zephyr Windon's hurtful appraisal of Aidan's personality, two years ago, when they first met in middle school. Zephyr and Aidan were friends now, but those words—"a personality like wet socks"—had etched themselves into his brain.

Aidan's walls were covered in posters for things like *Skyrim* and *The Witcher*. The bookshelves that weren't eyeball-deep in fat stacks of fantasy novels were stuffed with paraphernalia for Dungeons & Dragons, Magic: The Gathering, and LARPing—guidebooks, expansion packs, and cosplay.

But the overwhelming nerdiness wasn't the problem. The *problem* was standing before Aidan in the form of Zephyr Windon, *and* Terrance Adams, *and* Kai Pendleton.

The reason Aidan found himself in this predicament was that he was under the impression that his bedroom was entitled to any sense of privacy, and that his three best friends wouldn't barge in at any given moment like a pack of cackling, cross-eyed hyenas.

It was nice when your parents liked your friends, but it might have been nicer if they gave a bit of advance warning.

"Uh, nothing," said Aidan. "Homework."

Aidan cringed the moment he said it. It was summer vacation.

Zephyr, Terrance, and Kai seemed to think that was just the funniest joke ever told; they burst into a fit of laughter. He laughed nervously with them, simultaneously wondering if it would be better to hold on to the notebook for security, or to discreetly tuck it under his mattress.

Zephyr was the first to stop laughing; he turned it off like a light switch.

"Dude," said Zephyr. He pushed a pair of thick-rimmed glasses up his nose. "Are you looking at . . . ?" He proceeded to mouth something that rhymed with "doobies" but was somehow even more inappropriate.

Zephyr was the smallest of them—even shorter than Aidan—with neat black hair parted on the side like his mom combed it for him. At the very least, she made him comb his hair; she was very strict. Which was ironic because Zephyr was the biggest troublemaker of the four of them. He had a big mouth—both literally and metaphorically—which was filled with just way too many teeth, including two very big front teeth. If one of the four of them was going to say something stupid, it usually came out of his mouth.

"What?" said Aidan. "No. It's a notebook. Gross." His grip on it tightened. So much for discreetly tucking it away.

"Not that I endorse . . . *that*," said Terrance, "but if you *were* wanting to look at a dirty magazine, cutting out the pictures and gluing them inside an unsuspecting notebook and calling it 'homework'"—he air-quoted—"would be the way to do it."

Terrance was both the brains of the group and their newest member. His family moved from Brooklyn to Curtain Falls last year. He aced every class he was in, including PE, because he was athletic to boot, with a love for baseball and the Yankees. He was torn between pursuing forensic science and astrophysics, with documentary film-making as a sort of pipe dream. He dressed in button-down shirts and polos that he tucked into his pants, and he always wore a belt.

"Dude," said Zephyr. His eyes were bugging out, all but pressed against the surface of his glasses. "You cut out pictures of girls and glued them inside your notebook?" He smacked Terrance on the arm. "And here I thought *you* were the genius! Here, lemme look."

He made a grab for Aidan's notebook.

Aidan was not a violent person. But he hit Zephyr's hand, like a cat pawing at its own shadow—*bap!* And then he proceeded to stuff the notebook under his own butt. He weighed just barely one hundred pounds sopping wet, and he would use all one hundred to keep Zephyr from seeing this thing he had written.

"I am not looking at girls!" Aidan exclaimed. He looked desperately for someone to come to his rescue. With guilt in his heart, his gaze fell on Kai Pendleton. Aidan offered his most pleading look. Even though Kai was the *last* person he would want to read this notebook.

Kai had a cool haircut, shaved on the sides and long on the top, swooping over to one side. Kai was athletic. Kai was street-smart. Kai was a *ladies' man.* He flirted with just about every girl at school (including the most popular girl at Berkshires Middle School—and editor of the school newspaper, the *Berkshires Bulletin*—literal "Queen Bea," Beatrice McCarthy). They *all* flirted back. In fact, it was pretty safe to say that Bea had an *obvious* crush on Kai. Obvious to everyone except Kai, of course, because Kai was too cool for crushes. He dated NO ONE, which only added to his universal appeal. He was just this happy-go-lucky, easy to talk to, romantically unattainable all-American boy.

Aidan was in love with him.

Kai Pendleton wasn't Kai Pendragon, but he wasn't *not* him either. Just as Nadia (*Aidan* spelled backwards) both wasn't and *wasn't not* Aidan. Aidan certainly did not have an attitude problem, although sometimes he *wished* he did. It was just, sometimes this shy, quiet person he was on the outside felt like a lie. He *had* things he wanted to say. It's just, sometimes the words and feelings got tied up inside of him and never made it to the outside.

That's where his writing came in. The inside of this notebook was the one place Aidan was allowed to be himself. It was nice to invent a version of him that did and said the things that he was afraid to say and do. Also, Aidan was a little bit jealous that Kai flirted with just about every girl in existence—and by a fifty-fifty chance of fate, he fell into the biological category of genders that Kai did not flirt with—and this fantasy world was his creative loophole.

"C'mon, guys," said Kai. The sound of his voice made every muscle of Aidan's body decompress. "He's obviously writing another D&D campaign." Kai looked at Aidan, and Aidan felt it like a foot pedal, accelerating his heart. "Right?"

Aidan had no problem lying through his teeth. "Obviously. And no, you can't look at it yet."

Zephyr looked so bored by this revelation, his eyes retreated into his skull. "Ugh, you guys are so lame. When are you going to start caring about girls?"

"When are *we*?" said Kai. "When was the last time you even *talked* to a girl?"

"Bruh, I am just biding my time. Waiting for my growth spurt. Trust me, when summer's over"—Zephyr flexed his skinny arms and kissed the nonexistent biceps on each one—"the ladies will *flock* to this."

"I hate to burst your bubble," said Terrance, "but your mom is four feet tall, and your dad has a beer belly. If you have a growth spurt, it's going to be sideways."

"Oh yeah?" said Zephyr. "Well, joke's on you because I AM GOING TO HAVE A GIGANTIC—"

"La la la la la!" Aidan said, plugging his ears. "I'm not listening!"

"Nobody wants to hear about your weird little growth spurt," said Kai.

"You wear size five-and-a-half shoes," said Terrance.

"Just wait until I hit my growth spurt," Zephyr muttered, seemingly to himself. "*Then* you'll all be sorry."

"Bruh, I am *already* sorry," said Aidan. He stood up and cautiously patted Zephyr on the back, like one would a feisty chihuahua. Because Aidan was the least threatening presence in the room, Zephyr didn't swat his hand away, but rather, leaned into it.

"Bruh," Terrance and Kai agreed simultaneously.

There were many things Aidan, Zephyr, Terrance, and Kai liked to do on those lazy summer afternoons, and they each had their favorite. Aidan's was D&D night. Kai liked to hit the community pool. Terrance liked to ride bikes and explore the vast alien frontier of Curtain Falls, Shallowgrave County, Massachusetts, population 6,659. Zephyr was inclined to scary movie nights and video games because they were the two ways in which he consistently dominated the others, in both hand-eye coordination and psychological fortitude.

Despite their individual preferences, there was one thing they all could agree on: yeeting crap at the Witch House. It hit both the sweet spots of Terrance's need to explore and Zephyr's thirst for horror. It allowed Kai to exercise his pitching arm.

Aidan was the scaredy-cat of the bunch, but he had his own secret motive for wanting to go. Before leaving his bedroom, Aidan discreetly slipped his notebook into his backpack.

Yeet Street was an old, nondescript path made of dirt and gravel that veered off into the woods, careening wildly through the forest for a quarter of a mile. When it ended, so did your breath, because the thing standing before you was less a house than an entity. When you stared at the Witch House, it stared back.

When Zephyr, Terrance, and Kai invaded Aidan's room, it was with the express purpose of going straight to the Witch House. This had been decided, apparently. Naturally, they had their bags packed and pockets filled with projectiles ripe for the yeeting. They brought polished stones and aerodynamic sticks. Glass bottles, old baseballs, and expired fruit. Pebbles, coins, and marbles. Zephyr had a brand-new slingshot, and you'd better believe he was going to use it. (This was perhaps a safety oversight on the part of Mr. and Mrs. Windon.)

Since the windows were long since broken and shattered, the four friends had concocted an advanced game of sorts called Knock the Witch's Teeth Out. The "Witch's Teeth," in this scenario, were the glass shards that clung to every window frame in hungry, jagged rows.

Aidan, Zephyr, Terrance, and Kai dropped their bikes in the wild tangle where gravel became a jungle of tall grass and wiry weeds. There was a moment of silence. Not out of reverence or respect. The house had a way of sucking the air right out of you.

And then they unzipped their bags and unloaded their pockets and proceeded to do as the unfortunately named Yeet Street instructed: yeet.

"Do you think the ghost of Farah Yeet still haunts this house?" Kai asked. He wound his body up like a top, took aim, and let loose. The stone in his fastball grip shot out like a bullet. It missed the edge of a long glass shard by a hair. Kai seemed visibly disappointed, but to Aidan, it was poetry.

"Are you kidding me?" said Zephyr. "She's a witch. What else is she going to do while she's dead?"

"I mean, was she really even a witch?"

"It's *literally* in the title: Witch House. Stop asking stupid questions." Zephyr released a fierce marble from his slingshot. All velocity, no accuracy. It didn't even go through a window. "The better question is, do you think the ghost of *Gabby Caldwell* still haunts this house?"

Gabby Caldwell was a local teenager whose body had been found in the Witch House twenty years ago. She was something of an urban legend—maybe even more so than Farah Yeet because people *knew* her.

"Actually," said Terrance, "there's no such thing as ghosts, and witchcraft is the invention of feeble minds and religious misogyny." He grabbed his Yankees cap by the bill and adjusted it—a tic when conversations got stupid.

"*aCkShUaLlY*," Zephyr repeated mockingly. "Look, Terrance, just because you know big words and you're gonna study astrology at MIB doesn't mean you know jack about squat."

"Astro*physics*," Terrance corrected. "MI*T*. And *actually*—"

"No, Terry, shut your cakehole! Ghosts and witches are *real*, and it has been proven *numerous* times on the internet."

Terrance rubbed his eyes and shook his head.

"They even made a documentary about it! *The Blair Witch Project*? Ever heard of it?"

"Oof," said Aidan.

"Oh boy," said Kai.

Terrance did not hesitate for a second. He was a predator going in for the kill. He pulled his smartphone out, did not even type four whole words, and pressed go. He read aloud: "'*The Blair Witch Project*: It is a *fictional* story of three filmmakers, Heather Donahue, Michael C. Williams, and Joshua Leonard . . .'"

"What?" said Zephyr.

Terrance marched over to Zephyr and shoved his phone in his face.

"Bruh, get your dumb phone out of my face!" said Zephyr, swatting Terrance's phone away.

"There's only one dumb thing here, and it's not my phone."

Zephyr and Terrance stared each other down. Terrance was a head taller than Zephyr, but what Zephyr lacked in height, he made up for in spite.

Zephyr snatched Terrance's Yankees cap right off his head.

"Dude, give it back!" said Terrance.

It was too late. Zephyr took three running steps, then launched Terrance's Yankees cap like a Frisbee. It sailed. Wobbled ever so slightly as the bill threw it off balance. Curved. Then landed with immaculate precision through the shattered top-floor window of the Witch House.

The Eye of the Witch.

Zephyr had never made a perfect yeet like that. Not once in his tiny, growth-spurt-deprived life. It was as if Terrance's hat was carried inside by the very hand of the witch—Farah Yeet herself—as an act of divine intervention. Or whatever the witch equivalent of that was. Witchcraft?

"Bruh," said Aidan.

"Bruh," Kai agreed.

Zephyr turned and looked Terrance dead in the eye. If Zephyr felt any hint of remorse, it was nowhere present on his face.

"There," said Zephyr. "If the house isn't haunted, feel free to go in and get your stupid hat."

"Dude!" said Terrance. "My dad bought that for me at Yankee Stadium!"

"Yeah? Well, serves you right for wearing a stupid Yankees hat in Massachusetts."

Terrance's hands clenched and trembled with fury.

"Honestly, I did you a favor. Tell you what: I'll give you one of my Red Sox hats and we'll call it good. Whaddya say?"

"I don't want your damn Red Sox hat!" Terrance screamed.

Zephyr took a step closer to Terrance, until there was barely a breath between them.

"Then go get your hat," said Zephyr. "Unless you're afraid of ghosts or something."

Terrance turned one hundred and eighty degrees. Made a straight line for his bike.

"Ha!" Zephyr bawked. "That's what I thought. Ghosts are real. Go eat a Yankee Stadium wiener. I hear they're made of pigeons and sewer rats."

There was no hesitation in what happened next. Terrance spun on a dime. Marched back to Zephyr in seven deadly strides.

Punched him right in the bridge of his glasses.

"Crap," said Aidan.

Kai said basically the same thing, but the adult version. Aidan knew this because his dad said the exact same word at least ten times a day.

There was a slight delay on Aidan's and Kai's part, but once Terrance was on top of Zephyr—still hitting him, while Zephyr's hands were trying to wrap around Terrance's throat—they flew into action. Aidan was not one to take initiative, but adrenaline pushed the words out of his mouth.

"I'll get Zephyr, you get Terrance!" he said.

Kai seemed impressed that *anyone* would volunteer to "get Zephyr," let alone Aidan, but he nodded.

Kai put Terrance in a full nelson—his arms wrapped around Terrance's arms, locked behind the back of his head—and pulled Terrance off Zephyr. Aidan had no wrestling experience, so he simply fell on top of Zephyr and let his body weight do the work. He did not weigh a lot, but he weighed more than Zephyr.

"I'm fine, I'm cool, I'm fine!" Terrance yelled at a volume that seemed neither cool nor fine. But when Kai let go, Terrance walked away with his hands in the air. He was cool. He was fine.

Zephyr, meanwhile, was writhing and screaming and slobbering beneath Aidan. "I'm going to kill him! I'm gonna take a crap in his stupid Yankees hat, and I'm gonna smoosh it on his stupid head, and then I'm gonna kill him! You hear that, Terrance? I'm gonna kill you! And then I'm gonna kill every single one of the New York

Yankees, just to spite you! Even Gerrit Cole! You hear me? I'm gonna kill Gerrit Cole!"

"I think you should probably go," Kai told Terrance.

Aidan offered Terrance a sympathetic look while Zephyr writhed and howled like a demon beneath him.

Terrance glanced from Kai, to Aidan, to Zephyr. And for the briefest moment, Zephyr fell quiet. There was nothing but bloody murder in his eyes.

Terrance nodded, ran to his bike, and mounted it with a running start. He sailed smoothly down the gentle, forested curve of Yeet Street, then vanished behind the trees.

Aidan started to climb off Zephyr, but Zephyr pushed him off the rest of the way. Aidan fell on his back.

"Get off me, fatso!" Zephyr snapped. He stumbled to his feet and brushed off his pants. "Why don't you go on a diet? You weigh like a thousand pounds."

"Hey, c'mon," said Kai.

Aidan nodded thoughtfully, blinking away the sting of Zephyr's not-so-constructive criticism. It helped that his dad frequently gave him the *opposite* criticism, that he needed to eat more, or the wind would blow him away. He was honestly a little more worried about Zephyr's glasses. They were bent just enough in the middle that they couldn't sit on his face properly. The right lens was cracked, and the left had popped out entirely.

"I think we should *walk* you home," said Aidan, putting on a brave face. He emphasized the word "walk" because Zephyr was in no condition to ride a bike.

"*Kai* can walk me home," said Zephyr. "*You* can go eat a Yankee Stadium wiener you big, fat . . . fatso! You can eat ten of 'em!"

"Hey!" said Kai. "Don't snap at Aidan. He saved your butt!"

"I'm sorry!" said Zephyr angrily. And then his voice softened. "I'm sorry. I just want to walk home with Kai. If that's okay."

There were tears in his eyes. Coupled with his busted glasses that didn't sit on his face right, Aidan couldn't find it in himself to say no.

"Oh," said Aidan. "Okay."

Kai wasn't done with Aidan, though. He approached Aidan in a way that made Aidan's body go rigid. When Kai stopped, his right hand was extended, elbow down, palm open, like he wanted to arm wrestle. But this wasn't about arm wrestling, it was about the sacred art of the Man Hug.

Aidan grabbed Kai's hand, they brought it in, and they hugged it out.

Usually it ended in a couple good ol' slaps on the back. But Kai gave Aidan no slaps on the back this time. And he held the hug longer than Aidan had anticipated.

Aidan smacked Kai twice on the back—more violently than necessary, like he was tapping out of a WWE match—then pushed him away. And because Aidan was trying to make this as un-awkward as possible, he finger-gunned Kai and said, "I love you, bro."

Kai grinned wildly. "Not as much as I love you, bro."

"Oh my God, get a room!" said Zephyr. Under his breath, he muttered, "Maybe it's a good thing my glasses are broken."

Aidan felt himself blushing. Fortunately, Kai was already returning to Zephyr. They picked their bikes up off the ground—Kai with ease, Zephyr fumbling with his—then walked them slowly down Yeet Street. Kai waved back at Aidan. Even Zephyr offered a limp peace sign. Aidan smiled and waved back.

The smile on Aidan's face faded with each step they took until they disappeared from view.

Aidan approached the backpack he had left beside his bike. Crouched down, unzipped it, and retrieved a spiral notebook. There was no title on the front. Instead, he had drawn the alchemical symbols of the four classical elements in a straight line: fire ($\triangle$), air ($\triangle\kern-0.6em-$), earth ($\triangledown\kern-0.6em-$), and water ($\triangledown$). In his head canon, he called the story *Fire & Water*—a fantasy adventure, sure, but more importantly, it was a love story. A story of *forbidden* love.

No one could ever read this story.

Aidan tried not to think too hard about what he was about to do. If he did, he might change his mind.

He took three momentum-filled steps, then chucked his notebook. It flapped open and rattled its pages like the wings of a very large insect.

Landed barely—just barely—inside the shattered, top-floor window of the Witch House.

$$\triangle \qquad \triangle\kern-0.6em- \qquad \triangledown\kern-0.6em- \qquad \triangledown$$

There was a quiet little cove where a horseshoe of land hugged a tiny pool of sea, and it was here that Nadia Cross and Kai Pendragon would meet. Away from the bustle of village life. Away from the fire-spewing warships and the violent, hydromancy-controlled waves where Fyr and Meridia waged war. It came down to trade routes and territorial disputes, but years of bad blood turned the issue into something far worse. Meridians were known to sink Fyrian ships. Fyrians were known to harpoon unlucky merpeople. Who initiated the violence depended entirely on who you asked. It was rather barbaric, and Nadia preferred not to think about it.

This was very easy when Kai was around. And it was also very hard.

"Have you ever thought about running away from here?" Kai asked.

Nadia was snapped back from her unpleasant thoughts. "Run away? Where? How? You don't even have feet."

Kai gave a playful half-smile that made Nadia tingle. "You know what I mean."

They were lying on their backs–Nadia on the dry part of the beach, Kai on the wet part, where the tide ebbed and flowed into him–but now they rolled onto their sides, looking at each other. Nadia tried not to let her eyes wander. It helped that Kai had pretty eyes. Golden brown. Like tiger's-eye gems.

"What is there outside of here?"

Kai offered a breezy shrug. "Lots of places. The world is big."

"'*Lots of places*,' he says. '*The world is big*,' he says." Nadia imitated Kai in a low, dumb voice.

Kai simply smiled. Then he reached out and touched her face. Any chance Nadia had of playing it cool melted like butter over hot bread. She dissolved in his hand.

"Anywhere I can be with you," said Kai, "and *not* have to keep it a secret, sounds like a place I'd like to be."

Nadia rolled her eyes. Then rolled her entire body, her back facing him, so she could blush in privacy.

"I guess that doesn't sound terrible," she mumbled.

Kai chuckled in that easy-breezy way he did. "I'm glad you agree."

PART I

FIRE & WATER

CHAPTER 2

The Absolutely True Story of Farah Yeet

Say what you will about boys—and there were quite a few things one could say—but one of their stranger merits was how shockingly quick they were to forgive.

Aidan didn't know how it started. He could only assume Kai and Zephyr had a good talk on the way home, and somehow that led to Zephyr and Terrance talking again, because the next thing Aidan knew, Zephyr was texting him that they were all meeting at Terrance's house.

Zephyr also texted: **Sorry for calling you fat**

I only said it because ur a skinny little wiener and I was embarrassed I couldn't get you off me

You should consider pro wrestling

Weiner

And that, dear readers, was a Zephyr Windon apology.

Aidan went ahead and accepted it, and then proceeded to book it over to Terrance's house. This involved running downstairs, yelling vaguely for the entire house to hear, "HEY, I'M GOING TO TERRANCE'S HOUSE," at which point, Aidan's mom hollered from her bedroom, "Okay, sweetie, tell Aaliyah I said hi," then going outside, grabbing his bike off the front lawn, riding all 250 feet across the cul-de-sac, and dropping his bike on the Adams's well-kept lawn alongside Kai's and Zephyr's. The front door was already open, but Aidan knocked anyway.

"You come on in, Aidan," said Mrs. Aaliyah Adams, a tall woman with broad shoulders and braided hair. "Terrance and the boys are all in the living room doing something or other."

Aidan brushed past Mrs. Adams into the Adams's living room. He had no idea what he was walking into.

Terrance's dad, Mr. Adams, was a videographer, responsible for recording live events and small-scale video productions, which meant that, electronically speaking, he had all the newest tech. It also meant he had *way too much* tech. And for whatever reason, his friends were helping Mr. Adams sift through a half dozen totes filled with cameras, boom mics, and other film equipment.

Mr. Tekulvē Adams was a small, bald man who dressed sharper than the entire male population of Curtain Falls. Even on a lazy summer Saturday, he was wearing a floral button-down with sleeves rolled all the way up his biceps, slim-fitting black jeans, and low-top camel suede sneakers that exposed his ankle tattoo. The guy was *hip*.

"Ah, here we go!" said Mr. Adams. He pulled out a weird thing with multiple straps and a small, black device at its core. "The GoPro Chesty. Good visual quality and audio, and anyone can use it! Perfect for what you boys are doing. And as luck would have it, I have three!"

He tossed one to Kai, who caught it instinctively with one hand, then reached into the tote, pulled out two more, and tossed them to

Zephyr and Aidan. Zephyr barely caught his. The straps of Aidan's got tangled on one of his flailing arms, otherwise he would have missed it entirely.

"I figure *you*," Mr. Adams said to Terrance, "can operate the EOS C300."

Terrance's eyes widened as Mr. Adams pulled out an intricate-looking camcorder that was taller than it was long. There were a lot of buttons.

Terrance reached to grab it, but Mr. Adams pulled it just out of reach. "You swear on the Lord's name you're not gonna break it?"

Terrance nodded emphatically.

"You disrespect the Lord's name, your momma gonna have words to say."

Terrance nodded even more emphatically. He was practically vibrating.

"Oh, hush, Tekulvē!" Mrs. Adams hollered from the other room. "Me and the Lord got nothing to do with your overpriced camera."

"Overpriced ca—!" Mr. Adams exclaimed. "Of all the—! Terrance, can you put a price on the perfect moment caught in 4K?"

Terrance shook his head uncertainly. His eyes were still on the camcorder. He looked like he would say whatever it took for him to touch it.

"That's my boy," said Mr. Adams. He handed Terrance the camera, patted him on the head, and proceeded to leave the room. Then he turned back and said, "I'll leave you boys to it. Terrance, you'll put my totes back up for me?"

"Yes, sir," said Terrance. Even though there was no pulling his attention away from the camcorder, not now.

As Terrance examined the Holy Grail of camcorders, and Zephyr and Kai fumbled awkwardly with their GoPro Chestys, Aidan finally asked, "What is going on?"

"What?" said Kai. He dropped his GoPro in his lap and looked at Zephyr. "You didn't tell him?"

"Okay, so, here's the thing," said Zephyr. "I figured it'd be better if all three of us told him because we all know he's gonna be a little chicken-butt."

Aidan officially retracted his acceptance of Zephyr's apology. "Eat a Fenway Park wiener, Zephyr!"

"Hey," said Zephyr, pointing a finger at Aidan. "I'll have you know, Fenway Park wieners are *delicious*. Therefore, I'm choosing to accept your poorly constructed insult as a compliment. So *thank you, Aidan*."

"It wasn't a compliment! You are *not* welcome!"

"Okay, don't freak out," said Terrance, "but we're planning on going inside the Witch House tonight."

"What?" said Aidan.

"And we're spending the night there," Terrance added.

"WHAT?" Aidan screamed.

"Shushushushushushushush!" Kai placed a shushing finger on Aidan's lips which, Aidan had to admit, had an immediate sedating effect on him. Then Kai grabbed him by the shoulders and sat him down on the sofa. "This is actually a good thing! Remember just yesterday how Terrance and Zephyr were fighting? They're not fighting anymore! Zephyr gets to have a haunted house sleepover, which he's always wanted, and Terrance gets to film a documentary, which *he's* always wanted, and between the four of us, we'll be able to determine, once and for all, if the Witch House is haunted! BUT—" Kai turned and faced Terrance and Zephyr, both index fingers raised in warning. "Whoever is right and whoever is wrong about whether ghosts do or do not exist, there will be no sore losers. We're only in this for educational purposes, and for fun. Agreed?"

"Agreed," said Zephyr and Terrance.

Aidan stared back at these three idiots he called friends in open-mouthed terror. "And your parents are *okay with this*?"

He said it just loud enough that Mr. Adams peeked his head back into the living room.

Terrance laughed nervously. "Of course my parents know that we're camping out in your backyard," he said, all his teeth exposed. He gave his dad an enthusiastic thumbs-up. Mr. Adams reciprocated it and disappeared.

"Obviously our parents are not okay with it!" Zephyr hissed. "Well, except for Kai's mom. She's cool and lets him do whatever he wants."

"That's one way of putting it," said Kai unenthusiastically.

"That's why we have a foolproof backup story. Terrance's parents think we're spending the night at your house, yours will think you're spending it at mine, and mine think we're spending it at Terrance's. Foolproof!"

Aidan was sure Zephyr was confusing the word "convoluted" with "foolproof." Any one of their parents was capable of cracking this lie open with little effort.

Kai sensed that Aidan was not digging this "foolproof" plan, and so he attempted to appeal to Aidan's greatest weakness: his empathy.

"Oh, and I forgot the best part! We get to retrieve Terrance's hat! See? Everybody wins."

It took Aidan an eternal moment to let this last part process. To realize where exactly they were going. What they were doing.

And what *else* they might find there.

Aidan had made a fatal error. He *thought* he was getting rid of his notebook. Now it was coming back to haunt him. Ghosts and witches were the least of his worries.

He had only one strategy at this point: to lean into Zephyr's superstition.

"We cannot," said Aidan, "under *any circumstance*, spend the night there. It's haunted. It's possessed by a witch. A *dead body* was found there! If we stay the night in that house, WE WILL DIE."

Aidan did not need to pretend to be afraid because he was *terrified*. At least, socially speaking, Aidan would almost certainly die if his friends found a notebook that contained a love story about one of his best friends in the world reimagined as a merman. There was no recovering from that level of embarrassment.

This time, Mrs. Adams poked her head in the room wearing a Hail-Mary-full-of-grace look.

Terrance let out a fake laugh and slapped his knee. "Oh man! I can't wait to tell these scary stories when we're camping in your backyard!"

Mrs. Adams slowly retracted her head, snakelike.

Terrance's face turned serious as he hissed through his teeth, "Can we take this conversation *outside*?"

Aidan had half a mind to alert the authorities (Mr. and Mrs. Adams) of the debauchery set to go down tonight. Surely, *they* would tell everyone else's parents. Then again, he had seen firsthand how fast Terrance and Zephyr could turn on each other. Aidan knew he was not immune to their wrath.

He would have gone outside willingly, but Kai grabbed his right arm, Zephyr his left, and together they escorted Aidan to the sliding glass door leading to Terrance's backyard. Terrance led the way.

The backyard was a small, quaint square with a raised vegetable garden, a tiny patch of grass that took Mr. Adams exactly one minute to mow, and a koi pond. There was really nothing for them to do there except awkwardly stand and deliberate. Orange and white fish skittered to the surface of the pond to gape at them.

"Okay," said Kai. "What seems to be the problem?"

"Wh-what *seems* to—?" Aidan sputtered. "It *seems* like the three of you want to spend the night in a house where people *have died*."

"*Person*," Zephyr corrected. "One person died there. And according to Sheriff Jenkins, it wasn't even murder. It was more like an *Unsolved Mysteries*/cold-case sort of thing."

"*People!*" Aidan counter-corrected. "Do you guys even know the true story of Farah Yeet? *Multiple people* have died in that house!"

Kai looked at Terrance, Terrance at Zephyr, and Zephyr shrugged.

"I only know true stories that have been made into movies," said Zephyr. "Like *The Texas Chainsaw Massacre*."

"*The Texas Chainsaw Massacre* is *not* a true story," said Terrance.

"Is too!" said Zephyr.

"Guys!" said Kai. "Can we, just, not?"

Zephyr harrumphed. Terrance rolled his eyes. But a rare moment of quiet followed as Kai turned his attention to Aidan.

"So are you going to tell us this story or what?" said Kai.

Aidan sighed.

Farah Yeet was from a faraway land. Where, exactly, no one knows. Probably Europe. Or Russia. Or possibly the Scandinavian Peninsula. Anyway—not important. The *important* thing was that her homeland had stories, traditions, *rituals* that were passed down since the dawn of man. Some called it magic, but to Farah Yeet, these things were the essence through which the gods made the cosmos—ancient science, alchemy, pagan knowledge.

Zephyr raised his hand.

"Yes, Zephyr?"

"What's the Scandinavian Peninsula?"

"It's a peninsula in Northern Europe. It's where Sweden, Norway, and Finland are."

"What's a peninsula?"

"Oh my God, Zeph. It's a piece of land that sticks out into a body of water! Can I tell this story or what?"

"Oh. Okay. Keep going."

Farah Yeet came to America for the same reason that most did: for opportunity. She started her own business handmaking and selling curtains and drapes. Farah's drapes were *extraordinary*. She handwove each one, incorporating brilliant colors and breathtaking artistry. No two were the same. Some even speculated that she wove *literal magic* into the fabric.

Farah's business exploded in popularity. Her business was so successful, in fact, that demand far exceeded supply. Each new drape she made went straight to auction, always selling for more than the last. Word of Farah's curtains spread far and wide, bringing in the ultra-wealthy and elite, so they could be the ones to hang the newest Farah Yeet from their windows.

Farah had seemingly found everything she could ever ask for. But she also found something she had not expected: love.

She found that in a man—a window-maker—named Jesse Glass.

Terrance raised his hand.

"Yes?"

"A *window*-maker named Jesse *Glass*? C'mon. This is made up."

"Do you want to hear the story or not?"

"I do, but—ugh. Fine. Proceed."

Farah and Jesse dated in secret. *Why* they dated in secret is a bit of a mystery, but most speculate it was because Jesse came from shady roots. Like, a family of Satan-worshippers or something?

"*Satan-worshippers*?" said Kai incredulously.

Or, I mean, some people think that Jesse was hideously ugly?

"*Hideously ugly*?" Zephyr repeated.

Or maybe a kleptomaniac?

"This is getting ridiculous," said Terrance.

"Look, I don't know, okay?" said Aidan. "No one knows! All anyone can agree on is nobody liked the fact that Farah Yeet—whose curtains they loved—was dating some ugly, Satan-worshipping klepto or whatever. And the people of Curtain Falls unanimously agreed that this relationship tarnished the value of their expensive, magical curtains. And so, the townspeople got their torches and pitchforks, dragged Jesse in front of Farah Yeet's house, and murdered him right in front of her."

Zephyr, Terrance, and Kai stared at Aidan, open-mouthed. They were stunned into silence.

Farah never made another curtain after that. How could she?

They say that after that day, Farah Yeet turned herself over to spirits and powers known only in her homeland. She cursed every curtain she'd ever made.

But that wasn't the only thing Farah Yeet cursed. They say she cursed her own house so that the souls of the dead could never depart. So she could spend her days with the ghost of Jesse. So that even when she died, she could be with him. It's been called the Witch House ever since.

"Wait," said Kai. "Farah Yeet made curtains? Is that why Curtain Falls is called Curtain Falls?"

"*That*," said Aidan, "is why Curtain Falls is called Curtain Falls."

Kai looked at Terrance.

Terrance looked at Zephyr.

Zephyr said, "Bruh." And then his mouth curled the wrong way—into an elated smile. "I am so pumped for this sleepover!"

"I am going to debunk the *crap* outta this story," said Terrance.

Kai offered Aidan an apologetic look. This was *not* the reaction Aidan was going for. Kai placed a hand on Aidan's shoulder. "For what it's worth, that was some good storytelling. Have you thought about being a writer?"

"Yeah, man!" said Zephyr. "Aidan could be the next Stephen King, and I, Zephyr Windon, could be the real-life ghost hunter who all his stories are based on. Terrance could be our movie director, and Kai, um . . . since Kai is the good-looking one, I guess he can be the hotter but slightly-less-interesting fictional version of me. Bruh, we are all gonna be millionaires."

"I can be the *what*?" said Kai.

"I am *not* going to direct cheap horror," said Terrance.

"I am so dead," Aidan mumbled to himself.

△ ◬ ▽ ▽

Fyrgard was a vast, coastal city, and the capitol of Fyr. Lower and upper docks spider-webbed across each other over the Meridian Ocean, making way for both ships of the sea as well as airships with powerful, mounted balloons and steam-powered propellers. Farther inland, slums were stacked atop one another, bridged by rickety scaffolding and walkways. Built upon their backs were towering mansions. Great metal plates divided the classes, so the rich did not have to suffer looking at the poor suffer beneath them.

Nadia Cross lived above the plate. She should have been grateful. However, being born into a respectable household meant a great deal more was expected of her, being the daughter of a Fyrian judge (her mother) and the Grand Inquisitor (her father). Quite frankly, it sucked.

She was enrolled in the finest (most pretentious) all-girls' boarding school in Fyrgard: Madame Malevolencia's Academy of Magicks for Respectable Girls in Ankle-Length Skirts. What it lacked in humility and taste, it made up for in staggering comradery among the girls who hated the place. Also, school security was lacking. After curfew, Nadia had become quite proficient shimmying out her second-floor window via rope assembled from ankle-length skirts tied together.

Nadia had two roommates—both of whom were from out-of-country—who *always* covered for her when she snuck out: Terra and Zephanie. Terra was the smart one (from the western country of Westerran, meaning she was born with the gift of geomancy), and Zephanie was tiny and loud, with big glasses (from the southern country of Fengdu, born with the gift of aeromancy). Fyr got along just fine with Westerran and Fengdu. It was only Meridia that was a thorn in Fyr's side. Only water was a threat to fire.

"Are we ever gonna meet this man of yours?" said Zephanie.

"Yeah!" said Nadia, finishing the last knot on her skirt-rope. "Maybe? *Definitely* after we graduate."

Nadia had *not* told her roommates that "her man" was a *merman*.

"Well, that's a problem, because Zeph will never graduate," said Terra.

"You wanna fight, dork?" said Zephanie.

"No?"

"You know what a dork is, Terra? It's a *whale wiener.*"

"Interesting. You're still failing Cryptozoology."

"YOU KNOW WHAT, TERRA?"

The bickering continued. Meanwhile, Nadia fastened her rope to the nearest bunk-bed post, then tossed it out the window. She straddled the windowsill, waved vaguely, and proceeded to climb out the second-story dorm.

"Bye, Nadia!" said Terra.

"Bye, Nadia!" said Zephanie. "AND ANOTHER THING, TERRA—"

CHAPTER 3

Between a Ghost and a Hard Place

Aidan found that lying to his parents about his plans was as unpleasant as it was relatively easy. His mother, Jocelyn Cross, was a criminal defense attorney. Some would argue that she lied *for a living.* His father was a *private investigator*—hired by individuals or groups for investigative law purposes, often working with attorneys in civil or criminal cases. Before that, he worked for the FBI. He made the career change to be home more.

Aidan's father's name was Chris Cross, which sounded like a bad joke. He was a big guy, with hands like baseball mitts, and he was prematurely balding, with a thick, creased forehead like a rocky overhang sheltering eyes like burning coals.

He wasn't especially mean to Aidan. He was as kind and loving as anyone who resembled the fire demon, Balrog, from *The Lord of the Rings*, could be. But Aidan would be lying if he said his father wasn't the one person he was most afraid of.

Naturally, Aidan went straight to his mom with any and all questions and requests.

"Can I spend the night at . . . um . . . uh . . . Zephyr's house?" Aidan asked his mom as she washed dishes. He almost forgot whose house he was lying about spending the night at. Zephyr's stupid, foolproof plan.

Mrs. Cross was the antithesis of Mr. Cross: small-framed, with a cherubic face and a pantheon of facial expressions—most of them jovial—and overall, a beacon of joy to be around. If there was a reason she was such a good criminal defense attorney, it was because everything she did and said felt right.

Even so, Aidan was sweating like a pig eating a Baconator at Wendy's.

"Of course," said Mrs. Cross. Then she backtracked. "Just tell your father first. I'm sure he'll say yes."

"Can't you tell him?" Aidan pleaded.

"Your father likes it when you ask him for things. He likes *talking to you*. He's not the boogeyman, Aidan."

Aidan let out a small moan of dread and shuffled miserably out of the kitchen and into the hall leading to his father's study. He glanced back in case his sounds of suffering had any effect on his mom. They didn't. Her hands were back in a sink full of soap suds. How could she be so callous?

Aidan stalked timidly to the door of his father's study and offered three soft knocks. He quietly hoped his dad wouldn't hear, but he *did*, and he said, "Come in, Aidan," because apparently, he knew the sound of Aidan's knock. Or maybe Mrs. Cross just barged in without asking.

Aidan quietly entered.

Mr. Cross's study was a serious chamber, filled with tall shelves stocked with unfriendly-looking novels like *Crime and Punishment* and *War and Peace* and some straight-up antagonistic-looking textbooks. His blinds were slanted, allowing minimal lines of sunlight in. It was a bleak place that painted an unhappy picture of adulthood.

Mr. Cross sat behind his executive desk, reading paperwork under the light of his desk lamp, adjusting his reading glasses on the sharp bridge of his bladelike nose. He didn't look up as Aidan entered.

Aidan was in church mouse mode. He didn't dare speak until Mr. Cross gave permission.

After a small eternity, Mr. Cross removed and folded his glasses, tucking them into his blazer pocket. It was a Saturday, and the only casual thing about his outfit was the lack of a tie on his button-down shirt. Finally, he smiled. Although his smile was the sort you gave someone you were about to crack in an interrogation room. "How are you, Aidan?"

"Uh. Good?" said Aidan. It felt like a lie. *Was* he good? Could his dad tell if he *wasn't*?

"That's good," said Mr. Cross. "How are your studies coming along?"

Oh my God. Did his dad think he came in here to have a conversation? And it was summer vacation! Was this some sort of test?

"It's . . . summer?" Aidan said in the form of a question. "So . . ."

"Oh," said Mr. Cross. He chuckled to himself. "Silly me. Well, what can I do for you, Aidan?"

"May I spend the night at Terrance's . . . ehrm . . . I mean, Zephyr's house?" Aidan asked.

His dad offered a deep frown in response.

"I heard Terrance hit Zephyr," said Mr. Cross. "Broke his glasses. What was that about?"

Aidan took a deep breath. Let it out. It took every ounce of resolve to answer without having a breakdown.

"Zephyr threw Terrance's Yankees cap through the window of the Witch House," said Aidan. "He also said some mean stuff about the Yankees, so—"

"You were at the Witch House?" said Mr. Cross.

Crap.

"W-w-well . . . ," said Aidan. The stuttering had started. When it started, there was no stopping it.

"What were you doing there?"

"I m-m-mean—"

"You realize that's private property? You guys haven't been throwing things through the windows, have you?"

"Aside from Terrance's h-h-hat—"

"If Sheriff Jenkins finds out who's been breaking those windows, he's gonna make *you* pay for the repairs. Heck, he might even arrest you and send you off to juvie! Do you want that?"

"*N-n-nu-n-n-nuh-n-n-ngh*," said Aidan. He was trying to say "no."

"That goes on your permanent record. Do you *know* what they do to kids like you in juvie? Ever heard of a swirly?"

Aidan was on the verge of tears.

That's when his dad's face splintered, and he let out a half-amused gust of laughter. "I'm messing with you, bud."

Aidan blinked back the tears. Stared at his dad, shell-shocked.

The problem here was that his dad was what you would call a "heckler." Aidan, on the other hand, was a much more fragile thing, like one of those painted, hollowed-out eggshells his mom loved to collect. There was nothing wrong with being either of these. The problem was when you put the two of them together.

"Those windows were broken when I was your age," said Mr. Cross. "My buddies and I made sure of it. You all have fun at Zephyr's, okay?"

Aidan nodded again and backed away like a caged animal towards the door.

"Oh, and, Aidan?"

Aidan froze. He didn't even dare to breathe.

"I'm sure I don't have to tell you this, but don't go inside the Witch House. It's old and rotting. Don't want you getting tetanus."

Aidan was one spoken word away from crying. If he had to lie to his dad about going into the Witch House, he might crumble.

Fortunately, Mr. Cross didn't seem interested in receiving confirmation from Aidan—perhaps his dad was bored of him— because he retrieved his glasses, put them on, and returned to his paperwork.

"Shut the door behind you, please?" said Mr. Cross.

Aidan tried to say, "Yes sir," but the words lodged themselves in his throat. When they came out, it was a breathless whisper.

Aidan hurried out and shut the door.

The sun slipped into the soft, rolling edge of the Berkshires. Night fell over Curtain Falls, thick, heavy, and full of dreams.

Aidan packed for the sleepover. (Just not the sleepover his parents expected.) In addition to his sleeping bag and pillow, he packed a heavy-duty flashlight, bug spray, a multi-tool pocketknife, and even a Bible, which he intended to use more as a ghost deterrent, like holy water. (Aidan had seen too many possession/exorcism movies with

Zephyr.) Could you hit a ghost in the face with a Bible? Aidan might find out.

The boys convened in the middle of the cul-de-sac. There they dumped their stuff, and their bikes, until Zephyr arrived with his brother's bike cargo wagon for towing their sleeping bags and pillows. They loaded up, and then Terrance led the way—his bike had a clip-on headlamp—while Kai took up the rear.

Riding in the dark was spooky. But it wasn't the darkness—making the world look foreign, alien, otherworldly—that scared Aidan the most. It was the quiet. Everything was *too* quiet. The silence felt like a presence. That thought caused every hair on Aidan's arms to stand on end.

It wasn't long before they veered off the main road onto Yeet Street. The trees on either side of them stretched up into an infinite black ceiling, making the road feel like a tunnel.

The Witch House waited for them on the other side. It appeared ghostly, illuminated by the pale touch of moonlight, with walls like bone, and windows like eye sockets.

With sleeping bags and pillows in tow—and no one wanting to walk any amount of distance in the dark—they rode up to the front porch. Aidan, Terrance, and Kai dropped their bikes while Zephyr popped his kickstand out.

"Should we scope the place out before bringing our stuff inside?" said Kai.

"Yeah," said Aidan. "Scope the place out." He laughed nervously, even though he was crying on the inside.

"Let me know if you need to hold my hand, Aid," said Zephyr. "I do that for my baby sis at Screeemfest."

"I know you're being facetious," said Aidan, "but I will seriously grab your hand if something scary happens. Don't make promises you can't keep."

Aidan glanced at Kai as he said this, gauging his reaction. Kai didn't react. As if he didn't even hear. He was busy peering inside the nearest window with his flashlight.

"FYI, I get really sweaty hands," said Zephyr. "My mom says it's like holding a fish."

"You're holding hands with your mom too?" said Kai. His hand reached for the front doorknob.

"Wait," said Terrance. He slipped his backpack off, unzipped it, and removed the tangle of GoPro Chestys his father lent him. "No one goes in without their camera."

He proceeded to fit one on each of his friends, adjusting them to their chests, then powered each one on. Lastly, he unpacked the EOS C300—as delicate as a priceless artifact—and began recording.

In a surprising act of generosity—and perhaps a little bit of ego-stroking—Terrance turned the camera on Zephyr, and said, "Ghost Hunter Zephyr Windon, explain to our viewers what it is we're doing."

Zephyr's eyes lit up and he transitioned like the flip of a switch. Kid-in-a-candy-store glee one moment, cool-as-a-cucumber paranormal reality TV host the next.

"I'll *tell you* what we're doing, Terrance. Me and my cute little assistants, Aidan Cross and Kai Pendleton here, are not only *investigating*, but we're *spending the night in*, the most haunted house in all of Massachusetts: the Witch House of Yeet Street. There are more urban legends surrounding this house than the Lizzie Borden Bed and Breakfast and Salem combined. Just ask Aidan here. On a scale of one to ten, how haunted is this house?"

"I don't know about numbers, but we're probably going to die," said Aidan.

"There you have it, folks. Excited? I know I am. Kai, anything to add?"

"Call me your cute little assistant again, I'll murder you in your sleep myself," said Kai.

"I'm glad we have this on camera," said Zephyr. "Sheriff Jenkins, if I do not survive the night, it was *probably* Farah Yeet, or maybe the guy that murdered Gabby Caldwell, but do *not* rule out the possibility of Kai Pendleton. Wowie! A ghost hunter show *and* murder documentary. Isn't this thrilling?"

"I'm going inside," said Kai. And he went inside.

"And away we go," said Zephyr, following behind Kai.

"This guy is nuts," said Terrance, laughing to himself.

Finally, it was just Aidan outside.

Just Aidan and the ever-encroaching darkness, and a silence that watched. Waiting for stragglers to pick off one by one.

Aidan quietly whimpered and followed Terrance.

The entrance hall was a wide-open space with a tall, vaulted ceiling, a chandelier woven in cobwebs like cotton candy, and a crumbling, elegantly curved staircase to the right that became a wraparound balcony overlooking the entire foyer. The tile floor was littered with scattered rocks, loose bricks, and a cornucopia of every throwable object ever conceived: the Ghosts of Yeets Past.

Aidan found himself craning his neck back, observing the wrap-around balcony. Noting where the stairs continued to the second floor, leading to an inevitable third floor, and the room on the other side of that eye-shaped window.

Aidan needed to get to that room before anyone else. He had to retrieve his notebook without anyone noticing.

"Where to first?" said Zephyr.

"I need to use the bathroom," Aidan blurted out.

"Viewers, meet Aidan's bladder," said Zephyr. "It's the size of a teabag."

"I'll find it on my own. You guys keep exploring."

Terrance, Zephyr, and Kai stared at Aidan as if he'd announced he was planning to French the first ghost he saw.

"Are you sure?" said Kai. "I can come with you. Make sure you're, um . . . safe or whatever." He took a step towards Aidan, which made Aidan's heart do this thing where it forgot its own rhythm.

Aidan dug this idea, but it was out of the question. He needed these three preoccupied.

"I'd actually prefer some privacy," said Aidan. "If that's okay."

Kai seemed crestfallen that Aidan rejected his offer. It hurt Aidan's heart just to look at him. So he took a couple steps backwards, offering a pair of dorky thumbs-up to let everyone know he'd be okay.

"Don't die," said Terrance.

"Good talk, Terrance," said Aidan.

Zephyr, Kai, and Terrance wandered towards a pair of elegant double doors framed between a pair of aesthetic marble columns. Meanwhile, Aidan meandered off to the right, in a vague trajectory for the stairs.

Zephyr continued towards the door, hollering, "Here, ghosty, ghosty, ghosty!"

"Are we looking for a ghost or a dog?" said Terrance.

"Ooh, what if it was a ghost dog?" said Zephyr.

They disappeared behind the double doors.

Aidan crept up the stairs.

The Witch House was large on the outside, but something about the echoing emptiness made it feel even larger on the inside. The wraparound balcony encircled the entrance hall entirely, branching off into a puzzle of halls, chambers, and antechambers. The second-floor stairs continued where the first-floor stairs left off, continuing behind the east wall, with tall, narrow, oppressive walls on either side, and ascending into darkness.

Aidan hadn't needed his flashlight until now. Shattered windows allowed moonlight into the vast entrance hall freely. Here, there were no windows.

He switched his flashlight on. A hard beam of light punctured a hole through shadow.

Aidan continued upward.

Though the walls were bare, the square- and rectangle-shaped scars of picture frames remained. Some still had their nails. Memories haphazardly erased. Aidan's flashlight led his gaze, and his steps, as he climbed upward.

He stopped.

His flashlight fell on a single, bright red door at the top of the stairs—the most passionate, violent, blood-pumping red you had ever seen. It was almost cliché. Aidan was sure he had seen this exact door in half a dozen horror films at Zephyr's house: *The Sixth Sense, Insidious, It Comes at Night.*

It was not bravery, but curiosity, that carried Aidan forwards.

He reached the top step, with his flashlight shining into the center of the door.

There was no doorknob.

Aidan pushed on the door. It did not budge.

He moved his fingers along the edges, attempted to squeeze them in, to pull the door outward. It did not give.

Was this *not* the right way to the third floor? Was there *another* staircase? It wasn't unbelievable. Not as unbelievable as a staircase that led to a creepy red door without a doorknob and no conceivable way to open it.

A gentle slap sounded at Aidan's feet.

Aidan glanced down.

There, at Aidan's feet, was his notebook. The alchemical symbols for fire, air, earth, and water were hand-doodled on the cover in a straight line. He did not bend down and pick it up.

Aidan could feel the presence of someone standing behind him.

It wasn't a physical sensation. Somehow, he just *knew* someone was there. A body occupying space.

Aidan turned—rather abruptly—and standing there was a girl. She looked about sixteen, with blond hair and tan skin, and she was wearing a maroon tank top, white drawstring shorts, and flip-flops. But her casual wear took a back seat to her overall aesthetic, because from her scalp to her toes, she was dripping in blood.

And smiling.

Then she glanced down at herself. "Oh crap."

Aidan screamed, then panicked in the worst way possible. There was nowhere for him to go. He was trapped between a ghost and a hard place. So what he did was bolt headfirst into the red door, ricocheted off it, and tumbled down the entire flight of stairs.

Aidan was sure it was painful, but adrenaline coursed through his body like white water rapids. When he landed face-first at the bottom of the second floor, he exploded to his feet, screaming and running down the stairs to the first floor.

"Aidan, are you okay?" said Kai. He came from the west wing hallway into the vaulted foyer faster than anyone.

"What in the Jordan Peele heck are you screaming about?" said Terrance. He was already training his camcorder on Aidan like a pro. Whatever it was, he was determined to catch it on film.

"Please tell me it's a ghost!" said Zephyr.

As much as Aidan wanted to make Zephyr's wildest dreams come true, he needed to get out of this house, stat. Any and all explanations could wait until he was safely on the other side of—

"Hey, wait!" said a girl's voice. "I'm sorry!"

Every hair follicle on Aidan's body spiked.

Aidan, Zephyr, Terrance, and Kai rotated slowly. Standing directly behind them, in the dead center of the entrance hall of the Witch House, was the ghost girl, hands tucked timidly behind her back. Only now, she had no trace of blood on her.

Somehow, that scared Aidan even more. Anybody could cover themselves in blood and pretend to be a ghost.

No one could clean themselves off that fast.

"G-g-g-guys," said Aidan. He was shaking like a maraca. "We need to get out of here."

"Who are you?" said Kai.

"Dude, no way," said Zephyr. His jaw dropped. "You look *just like* Gabby Caldwell." He clapped slowly. "I almost crapped my pants. Bravo."

Terrance glanced between the ghost girl and the look of paralyzed terror on Aidan's trembling face. "Guys, this is weird. We should leave."

Upon hearing the name "Gabby Caldwell," the girl began crying. Clear streaks ran down her face that she attempted to wipe away with her wrist.

She sniffed violently, then looked directly at Aidan. "I'm sorry for scaring you. I thought what you wrote was beautiful." Then she looked at Terrance. "I have something of yours too."

She removed her hands from behind her. She held Terrance's Yankees cap.

There was just one problem.

She was no longer crying tears. She was crying blood.

Then her scalp split open, and blood seeped from it like a fountain down her face.

Terrance screamed. Zephyr screamed. Kai screamed. Everyone screamed, except for the girl. She just cried and bled profusely all over the place. She was a fondue of absolute terror.

The four friends ran outside. Hopped on their bikes, pedaled standing up, and booked it off the Witch House property and down Yeet Street.

They biked faster than anyone had ever biked anywhere in the lazy town of Curtain Falls.

CHAPTER 4

Seven Angry Parents (in a Sheriff's Station)

The Curtain Falls Sheriff's Department was a quaint, single-story rectangle painted fresh, earthy colors: brown and olive, with a forest-green trim. It had the cozy glow of a *fictional* sheriff's department from your parents' favorite '90s comfort show. In this show, solving murders took a back seat to drinking coffee, eating donuts, and friendly workplace shenanigans. There was probably a laugh track.

Sheriff Jenkins was hardly an intimidating presence. Despite his tallness, he had a formidable gut and a double chin that he attempted to hide beneath unshaven scruff. He was balding too, so that was great.

He was leaving the office late after an evening of paperwork—the needlessly busy kind. All Sheriff Jenkins wanted to do was order a Caniac Combo at Raising Cane's Chicken Fingers and watch some Netflix. He didn't even care *what* he watched. He'd recently taken to the "Surprise Me" button because in the time it took him to decide on something, he was done eating and ready for bed. If the Netflix algorithm thought he should watch a wholesome documentary series about children's toys from the 1970s, it was probably right.

Sheriff Jenkins was locking the door behind him, deciding between ordering a sweet tea or Dr Pepper, when the sound of bicycle wheels cut through the night, followed by the voices of four boys screaming at the top of their lungs.

"Sheeeeeriff Jeeeeenkinnnnns!" said Terrance.

"Gabby Caldwell!" said Kai. "She's alive!"

"No, she's not, you idiot, she's dead!" said Zephyr. "She's alive, but she's dead! She's *un*dead!"

"B-b-buh-b-b-bluh-b-b-b . . . ," Aidan stuttered deliriously.

He was trying to say "blood."

It was the dead of night, and the Curtain Falls Sheriff's Department had never been more alive.

Three and a half pairs of parents—with moods ranging from deathly worried to moderately disturbed—were clustered in the sheriff's department meeting room. Deputy Gonzalez had taken to calling it the "donut room" because it was where their secretary, Kimmy, laid out generous spreads of donuts. But right here, right now, it was the meeting room, for sure. It was the only room in the station big enough to fit everyone. Even then, there weren't enough seats.

That was okay. Not one of the boys could sit down, even if he wanted to. They took turns pacing in front of the whiteboard, explaining their story in erratic bursts and gestures.

Well, *three of them* did. Aidan stood in the corner, rocking on his heels and muttering to himself.

"We're not lying!" Kai exclaimed.

"How could you even *think* we would lie about this?" said Zephyr. He clutched his chest, emotionally wounded.

"Aside from you lying to us about where you were spending the night?" said Zephyr's mom. Mrs. Mei Windon was a short, rigid woman with a personality like a yardstick in the hand of an angry nun.

"Aside from you lying to us *every day* of your dishonest little existence?" said Zephyr's dad. Mr. Marty Windon's Boston accent grew stronger the angrier he got, and right now, he was ready to *pahk the cah in Havahd Yahd.*

"Mahhty!" said Mrs. Windon. Her Boston accent had a softer default setting. She placed a delicate hand on his hairy, meaty forearm, like a soft log covered in moss. "Your blood pressure."

"It's like 'The Boy Who Cried Wolf,'" said Terrance, detached.

"I'm telling the truth this time!" said Zephyr. "You have to believe me!"

"It's like *Chicken Little*," said Terrance, still mumbling to himself.

Zephyr cracked like an egg. "WHO YOU CALLING A LITTLE CHICKEN, TERRY?"

"Hey, hey, hey!" said Sheriff Jenkins.

"She read it," Aidan mumbled to himself. "She said it was *beautiful*. She was bleeding! There was blood everywhere—"

"I eat little chickens for *breakfast*, you Yankees-loving butt-snack!" said Zephyr. "Those little Chick-n-Minis at Chick-fil-A, ever heard of 'em?"

"Okay," said Sheriff Jenkins. "I said—I said okay!"

"Chick-fil-A is a homophobic institution, so no," said Terrance.

"Your mom is a homophobic institution!" said Zephyr.

That comment resulted in widespread disapproval from everyone in the room.

"Hey now, Zephyr, that was highly uncalled for," said Mr. Adams.

"I love *all* of God's children," said Mrs. Adams.

"Zephyr, when we get home, I'm shoving your Nintendo down the gahbage disposal!" Mr. Windon barked.

Zephyr seemed immediately apologetic. "I'm sorry, Mrs. Adams. I don't know why I said that. And it's an Xbox, Dad."

"That's okay, Zephyr, I forgive you," said Mrs. Adams.

"Xbox, Nintendo box, Atari box, whatevah," said Mr. Windon.

"I SAID OKAY!" Sheriff Jenkins boomed, silencing the room like a crack of thunder. "Okay," he said again, calmer. "I'm going to repeat this story back to you, just so *you know* that *I know* that I've heard this, um . . . this story . . . correctly. Okay?"

Zephyr, Terrance, and Kai nodded.

"Aidan?"

Aidan snapped up from his mumbling stupor. "Y-y-yuh-y-y-yeh."

Mr. Cross rubbed his eyes in secondhand embarrassment. "Just nod, Aidan."

Aidan nodded.

"Here, Aidan," said Mrs. Cross, standing and offering her seat. "Sit."

Aidan glanced at Sheriff Jenkins, to make sure he wouldn't be arrested for obeying his mom's orders. Sheriff Jenkins responded with a vague head movement that could have meant anything.

Aidan sat in his mom's chair. She stood behind him and kneaded the anxiety out of his vibrating shoulders.

"I wish someone would give *me* a shoulder massage," said Zephyr longingly.

"Shut your mouth, Zephyr," said Mrs. Windon.

"Okay," said Sheriff Jenkins, for the dozenth time. "So you boys

46

lied about your whereabouts tonight, when you were planning to spend it at the old Farah Yeet estate. You borrowed Tekulvē's camera equipment because you went there with the intent to *prove* the existence of ghosts."

"To prove *whether or not* ghosts exist," said Terrance.

"You told me you wanted to film a documentary about sleepovers," said Mr. Adams.

"I told you I wanted to film a documentary about sleepovers, *Blair Witch Project*–style," said Terrance. "Technically, nothing I said was a lie."

"No, nuh-uh. No, sir. Under our roof, that is not what telling the truth sounds like."

"What it sounds like to me," said Sheriff Jenkins, "is that you boys went to the Witch House with the *intent* to scare yourselves, and you succeeded."

The heads of all seven parents nodded in weary, sleep-deprived unison.

"Wait," said Kai. "What about the cameras?"

Zephyr's eyes lit up. "That's right. We have proof!"

"Oh snap," said Terrance, grabbing his head as if it were about to explode. "Am I not grounded?"

"Son," said Mr. Adams, "I don't care if you caught Casper and Patrick Swayze on that camera. You are grounded."

"But, Dad—!"

"Terrance Douglass Adams," said Mrs. Adams. "I don't care if you caught the *Holy Ghost in the form of a dove* on that camera! You are grounded."

Sheriff Jenkins interlocked his fingers together and leaned

forwards, thoughtful. "Supposing we were to corroborate your story by looking at your camera footage—"

"You can't be serious—" Mr. Cross scoffed.

"—whose camera would have captured the most convincing footage of this so-called ghost of Gabby Caldwell?"

Mrs. Cross looked genuinely upset at the mention of Gabby Caldwell. "Can we please not say that name?"

"*Oy vey*," said Mr. Windon, shaking his head.

"No, Marty, I will not be *oy vey*ed!" said Mrs. Cross defensively. "She was a real girl who lived—and died—in this town!"

"Whoa, hey, I'm not *oy vey*ing you, Jocelyn. I'm *oy vey*ing this entire cockamamie night. I should be watching Colbert right now."

Zephyr, Terrance, and Kai simultaneously looked at Aidan.

Aidan glanced between all three of them and violently shook his head. "I'm not watching that video."

"*None of you boys* are watching that video," said Sheriff Jenkins. "This is for adults only. We'll watch it on my office computer. Does anyone want to volunteer to babysit?"

No one volunteered right away. Then a slender, tattooed arm raised. It belonged to Kai's mom, Kalani—easily the youngest parent in the room at thirty-one. Honestly, she looked closer to Aidan and his friends' ages than that of, say, Marty Windon, who had just celebrated his fiftieth. Half a century had been kinder to disco.

"I'll babysit," said Kalani in a flat, bored tone.

Aidan never met Kai's dad. From the way Kalani—or even Kai—talked about him (or *didn't* talk about him), that was probably for the best.

Kalani dressed like she was auditioning for the 1987 vampire movie *The Lost Boys* (another Zephyr movie night): way too much black, cheap leather, cutoff vests, thrift store jewelry, and skin. She had a septum piercing. Aidan didn't know what a DUI was, but he'd heard she had one of those too.

It was with the slightest hesitation that everyone left their children in Kalani's care.

Mr. Adams collected the SD cards from each of the GoPro Chestys, which he had already gathered in a cardboard box. Together, Sheriff Jenkins, the Adams, the Crosses, and the Windons exited the meeting room.

The door hadn't closed all the way behind them when Kalani got up from her seat, popped open the nearest casement window, and pulled out a box of Pall Mall cigarettes.

"You boys don't mind if I smoke, do you?" she said.

She didn't wait for a response. She put a cigarette in her lips, pulled out a cheap Bic lighter, and lit up.

"I think I saw a No Smoking sign?" said Terrance.

Kalani took a long drag, made amused eye contact with Terrance, and then let it out. "I won't tell if you won't."

Terrence seemed unsure how to respond, so he didn't.

"Can I have a smoke?" asked Zephyr coolly.

"Zephyr!" Aidan exclaimed.

"Are you for real?" said Terrance.

"Mom, do *not* give Zephyr a smoke," said Kai. "He has asthma, and we are in a police station."

"You guys are such buzzkills," said Zephyr. "I do *not* have asthma! I *used to*, but I don't anymore."

"You literally have an inhaler inside your backpack right now," said Aidan.

"Which I have not needed to use in a *year*," said Zephyr. "Do you know how many days are in a year? Like, three hundred and something."

"There are three hundred and sixty-five days in a year," said Terrance. "We're going to be in eighth grade. How do you not know this?"

Zephyr plugged his nose with his fingers, and imitated Terrance in a cartoonishly nasally voice. "Hi, my name is Terrance. I'm so smart. I know quantum physics. I know how many licks it takes to get to the center of a Tootsie Pop."

Aidan pressed his fingers to his temples and groaned. He lowered his head and closed his eyes.

The problem was, every time he closed his eyes, all he could see was the ghost of Gabby Caldwell. Covered in blood. Crying.

"It's literally impossible to know how many licks it would take to get to the center of a Tootsie Pop," said Terrance. "It's totally subjective! How big is your tongue? How hard are you licking?"

"That's what she said," said Zephyr.

Everyone collectively groaned. Except Kalani. She choked on her own cigarette smoke, laughing.

And Aidan—still haunted by the image of the girl in the Witch House.

I'm sorry for scaring you.

Why was she crying?

I thought what you wrote was beautiful.

The background noise reached a fever pitch as Zephyr gloated at his gross joke, Kalani had a laughing/coughing fit, Terrance gagged, and Kai shushed his mother.

"ENOUGH," Aidan screamed. He bolted from his seat, pushing his chair back.

Aidan's voice silenced everyone.

"We literally *just saw* the ghost of Gabby Caldwell," said Aidan. "She was covered in blood. She was crying *tears of blood*. What is wrong with you?"

Kai frowned. Terrance lowered his head. Zephyr clucked his tongue awkwardly.

"Are you guys not worried for her?" said Aidan.

"I'm sorry, what?" said Kai.

"Worried *for* her?" said Terrance.

"Worried for the ghost that almost killed us?" said Zephyr.

"She did not *almost kill us*," said Aidan. "She scared the crap out of us, sure, but she didn't try to do that. She wasn't *trying* to bleed out the top of her head and her eyeballs. I think she was *sad* that that was happening to her. She apologized for scaring me, didn't she?"

Kalani's eyes were wide as she took another drag. She was riveted.

"Terrance!" said Aidan. "She tried to give you back your hat, didn't she?"

"I mean," said Terrance, "it could have been a trap."

"*Or*," said Aidan, "she wanted to give you your hat back because she's a nice ghost, and her spirit is trapped in that house, and she's just lonely."

Aidan had more evidence to go on. But it was evidence he was not ready to divulge. Maybe he never would be.

I thought what you wrote was beautiful.

"I think she's a nice ghost," said Aidan.

Zephyr, Terrance, and Kai stared at Aidan with varying degrees of skepticism.

Kai glanced at his mom and then rolled his eyes. "What, Mom? I know you're dying to say something."

Aidan felt his internal temperature rise. Somehow, he'd forgotten that a grown-up was present. (Kalani had that effect.)

"I think he's right," said Kalani, throwing her hands in the air. She took a quick drag, and then blew her smoke into the center of the meeting room table. "I think the ghost of Gabby Caldwell is probably nice. There. Happy?"

"*You* believe me?" said Aidan.

"Well, yeah," said Kalani. "I knew Gabby Caldwell."

Zephyr's jaw dropped. "You knew Gabby Caldwell."

The door to the meeting room opened. Kalani quickly flicked her lit cigarette out the window (undoubtedly a fire hazard), pretended to hawk a loogie, then closed the window.

"Whew!" said Kalani, adjusting her jacket. "It's brisk out, eh?"

The look on Sheriff Jenkins's face was harrowed. *All* the parents looked pale.

Aidan shouldn't have been surprised. This was exactly how they should look if they saw what he saw.

Sheriff Jenkins took three steps into the room, parents filing in behind him like zombies. Then he stopped and gave a resigned sigh.

"Everyone is free to go home," he said. Then he looked directly at Aidan. "Except for the Crosses."

Aidan's parents did not look surprised by this revelation. Christopher Cross looked the exact opposite of surprised. Jocelyn Cross was pale and completely shaken.

Aidan exchanged weary glances with Terrance and Zephyr. When he tried to meet Kai's gaze, Kai deliberately avoided eye contact.

Kai pushed through the last of the parents, and he disappeared.

Aidan was instructed to sit in Sheriff Jenkins's chair, while Sheriff Jenkins and his parents crowded on either side of the small office.

Sheriff Jenkins moved the cursor on Aidan's video footage and fast-forwarded to his ghostly encounter on the stairs. On-screen, Aidan's hands were on the mysterious red door, attempting to push and pull.

Aidan (the present Aidan) hadn't quite mustered the courage for what he was about to see, so when he heard the slap of his notebook fall at his feet, directly in front of him, he all but yelped and jumped in his seat.

When the version of him in the video turned around, the video warped and disintegrated into static.

"Wait, what?" said Aidan.

The video became clear again as Aidan toppled down the stairs, landing violently at the bottom. He scooped himself up to his feet with barely a moment to breathe and continued screaming, ambling down the steps to the first floor.

"Aidan, are you okay?" said Kai.

"What in the Jordan Peele heck are you screaming about?" said Terrance.

"Please tell me it's a ghost!" said Zephyr.

The audio crackled. The video wobbled. And the whole thing unraveled into a fit of static once more.

"No!" said Aidan. "She was right there! She was right behind us!"

Sheriff Jenkins grabbed the mouse and paused the video.

"Now I don't know what messed up your video," said Sheriff Jenkins. "But whatever it was, it messed up *everyone's* footage. Weird, but not unexplainable. That's what Tekulvē says anyway."

Sheriff Jenkins moved the cursor again, rewinding time. Aidan ran backwards up the stairs. Fell up the second flight of stairs, into a storm of static. When the static ended, the video was staring down on the notebook again.

Aidan—the present Aidan—swallowed against a knot in his throat the size of a secret.

"Now it seems that your hands were on that door when the notebook fell," said Sheriff Jenkins. "That part of the video freaked the other parents out a bit. What I need for you to do, Aidan, is to tell me that *you* dropped that notebook."

"What?" said Aidan.

"Maybe it slipped out of your backpack?"

"No! You're saying it fell out of my backpack and landed *in front of me*?"

"Or maybe it was tucked under your arm, or . . . I dunno, under your chin or something?"

"No!" said Aidan loudly. He was beginning to sweat.

"Why do you look so nervous?" said Sheriff Jenkins.

"Nervous?" said Aidan nervously. "I'm not nervous."

"But that's your notebook, isn't it, sweetie?" said Mrs. Cross.

Aidan felt the lie expand in his stomach. It was bloating, giving him a tummy ache.

"What?" said Aidan in a small voice.

"Your notebook," Mrs. Cross repeated. "I bought that notebook for you, didn't I? And you doodled those weird triangle things on the front, right? I've seen you writing in it."

"I . . . don't . . . um," said Aidan.

His mouth was too dry to speak, his brain too panicked to connect logical thoughts together. He had been cornered into his own lie. There was nothing left for him to do but disintegrate.

"Let me explain how this works," said Sheriff Jenkins. "If you tell me that a ghost dropped that notebook, I'm going to have to go into that house and look around. I won't be looking for a ghost, though. I'll be looking for someone who's living there when they're not supposed to. And the first place I'm looking is the top of those stairs, where I'm going to check out that notebook that's *maybe* yours, or *maybe* it belongs to the person that's living in there, who *maybe* bears a resemblance to Gabby Caldwell. So if you don't want me reading that notebook, I'm going to need some logical explanations right about now. You're not in trouble. I just want to know the truth. That's all."

It didn't *sound*, to Aidan, like Sheriff Jenkins wanted the truth. It *sounded* like he wanted to be let off the hook.

"*Please* just tell us the truth, Aidan," said Mr. Cross. His tone was bone-tired and empty of warmth. "This has gone on long enough."

Aidan felt the knife of those words cut in, and twist, and pull out, leaving him to bleed.

"I lied," said Aidan. The words crumbled out of his mouth.

"Okay . . . ," said Sheriff Jenkins, nodding.

"I think I just . . . spooked myself," said Aidan. "And then I fell down the stairs and got spooked even more. And when the others saw me, they got spooked and . . . I think we just scared ourselves. I'm sorry. I didn't mean to lie to anyone."

Sheriff Jenkins nodded thoughtfully. "And the notebook?"

Aidan felt the premonition of a stutter on his lips, but he pushed through it. "It's m-muh-mine."

Sheriff Jenkins prodded him with a look.

"I think it fell out of my backpack," said Aidan. "I guess that spooked me too."

Sheriff Jenkins folded his arms, leaned back, and exhaled. He was absolutely beaming with relief.

"Oh, sweetie," said Mrs. Cross. She planted a kiss on the top of his head. "Don't ever do this to us again. I love you. But please don't."

Aidan chanced a look at his father.

He immediately regretted it.

Mr. Cross was *simmering* with disappointment. He couldn't even maintain eye contact with Aidan. Mr. Cross pulled his gaze away, staring intently at nothing. As if *anything* was better to look upon than this genetic misfire whom he'd fathered.

The part of Aidan's brain that made him think bad thoughts took a permanent snapshot of this moment. Shelved it away as a "Core Memory"—like they called them in that one Pixar movie—for easy access. In case he ever started to feel too optimistic about life.

Aidan and his parents left the sheriff's department. Climbed into their black compact SUV. Aidan deliberately climbed in on the left side, behind the driver's seat, so he had as little chance as possible of meeting his father's gaze.

"Am I grounded?" Aidan asked, in a moment of unparalleled bravery. Every muscle in his body told him he should shut up and not say another word for the rest of the evening.

Mrs. Cross glanced sympathetically from Aidan to Mr. Cross.

"You won't be grounded," said Mr. Cross, "though you should be. And if you ever go into that house again, you *will be*. Do I make myself clear?"

Aidan nodded solemnly.

"I want you to know how disappointed I am in you," said Mr. Cross.

Aidan nodded again, slower and sadder. "I'm sorry, Da—"

"Don't talk. You've done enough talking tonight. No more."

Aidan felt the weight of those words. Let them process. Let them hurt. Aidan sealed his lips shut, irrevocably, like the Seven Seals of God in the Book of Revelation.

He was content not to speak another word.

Now or ever.

Aidan and His Darkness

Aidan fell down a deep, dark well that lived inside his head.

There, at the bottom, he lay broken and hurting for days.

He never left his house. Because it was summer vacation, there was no reason to leave. And because both his parents worked long, chaotic hours, there was never time for them to drag him outside against his will. He never left his room, except to eat dinner with his family.

It wasn't the first time Aidan had gotten like this.

It happened two years ago, at the start of middle school, when Zephyr and Kai hit it off. Aidan and Kai had been best friends since first grade. Friendship that stretched that far back was a special sort—one that transcended middle school superficiality and hierarchies, dictating that guys like Kai Pendleton and girls like Beatrice "Queen Bea" McCarthy belonged together, and people like Aidan Cross existed far in the outer margins, like trash floating in the gutter, out of sight.

Aidan never had to work hard to be worthy of Kai's friendship. He *cared* about Kai, and so it all came naturally.

And then Zephyr came along.

Suddenly, here was this tiny kid with a big mouth who was kind of dumb, but extremely funny, and cool in all the ways that counted at the beginning of sixth grade. Zephyr Windon radiated confidence, and so did Kai Pendleton. It was only natural the two of them would strike up a friendship. You know who did not radiate confidence? Aidan. Also, he had a personality like wet socks. At the time, it seemed inconceivable to Aidan that the three of them could be friends *together*. It certainly didn't happen all at once. Aidan was a little fuzzy about what changed, and how it all clicked into place. When Aidan fell into one of his depressions, details tended to go murky in his peripheral. There was only Aidan and his Darkness.

His friends had tried to contact him in their group chat, but he hadn't responded to any of their messages. Not yet, anyway. It was easy to do this because not one of them seemed happy about his existence.

Zephyr: **Did you SERIOUSLY tell sheriff jenkins you lied about seeing a ghost???**

Terrance: **My parents think I lied to them too now. Thanks a lot, Aidan.**

Kai: **Seriously aidan what the ****?**

Kai typed an actual word there, but Aidan was forbidden by his father from ever speaking that word, typing it, or even *thinking* it.

It was easy for Aidan to ignore these messages. It was easy for him to ignore a lot of things when he slipped into his Darkness.

Mrs. Cross was anything but oblivious.

It may not have been her Darkness, but if Aidan's mom had one superpower, it was seeing things that were invisible to others. Aidan assumed it was part of what made her such a great lawyer.

"How would you feel about meeting with Doctor Jozwiak again?" Mrs. Cross asked.

It was four days after that night at the Witch House. One hour before another dreaded Cross Family Dinner. Mrs. Cross cornered Aidan in his bedroom to ask him this. Normally, she might have caught him trying to scribble another chapter of *Fire & Water*—his favorite thing to do in his alone time. But since he no longer had the notebook, he was more often than not doom-scrolling on his phone—a surefire way to feed his Darkness.

Dr. Jozwiak, pronounced *YAAZ-vee-ak*, was a different sort of doctor. She specialized in things inside Aidan's head, like his thoughts and feelings. Aidan liked her. What he *didn't like* was talking about the things that made him sad. Dr. Jozwiak had told him that to heal, it was necessary to dredge up the things that made him sad—that he didn't want to talk or think about. But the problem was, whenever Aidan tried to comply, he always cried and came out of the meetings feeling the worse for wear. It never took much convincing from Aidan for Mrs. Cross to cancel the next appointment.

"I'm fine," said Aidan. He sat upright on his bed and forced a smile. It felt like the biggest lie he'd ever told.

Mrs. Cross frowned and gently sat down on the bed beside him. "You don't look fine. When did you last eat?"

The last time was twenty-three hours ago, when they ate dinner.

"I had a frozen burrito for lunch," Aidan lied.

Mrs. Cross folded her arms. She didn't believe him.

"I microwaved it first," Aidan added, as if that made his lie more believable.

"Tell me what I can do to make you happy," said Mrs. Cross.

Aidan frowned.

"Ask me for anything," said Mrs. Cross. "Go crazy. Try me."

"I don't know," said Aidan. Even though he did know, just a little bit. "I guess I'd be happier if I had my notebook."

"The one you dropped in that old house?"

Aidan nodded feebly.

Mrs. Cross grimaced. The Witch House was obviously a sore subject in the Cross household. "Would it help if I got you a new one?"

Aidan shook his head. "Not really. It's not the same. I'm s-s-suh . . . I'm s-s-sor-r-r—"

Aidan was not sure which was harder: to get the word "sorry" out of his mouth, or not to cry while trying. Tears were already welling up in his eyes.

"Oh, baby," said Mrs. Cross. She pulled him into her and kissed the top of his head. "I get it. That notebook was special to you."

Mrs. Cross huffed.

"All right," she said. "Okay."

Aidan did not know who she was saying "all right" or "okay" to. It sounded like she was psyching herself up.

Mrs. Cross grabbed Aidan by the shoulders and looked him in the eye.

"It'll be an hour before your father gets home," she said. "That gives us an hour to drive to the Witch House, get your notebook, and be back in time for dinner."

The tears were gone. Now Aidan stared at his mom like she had proposed a quick trip to the moon to see if it was made of cheese.

"Who will make dinner?" Aidan whispered. Even though food was the absolute last thing on his mind.

"I'll order pizza," Mrs. Cross whispered back.

"With stuffed crust?" said Aidan. He only now realized just how soul-crushingly hungry he was.

"With stuffed crust."

"And pineapple?"

"Let's not go *too* crazy."

The Crosses' black Mazda CX-5 rolled up to the Witch House where gravel disintegrated into a tangle of unkempt grass and weeds. They parked underneath the shade of a single black locust tree in the clearing.

The front door was still hanging open from four days ago. Like an open mouth. Like unfinished business. Aidan and Mrs. Cross stepped out of the car, and then just sort of stopped and stared, breathless. The Witch House had that effect on everyone—adults included.

"Okay . . . ," said Mrs. Cross.

Aidan nodded, mouth agape.

"All we have to do is go inside and get your notebook," she said.

"That's all," said Aidan.

They continued to stand and stare. Aidan felt dizzy.

"Okay!" said Mrs. Cross, more invigorated. She clapped her hands. Aidan perked upright. "We're going to do this running, okay? But you know the layout of the place, so I need you to take the lead. Just know that wherever you run, I'll be right behind you."

Aidan inhaled, exhaled, and nodded.

"On your mark," said Mrs. Cross.

She and Aidan dropped into a starting position—one leg back, one leg forwards, hands touching the ground.

"Get set," said Mrs. Cross.

Aidan and Mrs. Cross lifted their hips, legs taut, ready to explode. "Go!"

Aidan launched off his forwards foot and flew. His arms cut back and forth, legs chugging, feet barely touching the ground. He cut across the grass, up the front porch, through the front door, into the mouth of the beast.

Aidan's first thought was how much brighter and un-scary the inside of the Witch House appeared in broad daylight. It was almost enough to make him pause, to stop and look around in wonder at details that were invisible four nights ago. But Aidan didn't stop running. Instead, he flew up the stairs, two steps at a time. When he reached the top, his sneakers squeaked as he flipped a U-ey, and he peeled up the next flight of stairs, behind confined walls.

Those empty walls, littered with nails and the ghostly squares of picture frames past, were still claustrophobic, but in daylight, were hardly scary. Even the red door at the top somehow looked *less red*— dull and tired and pale—like an ordinary door. It . . .

. . . had a doorknob.

Aidan stopped.

He expected his mother to run into him—or say something—but neither happened.

Aidan turned. His mother was not there.

Either one of three things happened: 1) A ghost had gotten his mom. Although this seemed unlikely, because in broad daylight, this house felt incredibly *un*haunted. 2) His mom wanted Aidan to do this on his own. 3) His mom had chickened out. This felt most likely because even though his mom was intelligent, and strong, and emotionally brave, she was also a chicken. Unlike Zephyr, she was terrified of horror movies. She was scared of the movie *Coraline*, for Pete's sake.

Whatever the case, Aidan was feeling daring. He faced the red door, marching up to it with confident steps.

His notebook was not in front of the door.

But he had a sneaking suspicion of where he might find it.

Aidan opened the door.

On the other side was a big, spectacularly empty attic space. The wooden ceiling was a slanted triangle, its spine running from a single broken window in the shape of an eye—from which daylight poured in—to the back of the room. This illuminated a part of the back wall that appeared swollen and waterlogged. The water damage looked vaguely human-shaped. (Nope. Aidan did not like *that*.) The floor, like the rest of the house, was littered with projectile debris: rocks, sticks, pine cones, and a New York Yankees baseball cap. And underneath the window, a notebook, doodled with the alchemical symbols for fire, wind, earth, and water.

Aidan collected Terrance's hat first, and then his notebook. Through the eye-shaped window, he noticed his mom, sitting in the scraggly, unkempt grass, with her left shoe off.

Was her foot bleeding?

"Mom!" Aidan exclaimed. "Are you okay?"

Mrs. Cross chuckled uneasily. "I'm okay. I stepped on a thorn from this black locust tree. It went through my shoe and into my foot."

Aidan grimaced. That did not sound okay.

"Don't be mad," said Mrs. Cross, "but I called your father. He's on his way."

Aidan's blood ran cold.

But only slightly.

Aidan conquered a larger fear today and had reaped the rewards. He had his notebook. He had Terrance's hat. What was the worst his dad could do to ruin this day?

Aidan tried not to let his mind linger on that question.

He retraced his steps: out of the attic, and down the first flight of stairs. He stopped before the stairs leading down to the first floor, and instead leaned over the walkway railing that wrapped around the foyer.

"Gabby Caldwell?" Aidan called out. "Are you here?"

Aidan waited—listening patiently for anything that could be a sign from the other side.

There was nothing.

Aidan opened his mouth to try once more. But in that exact moment, he heard a vehicle pull up outside. The engine stopped, and with it, the beating of Aidan's heart.

Aidan exited the house as sunlight slipped behind the Berkshires. Mr. Cross was preoccupied with Mrs. Cross's foot, cleaning off blood with a disinfecting wipe.

"You really punched a hole in this thing!" said Mr. Cross.

"You're telling me!" said Mrs. Cross. "I'm opening a bottle of wine when we get home."

"Are you sharing?"

"If you're really nice to me."

Christopher and Jocelyn Cross were definitely flirting. Apparently, love was not dead.

Mr. Cross bandaged Mrs. Cross's foot. Then, to Aidan's surprise, he beckoned Aidan over, and together they assisted her into the car—even though she claimed she could get in just fine.

"Stop it, we're being nice to you," said Mr. Cross. "I want that glass of wine."

"Do I get wine too?" Aidan asked.

His parents laughed. Hearing their laughter—especially at something *he said*—made him smile. He couldn't remember the last time they were all laughing and smiling like this.

"Nah, buddy," said Mr. Cross. "One of us needs to be sober, make sure nothing crazy happens. Your mother has two glasses of wine, and she starts dancing on the table and swinging from the chandelier."

"I do not!" said Mrs. Cross.

"Just wait," said Mr. Cross, winking at Aidan. "She will."

Once Mrs. Cross was safely packed away in the driver's seat of the CX-5 (she did not need her left foot to drive), Mr. Cross glanced down at the Yankees hat in Aidan's left hand, and the notebook in his right hand. Aidan felt a pang of guilt and regretted not hiding these things in the car.

"You went in the house?" said Mr. Cross.

Aidan opened his mouth but floundered for a response.

To Aidan's surprise, his father pulled him into a hug with one hand and ruffled his hair with the other. "That was very brave. I'm proud of you, Aidan."

Aidan wasn't sure what his mom might have said over the phone to paint this in Aidan's favor, but he wasn't taking it for granted. He hugged his dad back and resisted the very strong and delicate urge to sob into his dad's shirt.

"Want to ride home with me, chief?"

Aidan wiped a wrist across his eyes and nodded. Yes, he did.

Aidan rode with his dad while his mom drove the CX-5. They arrived home at the exact same time as their pizza delivery driver. Mrs. Cross paid the driver while Aidan and Mr. Cross relieved him of the pizza—a half pepperoni, half pineapple Canadian bacon stuffed crust. It was the best meal Aidan could remember eating. What it lacked in nutritional value, it made up for in love, and Aidan could feel *that* nourishment in every part of his slightly malnourished body.

When dinner ended, Aidan retreated to his bedroom with his notebook and Terrance's hat in tow. He'd give it back to Terrance tomorrow. But first, he wanted to *write*. He *needed* to write.

It was only as he opened the notebook that he noticed a strange texture on the last page. As if it had been painted on. The notebook opened easily to that page.

This time, Aidan's blood really did turn cold.

The last page was written in what appeared to be blood, finger-painted in large, sloppy letters:

I ONLY APPEAR AT NIGHT.
I'M TRAPPED HERE.
HELP ME.

CHAPTER 6

Pinkie Promise with Blood on Top

Aidan's friends all had defining characteristics. Terrance was smart. Zephyr was funny. Kai was athletic. Each was brave in his own unique way—intellectually, psychologically, *literally*. These were the boys who wanted to spend the night in a haunted house—for fun! For science! To repair a friendship.

Then there was Aidan.

What was Aidan's defining characteristic, other than being the *exact opposite* of brave?

Sure, his dad *called* him brave, but that only made Aidan hyperaware of the contradicting facts. Aidan had only entered the Witch House because he thought his mom was behind him. He didn't do it to help the ghost of Gabby Caldwell. He did it for selfish reasons. For his notebook. For himself.

Well, now he knew for a fact—a fact handwritten in blood—that the ghost of Gabby Caldwell needed help.

And Aidan wanted nothing to do with it.

He took one look at those words, and the blood, and he was incapacitated with fear. He tossed the notebook into his closet, closed the sliding mirror doors, crawled underneath his bedcovers, and coiled into the fetal position.

He was still facing the closet.

He rolled onto his other side, facing the wall.

I only appear at night.

What could Aidan do to help her? How do you help a dead person?

I'm trapped here.

One thing Aidan had learned from watching horror movies was that ghosts had unfinished business. Once that business was finished, they could go wherever dead people are meant to go. *Be* whatever they're meant to be. Angels? Hopefully not Biblically accurate angels. Aidan shuddered at the thought.

Help me.

Maybe Aidan Cross was not brave.

But Nadia sure was.

Aidan kicked his covers off and jumped out of bed. He opened his bedside table and pulled out his journal and a pen tucked into a leather loop on the spine. His journal was a completely separate, vaguely neglected writing apparatus from the notebook in which he wrote *Fire & Water*. He'd stopped writing in it ages ago because rereading his cringey past entries made him want to set himself on fire.

He had only done what he was about to do a small handful of times. Only when he was faced with an important decision that he did not trust himself to make.

Who he *did* trust was Nadia. Nadia was cunning. Nadia was fearless.

It just so happened that everything Nadia said, did, and thought was a product of Aidan's mind.

Aidan opened to a blank page and wrote: *Nadia, what would you do?*

And then he waited.

He always felt like an idiot at this part, but the trick was patience. Like any creative writing, you had to push through the awkward emptiness and the stupid feeling of staring at a blank page without a clue. You had to wait for that elusive creative genius to come fluttering by, and you had to snatch it on your pen and engrave it on the page before it vanished like a wisp. Writing was a real booger sometimes.

The muse entered Aidan, like a tiny voice, and he proceeded to scribble madly.

Nadia: *What a stupid question. You obviously have to save her, dummy. What are you asking me for?*

Aidan allowed that slightly hurtful response to process. Let the sting settle. Nadia was always brash but never ill-intentioned.

Aidan replied: *What can I even do? She's already dead.*

Nadia's words exploded out of him: *And she's hurting! And she's scared! And she asked YOU for help!*

Aidan: *But how can I even help?*

Nadia: *You can help by trying. I never know what I'm going to do, or how I'll do it, but I at least try. Do you want to be the person who doesn't help someone in trouble? If so, I'm ashamed to be a character inside your head. I oughta move out. Maybe I'll move into Neil Gaiman's head. Neil Gaiman is actually cool.*

A teardrop fell onto the page in a messy splat.

Aidan was officially hurting his own feelings. He wiped his eyes, gave a gross little snort, and sniffled the mucus away.

Aidan: *But I'm scared.*

Nadia: *Being brave doesn't mean you're not scared. It means doing things even though you're scared.*

Aidan set his pen down—cautiously—like it was a smoking barrel. Let the words cool on the page. He could be scared *and* brave at the same time? It sounded like baloney, but if Nadia said so, who was he to argue?

Nadia was the bravest girl in all of Aether.

Spools of twilight unraveled in oranges and pinks. Night fell darker than usual. Thicker, almost soupy. Stars were blacked out by a heavy sky full of invisible clouds. The possibility of rain was real.

Aidan geared up for the worst: rain boots, waterproof jacket, water-resistant flashlight. He packed his backpack full of all the things one might require on a haunted rendezvous: duct tape, his dad's old camera with infrared capability, a 26-ounce carton of Morton iodized salt in case he needed to make a protective salt circle. All those horror movie nights with Zephyr had prepared him for this moment.

As a last-minute thought, he wrote a brief message on a sticky note. He stuck it to the rim of Terrance's Yankees cap. He had a small errand to run first.

Stealth was not necessary sneaking out of Aidan's home. His dad slept like a coma patient and snored like the deforestation of the Amazon. As a result, his mom slept with the sort of earplugs you wear on a construction site.

With bike in tow, Aidan exited with extraordinary ease.

Aidan did not have a clip-on bike headlamp, but he did have ingenuity. He removed the duct tape from his backpack and fastened his flashlight onto the center of his handlebars. He looped the roll of tape several times over, crisscrossing for stability. Voilà! Headlamp à la mode.

Aidan mounted his bicycle and kicked off. With his slightly askew, heavy-duty flashlight illuminating the path ahead, he sailed off like a ship over a waveless sea.

Directly across the cul-de-sac to Terrance's house.

Aidan rolled up the driveway to the Adams's front porch and removed Terrance's hat from his backpack. He deliberated for a moment, then decided to hang it on the doorknob over leaving it on the welcome mat. It was less likely to be seen right away, but it was also less likely to be stepped on accidentally. Attached to the bill was a sticky note that said:

> Sorry for everything.
> —Aidan

Satisfied, Aidan mounted his bike again and stole off into the night.

The little sounds of summer darkness were a quiet orchestra. Trees rustled hauntingly in the wind. Crickets harped, and cicadas sang. Aidan's tires hummed against the cold asphalt.

That hum became a growl as he turned onto the gravel of Yeet Street.

The trees of that narrow, winding road clustered together like walls closing in. The darkness felt solid. Aidan felt claustrophobic despite being outdoors. With every turn, it seemed the trees might narrow into a sliver of road, and eventually, a dead end.

But the road ended the way it always did: in a wide-open field, interrupted only by the shadowy husk of a black locust tree, and the Witch House—pale, ancient, ever watching.

Aidan rode to the front porch and leaned his bike against the nearest pillar. Wrestled his flashlight out of what he realized was *too much* duct tape.

Once the flashlight was free, Aidan gave a nervous tug of his backpack straps.

He entered the Witch House. He did not close the door behind him.

Moonlight poured generously into the cavernous foyer, illuminating debris and the sparkle of broken glass. There were unexplored pathways on two separate levels—first and second floors—branching north and east and west. There was essentially everywhere to explore. All Aidan had really traveled was up.

"Hello?" Aidan called out uncertainly. "Gabby Caldwell? Are you there?"

There came a sound from deep within the house—like weight on a loose floorboard. Or a creaky door hinge. Perhaps it was just the old bones of the house settling. Either way, it sent a shiver up Aidan that started at his toes and zigzagged up to his scalp.

And then there was nothing.

Aidan waited for another sound, but the longer he waited, the more he was overwhelmed by the urge to get out. If he was going to do this, he had best do it already.

In video games, when exploration was involved, Aidan had a methodical approach: start left and explore in a clockwise motion. The method wasn't perfect, and it grew harder the larger the area was—sometimes he had to move clockwise in sections—but it was a start.

Aidan ventured left into the west wing.

The hallway was echoingly tall, making it appear narrower than it was. In reality, it was gargantuan, with doorways like arches under a bridge. The first room he came across was the library. Rolling ladders on fixed tracks reached higher-up shelves. Most books were rustic hardcovers made of leather, stamped in gold and silver foil. Some were in English—like an ancient copy of *The Wonderful Wizard of Oz*, laid out on a coffee table in the middle of the room, the cover and spine of which were hanging together by threads. Others were in a language Aidan did not recognize.

Next was a weaving room, filled with looms ranging from old to ancient—undoubtedly where Farah Yeet made her cursed curtains. A large power loom the size of an upright piano was strung with yarn where ivory keys might have been. Shelves were built into the walls, filled with color-coded spools of wool and cotton. The thing that stole Aidan's attention, however, was an unfinished tapestry hanging on the far back wall, ending in lines of unwoven yarn. The image it depicted was the silhouette of a man standing in a deep, dark forest. He was woven in such a jarring shade of black, he appeared to be cut out of the very fabric of shadow. Above him, written in the shape of the branches, were two words: *Blue Hill*. Below him, written in the roots of the trees, a single word that writhed like a worm beneath Aidan's skin: *Blåkulla*.

Somewhere in the vacuum of the Shadow Man's face, Aidan could almost feel his invisible eyes on him.

Yeah, no. Moving on.

Next was what was undoubtedly Farah Yeet's bedroom. The walls were painted as red as freshly spilled blood. Long black curtains swooped shadowlike over windows as tall as trees. A massive canopy bed was carved out of wood as dark as night. A full-body mirror was against the wall beside it. There was a cold, breathless fireplace, and above it, another tapestry. Aidan was unsure of its exact measurements, but he wanted to call it "life-size" because the woman depicted was the size of a real-life woman.

She was woven in excruciating detail, each threading as deliberate as a pixel, as poetic and refined as a brushstroke. She wore a long white dress with a mock neck, gathered sleeves, and layered ruffles all the way to her shoes. Her fiery red hair was cut into an almost boyishly short bob, with freckles speckled across the soft curve of her nose. She looked a bit like an older version of Aidan with enough confidence for them both. She posed in front of a tree that Aidan realized was the black locust tree out front. It was smaller here, but it bloomed behind her like a gentle green parasol.

Aidan felt drawn—mothlike—to the tapestry of the woman with hair like fire. There was just something about it that eluded words or reason. The mantelpiece was not so high that he could not touch its hem. He just wanted to feel the intertwining mosaic of texture beneath his fingertips. To see if it felt like it looked: like woven starlight.

If this was Farah Yeet, she looked nothing like Aidan imagined. She looked happy. Uncalloused by the world. She looked—

When his fingers touched the fabric, he felt an electric piercing, like a static shock. A long, cosmic needle threaded through Aidan's mind.

Aidan almost tripped backwards and fell. But whatever it was that snapped inside of his brain, the signal did not reach his fingers, telling him to break contact. In fact, it was quite the opposite, like an electrical current that refused to let go.

That's when Aidan heard the shadow of a breath and noticed the slightest movement—a twitch, a blink—in his right peripheral.

There was *someone else* in the room, hiding in the far back corner. Tucked behind an artificial potted plant with fronds and a decorative table littered with unlit candles of varying heights.

She was crouching low, peering over the edge of the table between fronds like some jungle explorer. She was staring right at him—eyes wide and full of interest.

When she realized she and Aidan were making eye contact, she jumped back with a start. Then she waved timidly. "Oh, hey."

Aidan let go of the tapestry and ran for the door.

He ran down the towering hallway and into the foyer faster than he could take a breath.

Aidan came to a breakneck halt. What was he doing? He came here to *help*. Was he really running away?

Slowly, Aidan rotated until his back faced the open front door.

"Gabby Caldwell?" he said.

"Hello," a girl's voice replied nervously.

A disembodied voice.

It seemed to come from the very fabric of the house, everywhere and nowhere all at once.

Aidan tripped over his own feet and landed on his tailbone. Spider-crawled backwards until he was outside the front door, at the edge of the porch.

"Please don't go!" said the voice. It sounded close—as if the body it belonged to was standing just inside the doorway. "I'm not bad. I promise you, I'm not."

Aidan didn't dare move. He repeated in his mind, over and over: *What would Nadia do? What would Nadia do?* But he couldn't form an intelligent response to that question.

He was distracted by how sad the voice sounded.

"Why can't I see you?" said Aidan.

"I didn't want to scare you," said the voice. "Sometimes I'm covered in blood, sometimes I'm not. I don't really have control over it."

Aidan nodded slowly. That seemed like a reasonable enough explanation. Slowly, he climbed to his feet. Dusted his pants off. "I'd like to see you."

There was a heavy, tangible pause in response.

"It's okay if you don't feel comfortable—" Aidan started to say.

What happened next was like a magic trick. There was a quiet sound, like the ripple of fabric, and then Gabby stood not three feet inside the doorway. Hair like moonlight, with tan skin that looked like it'd never missed a day in the sun. She was wearing the same maroon tank top, white drawstring shorts, and flip-flops he'd seen four days ago. She was *not* wearing a bucket of blood, thank God. She looked anxious but also eager.

"You're not covered in blood," Aidan observed stupidly.

Gabby glanced down, confirming for herself, then nodded. "For now."

Aidan nodded slowly.

"Do you promise not to run away if I start bleeding?" Gabby asked, perhaps a little too eagerly.

"Oh," said Aidan awkwardly. "I mean, um."

"I promise I don't do it on purpose. Bleeding out of your skull is bad enough. Having people scream and run away from you is way worse."

"Does it hurt?" Aidan asked.

Gabby bit her lip, considering. "Kind of? It's like you hurt yourself a long time ago, and you're not in physical pain anymore, but you're haunted by what the pain felt like. Like a ghost pain. But, um. Not a literal ghost. I realize *I'm* a literal ghost. I mean it more in a metaphorical sense. If that makes sense." Gabby cocked her head slightly. "Does that make sense?"

Aidan continued to nod slowly.

"I feel like I'm talking a lot," said Gabby. "If you want me to stop, I can totally stop. It's just been a long time since I've talked to another person, so if you want me to shut up, just say the word, and I will totally shut up. You know what? I'm going to shut up. Okay. Shutting up now."

"No no no," said Aidan. "What you said makes sense. And I don't think you're talking too much. Sorry. I've just never talked to a ghost before, and it's not what I expected."

"*Good* not-what-you-expected, or *bad* not-what-you-expected?"

"I mean, I was worried you might try to kill me, so definitely more *good* not-what-I-expected than bad."

Gabby smiled. It was a nice smile—like Aidan's mom's smile—honest, and simple, and full of joy. It radiated something warm and contagious.

"Are you really Gabby Caldwell?" Aidan asked.

Gabby nodded. Then hesitated. "I think so? It feels like my name."

"*You think so?*"

Gabby looked a little sad. "I think my memory's fading. I don't remember much."

"What don't you remember?"

Gabby shrugged. "Who was I? How did I get here? Why?"

Oof, Aidan thought. That was a lot not to remember.

"I remember I was born in 1988," Gabby mused hopefully. "And it was 2004 when I died. That's when the new Usher album came out." She frowned. "Which I don't remember anything about, but I *feel like* it was good? Anyway, that would make me . . ." Gabby scrunched her face, doing the math in her head. "Sixteen years old!"

Gabby looked positively proud. Aidan hated to ask what he was about to ask.

"Do you remember how you died?" he asked timidly.

Gabby shook her head. She didn't hesitate. She simply did not know.

"Can you leave the house?" Aidan asked.

Again, Gabby shook her head. This time, she looked sad.

"What happens if you try?" Aidan said.

Gabby observed the doorframe reluctantly. Looked straight ahead, resolute.

Reached her hand out and took several small steps forwards.

The moment Gabby's index finger reached an invisible line that separated outside from inside, her fingertip disappeared. To Aidan, observing from outside the door, her finger looked hollow, like a hologram that became transparent at certain angles.

Gabby pulled her finger back with a subtle *whoosh.* Everything was intact—although she and Aidan stared at her hand to assess the damage.

"Weird," said Aidan, breathless.

"It feels even weirder," said Gabby. "Like dipping your finger in water, but without the wetness."

"What happens if you go all the way?"

"I disappear."

Aidan's eyes widened in alarm.

"Not forever," Gabby clarified. "It's like . . . how I disappear every day when the sun comes up. When I do, it feels like it takes up time. Like sleeping. When you sleep, it feels like time has passed, right? When I leave the house fully, it's like how I disappear every morning, except sooner. Sometimes, when I get really sad and lonely . . . I just walk outside and disappear. It's like sleeping to escape your problems."

Gabby gave a sad little laugh.

Awkward silence ensued.

"Okay, enough about me," said Gabby. She sat down cross-legged inside the front door. "I want to talk about you."

"Me?" said Aidan. "Oh, I dunno. I'm not interesting. You're a ghost trapped inside the Witch House. I feel like we should be talking about you. So we can figure out your unfinished business and free you from this house or whatever."

"Unfinished business?"

"Yeah. I mean. Don't all ghosts have that?"

Gabby rolled her eyes. "Bro, I don't know *anything* about that. I don't know my own Social Security number. All I know is that talking about me is depressing, and you're an author, and I want to know what happens next with Nadia and Kai."

Aidan's eyeballs inflated like tiny balloons outside his skull.

"Sit down!" said Gabby, patting the floor in front of her. "I get to ask you three questions. Then we can keep talking about how dead and cursed I am."

The only thing more worrisome to Aidan than the ghost of Gabby Caldwell having read his most private creative writing was how eager he was for *feedback*. Secretly, *everyone* wants feedback on their writing. The trick is that everyone only wants praise and not soul-crushing criticism. However, Gabby had already told Aidan that she thought what he wrote was beautiful, so feedback from Gabby seemed like the best place to start. It also helped that she was a ghost and had been dead for twenty years, which somehow made her feel less threatening, critically.

"Okay . . . ," said Aidan. He cautiously folded his legs and sat down. "What do you want to know?"

"Is the story complete or is it ongoing?" said Gabby.

"Ongoing. I don't know how to end it."

Gabby pumped her fist and grunted, "Yes!"

"How far did you get?"

"Oh, I read the whole thing."

"You *what*?"

"I actually started *rereading* it, I was so into it."

Aidan's jaw hung open like a drawbridge.

"Dude, why are you surprised?" said Gabby. "It was good! My only complaint is that I want more, and I need it, stat. So if you don't mind . . ." Gabby made a gentle shooing motion with her hand. "Shoo, shoo! Don't come back until you have more. More pages, please."

"Oh, um . . . okay?" Aidan started to stand.

"I'm kidding!" said Gabby, laughing. "Please don't leave. I'm so lonely. Sit back down. I have more questions. Please sit."

Aidan sat back down nervously. Gabby Caldwell was . . . not what he expected. Aidan wasn't sure if that came from her being three years older than him, or being born in 1988, or being dead for twenty years. Maybe all of the above?

"So Nadia and Kai end up together, right?" said Gabby. "No, wait—don't tell me. Okay, tell me. That's not a spoiler, right? They *have* to end up together."

"I mean, I'd *like* for them to," said Aidan, blushing. "But it's complicated—"

"What?" said Gabby. She grabbed her head with both hands. "You're telling me there's a possibility these beautiful, star-crossed lovers *won't* end up together?"

"It's just, there are external factors to consider . . . ," said Aidan. The external factors were Aidan's very real feelings for Kai—the real Kai. And if Nadia and Kai "got together," then . . . they were together! And then what was the point of Aidan writing this story anymore?

The truth was, Aidan needed this story. He needed the open-endedness of it all. If Nadia and Kai had hurdles to overcome, then it was okay for Aidan to be where he was. There was hope.

"External factors?" said Gabby, scrunching her brow.

Aidan held up two fingers. "You've asked two questions. You get one more. Then we talk about you. Deal?"

Gabby smiled slyly. "Deal."

Why did Aidan feel like he'd walked into a trap?

"This is a *very* romantic story," said Gabby teasingly. "I've *never* met a romantic, sensitive boy like you who could write something like this."

"Is that a question?" said Aidan impatiently.

"My question is: Do you have someone *you* love? A girl? Or maybe . . . someone else?"

Aidan started to sweat.

"Maybe a"—Gabby leaned forwards and whispered—"mermaid?"

"Okay." Aidan climbed to his feet. "That's enough of that. It's late. I need to get home."

"Oh, c'mon." Gabby pouted. "I was just teasing. I'm sorry."

"I'll come back tomorrow," said Aidan.

Gabby perked up. "Really?"

"I'll bring my friends."

Gabby's eyes grew wide, and she nearly tipped over backwards. "All of them?"

"I need their help if I'm going to figure out how to help you. Terrance is smart, Zephyr knows about ghosts, and Ka-*uhhhhh* . . ." Aidan trailed off when he realized that he was about to say the name of the love interest of Gabby's new favorite book. Crap. "Gabby, I'm going to make a deal with you: I will keep writing chapters of this story and bringing them over for you to read *if*—and only *if*—"

"Deal," said Gabby.

"I haven't even finished," said Aidan.

"Right. Sorry."

"You cannot," said Aidan, "under any circumstance, tell my friends about this story, okay? Not Zephyr, not Terrance, not . . . none of them."

"*Pfft*," said Gabby, rolling her eyes. "Boys are so weird. Deal, bro. I will tell *not none of* your bros about your cute little romance story. Although it is their loss because they would *swoon*."

"I'm serious. I want to hear you swear."

"What, like the f-word?"

"What? No! Like, swear on a Bible or something."

"I'll be honest, I've never been a big fan of the Bible," said Gabby. "You'd have better luck having me swear on a Harry Potter book—like *Order of the Phoenix*! Hey, did J. K. Rowling ever finish writing those?"

Aidan didn't want to talk about J. K. Rowling. "How about a pinkie promise?"

Aidan stuck out his pinkie as he said it. Only then did he find Gabby staring just a little too intently at his pinkie. A second later, he realized he was wondering the exact same thing she was probably wondering.

"I've never touched someone before," said Gabby. "I mean . . . you know what I mean, right? Not since I've been dead."

Aidan nodded, sort of breathlessly. "Can you touch things?"

"I wrote inside your notebook, didn't I?" said Gabby defensively. And then she softened. "But it takes concentration. Otherwise, my hand goes right through things."

Aidan took a step towards the open doorway. Raised his pinkie so that it was inside the invisible house perimeter.

"Promise?" he said.

Gabby swallowed. Raised her hand until it was barely a touch away.

Hooked her pinkie in his.

Her touch felt less like skin and more like energy, thrumming. Aidan had anticipated coldness, but her touch was cool, like a breeze.

"You feel so warm," said Gabby.

When Aidan met her gaze, he nearly jumped. A single red line streamed down her face. A tear made of blood.

Aidan was surprised to find he was more concerned than afraid. "Are you okay?"

Gabby wiped her wrist across her face, smearing the blood. She did a double take when she saw red.

"Great," she muttered. "I'm sorry. This is so gross."

She cried harder.

It reminded Aidan of those quiet times when he caught his mom crying alone. She always pretended that she hadn't been, and Aidan played along.

Aidan was not a brave person. But it didn't take bravery so much as heart to do what he did next. If there was one thing Aidan was not short on, it was heart. He stepped inside the doorway and wrapped his arms around Gabby Caldwell—wet and sticky and cold—and hugged her.

Gabby at first seemed horrified. She was bleeding all over the first living person she had met in twenty years. Any semblance of dignity crumbled as she hugged Aidan back—squeezed him fiercely—and sobbed.

"I don't want to be here," she cried. "Please help me. I can't do this anymore."

"I'm going to help you," said Aidan. Even though he had no idea how. "I promise."

After a long, hard cry, and a hug that absorbed hurt like a sponge, Gabby released Aidan and wiped her face. She was no longer covered in blood. Aidan glanced down at himself, shocked to find no trace of blood on him either.

When he met Gabby's gaze again, she was misty-eyed, but smiling.

"I feel so stupid," she said. "I don't even know your name."

Aidan blinked and realized he was teary as well. He sniffled, shamelessly wiped the evidence away, and said,

"My name is Aidan."

CHAPTER 7

Pineapples (without Sunglasses)

Aidan *tried* to change into his pajamas. He only made it halfway. He sat on his bed for a second, just to process everything.

The next moment, he was fast asleep.

He slept until noon the next day. When he opened his eyes, rolling over to glance at his phone in a groggy haze, his friends had all but blown it up with dynamite.

Terrance: **Dude, why is my Yankees cap on my front doorknob with a note with your name on it, Aidan?**

Zephyr: **Did you go into the witch house AGAIN? WITHOUT US??**

Kai: **Aidan can you return our calls? We're worried**

Kai: **Btw sorry for being a butthole. You didn't deserve that**

Aidan exited his texts and looked at his missed calls: one from Terrance, one from Zephyr, and—Aidan had to collect his jaw from the floor—*fourteen missed calls* from Kai Pendleton.

Aidan *wanted* to be excited about receiving this much attention from Kai. Instead, it just gave him anxiety.

He barely had a moment to process it all when there were exactly two and a half knocks on his bedroom door. Before that third knock could fully register, Zephyr, Terrance, and Kai barged into his bedroom like federal agents on a drug bust.

In that instant, Aidan was acutely aware that he was wearing nothing but bright pink boxers with pineapples on them. He yelped and pulled his blanket around his waist.

"Whoa, hey!" said Aidan. "Am I allowed to have just a modicum of privacy in my own bedroom?"

Terrance rolled his eyes impatiently. "Come on, Aidan. We're all boys. You don't have anything we don't."

"I mean, I don't know about you guys, but I'm circumcised," said Zephyr, "so he *might* have something I don't."

"Ew, gross!" said Kai. "Nobody wants to hear about your weird little circumcision."

"I also don't have pink boxers with cute little pineapples on them," said Zephyr. "They *were* pineapples, right?"

Aidan pulled his blanket all the way over his head like a burial shroud.

"Were the pineapples wearing sunglasses, or did I just imagine that?" said Zephyr.

Aidan inspected his underwear underneath the blanket. No, the pineapples were not wearing sunglasses. Thank God.

"The level of attention you're paying to Aidan's underwear is miraculous," said Terrance. "Can you imagine if you had this much focus at school? You'd have good grades!"

"Hey, it's not my fault Aidan's underwear is more interesting than integers and rational numbers."

"Zephyr?" said Kai.

"Yeah?"

"Can we stop talking about Aidan's underwear?"

Zephyr rolled his eyes and gave an exasperated sigh.

"The pineapples do not have sunglasses," Aidan announced from underneath his blanket.

"What?" said Zephyr in disbelief. "No way!"

Aidan pulled the blanket off his head. "But I'll give you an A-minus for effort."

"Yes!" Zephyr pumped his fist. "I got an A-minus in Underwear, booyah!"

"Can I *please* get dressed now?" said Aidan.

Once Aidan was dressed, he was painfully aware that he had some explaining to do.

The thing was, there were certain parts of the truth that Aidan was not comfortable disclosing: spiraling into his Darkness for the better part of a week. His notebook. And by association, the message *inside* of his notebook. Aidan decided to omit his *first* trip to the Witch House yesterday—the one with his mom—and skip straight to his middle-of-the-night trip.

What he *did* tell his friends was: he went to the Witch House in the middle of the night because he was worried about the ghost of Gabby Caldwell. They talked. She was actually really nice, if a bit talkative (for a ghost). Aidan explained the apparent mechanics of the curse: she only appeared at night, she couldn't leave the house, and her memory was shot. Aidan pinkie-promised that he would help her, they hugged, and they said goodbye. Aidan came home and slept in until noon. Which brings us to—

"Okay, tell me what you're thinking," said Aidan. "You're looking at me weird."

"I mean," said Kai, "I dunno, man."

"It's a lot," said Terrance.

"Are you *sure* that's how things went down?" Zephyr asked.

Aidan couldn't believe not a single one of his friends believed him.

"You saw her!" Aidan exclaimed. "You *literally* saw a ghost. What exactly is it that you have such a hard time believing?"

In that moment, Aidan decided that he didn't care. Or rather, he *refused* to care. Gabby had asked *him* for help. And Aidan was going to help her—with or without his friends.

Aidan stormed into his closet, pulled out his notebook, and opened to the last page—only to rip it clean out. He shoved the page in his friends' faces.

"Do you think I made *this* up?" Aidan demanded.

All three boys read and then reread the same horrific cry for help handwritten in blood: *I only appear at night. I'm trapped here. Help me.*

The mood in the room softened rather than intensified. While there was a lot to find alarming on that page, Zephyr, Terrance, and Kai all seemed to realize that maybe they had misjudged the situation.

"So," said Kai, "you made a pinkie promise with the ghost of Gabby Caldwell?"

Aidan offered a feeble nod. "Not that I know how to help her."

"You *hugged* the ghost of Gabby Caldwell?" said Zephyr, wagging his eyebrows.

"It wasn't that sort of hug."

"So what now?" said Terrance.

Aidan shrugged. "What are you guys doing tonight at, say, midnight?"

CHAPTER 8

The Backwards Lady

Aidan answered the incoming call. "Zephyr, where are you?"

"The good news is, I'm out of my house," said Zephyr, laughing uneasily.

"What's the bad news?"

"What if I told you I was stuck in a tree?"

"Good grief," said Aidan. "Okay, we're coming."

Aidan hung up.

"What's the holdup?" said Kai.

Aidan, Terrance, and Kai were gathered at their agreed meeting spot—Curtain Falls Park, which convened in the triangle between Aidan and Terrance's cul-de-sac, Zephyr's house, and the trailer park where Kai lived.

"He's stuck in a tree," said Aidan.

"Of course he is," said Terrance. "Where else would he be?"

Aidan, Terrance, and Kai mounted their bikes and booked it over to Zephyr's house.

Zephyr had the biggest house of all, on the corner of Ivy Lane and Dominion Drive—a five-bedroom, four-bath lakeside property with aged white cedar siding, white trim, and a guesthouse. Zephyr had four siblings—Winston (twenty-two), Xavier (eighteen), Yvonne (sixteen), and happy little accident Adelaide (ten), with whom they had to start the alphabet over. Mr. Windon was owner and CEO of

Fuhgedaboudit Furniture, a New England retail chain. "Mattress Marty" was a local celebrity, known for starring in his own TV and radio spots, making outrageous sports bets, and giving away free mattresses when the Sox win big.

Aidan, Terrance, and Kai hopped the curb, rode across the Windons' manicured lawn, and stopped beneath an oak tree with an easily accessible branch growing outside Zephyr's second-floor bedroom window. To be fair, it was truly massive. Zephyr had bitten off more than he could chew.

"Hi, guys," said Zephyr, cheerfully, twenty feet above them. "How's it going?"

"You're stuck in a tree, Zephyr," said Terrance. "That's how it's going. We're wasting precious ghost-hunting hours rescuing you like a cat."

"Terrance." Zephyr placed a tender hand over his heart. "Are you actually *excited* about ghost hunting?"

"Oh my God," said Terrance, rolling his eyes.

"Look at Mister Science over here." Zephyr pretended to wipe away a proud tear. "Look how far he's come."

"That's back when ghosts were *pseudo*science. But now we know that they're *actual* science. Zephyr Octavius Windon, what I'm actually doing is *important, scientific work*."

"Okay, guys," said Aidan. "I think we're getting a little off track—"

"Listen here, you little buttsnack!" Zephyr exclaimed. "You know how much I hate my middle name!"

Terrance cradled his arms like he was holding an invisible baby, rocking them as he sang, *"Zephyr Octavius in the treetops / When the bough breaks, Lil Zephyr will drop—"*

"I'm going to murder you," said Zephyr. He climbed down the tree angrily. "Then you can be dead buddies with Gabby Caldwell and do all the dead science you want from beyond the grave."

Terrance continued to sing, only now he was doing a little dance along with it. *"Zephyr Octavius sitting in a tree / K-I-S-S-I-N-G—"*

"That doesn't even make any sense!" Zephyr screamed. He descended branches like a squirrel with a death wish. "Am I kissing myself?"

"Zephyr, you are doing that very fast," said Aidan anxiously. "Please don't hurt yourself."

"Terrance, stop provoking him!" said Kai.

Terrance was now singing to the tune of the *George of the Jungle* theme song. *"Zephyr, Zephyr Octavius, small as he can be—"* He imitated George's ululating call. *"Watch out for that tree!"*

Zephyr dropped from the bottom branch onto the lawn and exclaimed, "YOU'RE DEAD."

Terrance pumped his arms in the air and exclaimed, "We did it!"

Zephyr came to a dead halt, mid-lunge, arms extended with malintent. "We did it?" He looked down at the ground beneath his feet. Stepped in place to test the integrity of the terrain. "We did it!"

Terrance and Zephyr clapped hands and proceeded to do what appeared to be their very own secret handshake. Either that or they were making it up as they went along. There were lots of steps, slaps, spins, and some mild choreography involved.

"Can we go now?" said Kai impatiently.

Zephyr had planned ahead, parking his bicycle discreetly behind the hollies underneath his bedroom window.

From there, it was smooth sailing to the Witch House.

The air felt different tonight. Like when the temperature drops before a storm and the sky turns green and strange. They rode their bikes to the front porch of the Witch House, dropping them in the tangle of grass. When Aidan reached the front door, he wondered if he should offer some sage advice before they had their first conversation with a ghost.

"She's really nice," said Aidan. "If she starts bleeding out of her head, try not to freak out." To Aidan's own surprise, he added, "I think it happens when she's emotional."

How Aidan came to that conclusion was beyond him. But it *felt* like the truth. His friends nodded in varying degrees of acceptance. Who were they to argue?

Aidan started to open the door.

A pair of hands grabbed the door from the other side, stopping it.

Visible fingers wrapped around the edge of the door. Slowly, a head peeked from behind. It was Gabby—but her usual tan glow was gone. She looked pale. Afraid.

Aidan jumped with a start, and Terrance and Kai screamed, and Zephyr did both, then prayed Hail Mary under his breath.

"This isn't a good time," said Gabby, glancing sideways. "You should go."

"What?" said Aidan. "Why?"

"She's here," said Gabby, terrified.

"*Who's* here?"

"The Backwards Lady," said Gabby in a whisper.

There was a sound from somewhere deep within the house, probably an upper floor—singular and indistinct—like the crunch of several small twigs being broken in half.

"I have to go," said Gabby. "I'm sorry. Please don't come inside."

Gabby appeared to have ditched her flip-flops in the name of stealth as she abandoned the front door. Her bare feet slapped across the tile floor, off into the distance.

The front door creaked slowly open, revealing an empty, moonlit foyer, littered with broken glass and debris.

"The *Backwards* Lady?" Kai repeated.

"Nope," said Terrance, shaking his head. "I'm out."

"Yeah, I'm pretty sure I've seen this movie," said Zephyr. "If we go inside there, we all die."

"I'm going inside," said Aidan.

Once again, Aidan surprised himself with his own words.

"You're doing *what now*?" said Terrance.

"Yeah, no," said Kai. "I'm not letting you do that."

"It sounds like she's in trouble!" Aidan protested. "Besides, I promised I'd help her."

"You promised you'd break a curse," said Kai. "Not fight some Backwards Lady!"

"What if this Backwards Lady is part of the curse?"

Kai opened his mouth. Then closed it and made an exasperated, angry sound through his teeth.

"I'm not going to fight her," said Aidan. "I just want to see her.

Maybe talk to her. If she's somehow keeping Gabby prisoner here, maybe I can negotiate with her."

"Aidan, I swear to God," said Kai. "If you go into that house, I am *not* going in there to protect you. You'll be on your own."

"Good!" Aidan shot back. "I don't want you to."

Aidan briefly wondered if he was actually Aidan, or if Nadia had somehow taken control.

"I don't want to put you guys in danger," said Aidan, softer. "You didn't make a promise to Gabby. I did."

"Aidan—" Kai protested.

"It'll just be a minute. I'll poke around and come right back out. If the coast is clear, I'll let you know."

Kai pursed his lips.

"I'll be fine—" Aidan started to say.

"If anything happens"—Kai cut him off—"and I mean *anything*—I want you to yell for help. I'll be right here. You promise?"

"I promise."

There was a moment of tangible tension. Aidan wasn't sure what it felt like to everyone else, but to *him*, it felt like a hug would have filled the pause nicely. The longer he stood there, the more he longed for one. So he quickly turned and marched into the house.

Aidan stopped in the middle of the foyer.

"GABBY?" Aidan called out.

There was—unsurprisingly—no response.

"She obviously doesn't want to be found," said Kai impatiently. "Can we go now?"

"BACKWARDS LADY?" Aidan shouted.

"Jesus Christ," Kai mumbled to himself, then mimicked Zephyr in crossing himself, even though he wasn't Catholic.

Aidan glanced between the first and second floors. He looked up at the part of the balcony where the stairs to the second floor ended and the stairs to the third floor ascended behind the east wall. And there—for a fraction of a moment—Aidan saw the hem of a white gown, and a pale foot step backwards behind the wall.

"Holy crap," he said. "I think I just saw her."

"Nope," said Terrance, shaking his head. "Nuh-uh."

"Aidan, get out of there," said Kai. He looked scared. "Please."

"Holy Mary, Mother of God, pray for us sinners, now and at the hour of our death, amen . . . ," Zephyr mumbled.

Aidan was about to relent. This was officially scary. Even Nadia would tell him to eff this noise.

As Aidan started to nod, turning back towards the front doorway, the door slammed shut—completely on its own.

Aidan's stomach dropped.

"Aidan!" Kai screamed.

"Oh my God," said Terrance. "OH MY GOD."

"Hail Mary, full of Grace, the Lord is with thee—!" Zephyr prayed frantically.

Kai and Terrance banged on the front door.

When Aidan's body finally caught up to the horror that his brain was comprehending, he ran to the front door and wrestled the doorknob violently. The door did not give. It gave no indication that it was even *capable* of opening. It was the Red Door all over again.

"G-g-g-g-g-guys!" said Aidan. "I'm s-s-s-s-scared!"

"Find a window!" Kai exclaimed. "They're all broken, right?"

"You guys," said Terrance nervously. "Something's wrong with the windows."

"Blessed art thou among women and blessed is the fruit of thy womb, Jesus," prayed Zephyr.

Aidan noticed it the moment Terrance said it.

All the windows.

Every single window in the house.

They were whole again. Not a single window was broken.

He ran to the nearest window, which Kai slammed with the palms of his hands. Aidan ran his fingers along the edges, searching for a latch or lever.

There was nothing.

"Aidan, back up!" said Kai.

When Aidan looked up, Kai had a bike. He held the handlebars with one hand and the bike seat with the other. He wasn't going to ride it. He intended to throw it.

Aidan backed away and not a moment too soon. Kai spun one hundred and eighty degrees, lifting the bike off the ground with sheer momentum, then releasing it. The bike hit the glass with an expensive-sounding crash.

It didn't break through, but it did leave a spiderweb of cracks.

The sound of cracking continued, and for a second, Aidan was flooded with relief. He was saved.

Then he realized the cracks in the window were retracting.

Resealing.

Disappearing.

"No," said Kai. He pounded on the glass with both fists. "No!"

Aidan was going to die.

No sooner did Aidan have that thought than he heard a sound, like sticks breaking. He turned around slowly.

At the top of the stairs was a woman. She wore a white dress with long sleeves. Long black hair reached halfway down her back. Aidan saw this clearly because her back was facing him.

She took a step backwards. Down the stairs.

The way her leg moved was all wrong. It bent backwards at the knee, and her leg made a crackling sound. She took another step, and her other leg broke backwards as well. Then her arms broke at the elbow, bending backwards, and each of her fingers snapped backwards, one at a time, so that her palms faced outward.

Aidan now fully comprehended Gabby's fear of the Backwards Lady.

His heart was beating so hard, he expected it to explode.

His leg felt warm and he realized he was peeing his pants. Never, in all his days, did he expect peeing his pants to be the least of his worries.

He felt woozy. Little black dots and squiggles littered his vision like microorganisms in a petri dish. The world faded to black around the Backwards Lady. Aidan floated in a void of space.

As the Backwards Lady descended upon him, she parted the black waterfall of hair from the back of her head. Behind the hair was a face Aidan recognized.

His.

Aidan was stiff as a board as he vomited. He fell backwards into a blackness that swallowed him whole.

CHAPTER 9

Happy Fun Times at the Witch House

Aidan awoke to four people standing and kneeling over him. Among them was Gabby Caldwell, kneeling the closest to him and crying.

His friends stood farther back. Only Kai looked directly at him. Zephyr and Terrance were preoccupied by the presence of the *actual* ghost of Gabby Caldwell. Their eyes were like golf balls.

"I told you not to come in, Aidan!" Gabby sobbed. "I *told* you! Why didn't you listen?"

Kai sniffled. Aidan noticed the glint of wetness under Kai's eyes before he rubbed his face discreetly. Had *he* been crying?

Aidan sat up, feeling a pantheon of pains across his body—specifically where he must have hit the ground when he fainted. Then he realized his clothing felt weird, and he glanced down.

He was wearing a dress.

An ancient-looking white dress with a mock neck, gathered sleeves, and layered ruffles. It was slightly too long, extending to his high-top sneakers—the only article of clothing he'd come here in.

"WHAT AM I WEARING?!" Aidan exclaimed.

His friends shuffled awkwardly in response.

Gabby Caldwell, however, cracked a grin, despite her tears. "Oh, that old thing? Just something lying around."

"Okay, but *why am I wearing it*?"

"Well, *Aidan Cross*, there's no need for embarrassment, but you peed your pants, and you puked all over yourself. Death has not taken away my sense of smell, and you did *not* smell good."

If Gabby was trying to convince Aidan there was no need for embarrassment, she was failing spectacularly. He was mortified.

"Don't worry, I didn't change you myself," she said, smiling slyly. "I asked your friend Kai Pendrag—I mean, *Pendleton*—to clean you off and change your clothes."

To Aidan's absolute horror, Gabby winked.

She knew. Of course she knew! She'd read everything he'd written of *Fire & Water*! How could she *not* know?

Fortunately, Kai didn't notice her winking. He was too busy blushing. "Don't worry, I didn't . . . um . . . look at anything. Or do anything weird." Kai seemed to realize he was making things worse with every word he said. Naturally, he kept talking. "Gabby told me to. I would have left you in your puke clothes."

Aidan felt his own face turn into a space heater.

"Thanks for changing my puke clothes anyway," said Aidan—mostly to shut Kai up. But he also meant it. The smell of puke made Aidan want to puke. The *thought* of the smell of puke made Aidan want to puke. Just thinking about it, *Aidan wanted to puke*. He had a sensitive gag reflex.

Aidan had the terrible idea to sniff the dress, and he cringed. It may not have smelled like puke and pee, but it *did* smell like dust and mothballs. "This is Farah Yeet's dress, isn't it?"

"I mean, they could be *anyone's* clothes," said Gabby. "This house has been around since the 1920s. Although if it *is* Farah Yeet's dress, she must be a woman of incredibly modern tastes. The tag says it's from Wet Seal."

Aidan, Zephyr, Terrance, and Kai blinked slowly. Between the four of them, they had not one single clue what a Wet Seal was.

"Hey, don't worry!" said Gabby. "You look cute. Right, Kai? Doesn't he look cute?"

Kai's face turned the color of Mars. "What?! I mean, um. He looks fine." He looked at Aidan directly and blushed even harder. "You look fine. It's fine."

Gabby was smiling so big, it threatened to split her face in two. This might have been the single greatest moment of her life. Or death. Whatever.

"Aren't you going to ask *me* if *I* think Aidan looks cute?" asked Zephyr. "Because *I'm* comfortable enough in my masculinity to admit Aidan looks cute."

Aidan buried his face in his hands, wishing he could disappear.

"What about you, Terrance?" said Zephyr. "Don't you think Aidan looks cute?"

"Personally?" said Terrance. "I think he looks like one of my grandma's creepy porcelain dolls. No offense, Aidan."

"None taken," Aidan sobbed into his hands.

There was a moment of silence as everyone gestated the fact that Aidan was not dead—Aidan included. When Aidan finally removed his hands from his face, he realized the windows of the foyer were once again shattered. The door was wide open. The Backwards Lady *felt* like a dream.

"Did that really happen?" said Aidan.

"Which part?" said Kai. "The part where you walked into this house like an idiot, and the door slammed behind you, and we couldn't open it?"

"Or when all the windows fixed themselves, and we couldn't break them?" said Terrance.

"Or when a *literal* Backwards Lady came *Snap, Crackle* and *Pop*ping down the stairs like a Rice Krispies Treat?" said Zephyr, shuddering.

"Did you see the face on the back of her head?" said Aidan.

"What, like Voldemort?" said Gabby.

"Sort of," said Aidan. In truth, the face he saw was much more upsetting than He-Who-Must-Not-Be-Named.

Kai shook his head. "I didn't see that. Once you fainted, everything went normal. The windows were broken, the door could open, and the Backwards Lady just . . . disappeared."

"So the Backwards Lady has a Voldemort on the back of her head?" Zephyr asked casually. "What'd it look like?"

Aidan didn't want to talk about that. Instead, he attempted to stand. His legs wobbled, but he managed. The hem of his dress touched the floor.

"When did you have time to change my clothes?" said Aidan.

"Dude, you've been out for a hot minute," said Terrance.

"A hot minute?" said Zephyr. "Try *fifteen* of 'em! We were this close to calling nine-one-one." He held his index finger and thumb a centimeter apart. "*Thisssss* close. Like the size of a Yankee Stadium wiener close."

Terrance rolled his eyes but chose not to take Zephyr's bait.

Aidan patted the ruffles of his dress for his phone—which was obviously not there. This thing didn't even have pockets.

Terrance was one step ahead of him. He'd apparently pocketed Aidan's phone for safekeeping. He handed it back. Aidan looked at the time.

"Oof," said Aidan. "It's late."

Zephyr gave a dazed nod. Self-proclaimed ghost hunter or not, he looked tired.

"We should go home and recoup," said Kai.

Gabby pouted. Now that the Backwards Lady was gone, she looked like she could talk the night away. "Oh. Okay. Yeah, you guys need to sleep, huh?"

Terrance stared at Gabby like the anomaly she was. "How are you real?"

"What?" said Gabby. "You mean as a ghost?"

"Sure."

Gabby shrugged sheepishly. "I dunno. I honestly don't know a lot of things. Like how I died. Why I'm stuck here. Why there's a Backwards Lady who lurks around sometimes. Or . . . *anything*, really. I was hoping you guys could maybe help me figure all that out."

Aidan glanced between his friends as they processed this rather big ask. Sure, Aidan had promised to help Gabby—and he would—but it'd be so much easier with the help of his friends.

"Well, you're in luck," said Terrance. "Because I was voted in our school's yearbook as Most Likely to Solve a One-Hundred-Year-Old Mystery. Which, at first, I thought was stupid. But now I think it might be destiny. *Metaphorical* destiny. Real destiny is fringe theory and scientifically unsound."

"You're *also* in luck," said Zephyr, "because there are some who call me the resident ghost expert."

"Literally no one has ever called you that," said Terrance.

"Name one other person who's hosted a ghost-hunting documentary here!" Zephyr shot back. "Name *one*!"

"My mom knew you when you were alive," said Kai quietly.

Everyone looked at Kai.

"Maybe she knows something," he added solemnly. "It's gotta be worth a shot, right?"

Gabby sniffled, overwhelmed by this outpouring of support. "Thanks, guys. This means a lot to me."

There was a moment of quiet hopefulness. They were going to help Gabby. Or at least try.

In that instant, Aidan glanced from Gabby to Kai.

Back to Gabby.

Back to Kai.

"Hey, guys, is it okay if I have a conversation with Gabby, um . . . privately?" Aidan asked.

Zephyr, Terrance, and Kai stared at Aidan as if he'd asked what the square root of a Yankee Stadium wiener was.

Zephyr grinned and waggled his eyebrows. "Look at this guy! He's wearing a dress and *still* killing the ladies."

Terrance elbowed Zephyr and said, "Dude, you can't say that when the girl is dead."

"Oh my God, you guys," said Aidan. "This is definitely not that sort of conversation."

Gabby, however, fully leaned into the speculation. She wrapped a long arm around Aidan's shoulders, grabbed his chin with her free hand, and tilted his head sideways. "He sure is cute, though. Look at that profile. That is a *good* profile."

Aidan grabbed Gabby's hand and dragged her towards the double doors at the back of the foyer. "Okay, Gabby and I are talking now. Feel free to go on without me. Good night, everyone. Sweet dreams. *Byeeeee.*"

Aidan and Gabby barged through the doors, which Aidan closed behind them and threw his back against dramatically.

The room turned out to be some archaic dining hall. At its center was a banquet table—the sort you see in movies with mansions and rich couples who no longer love each other sitting at opposite ends. Chairs were strung together by cobwebs. A stone fireplace jutted from the wall with a cold, dark mouth that hadn't tasted fire this century.

"You okay?" said Gabby. "You seem . . ."

Aidan was straddled in front of the double doors, arms out, like some unhinged starfish.

". . . on edge," Gabby finished.

"When I told you not to tell any of my friends about my notebook," said Aidan, choosing his words carefully, "there was a reason for that. And that reason is . . ."

The reason became lodged in the back of Aidan's throat. He couldn't say it out loud—even though it was painfully obvious. Aidan had never spoken this part of himself aloud.

"Dude, I get it," said Gabby.

Aidan blinked. "You do?"

"Yeah, man. You like Kai."

She said it so casually—so freely—it knocked the wind out of Aidan.

"He's cute," said Gabby. "He's kind. And maybe I'm wrong, but do I detect just a *hint* of bad boy flair? But it's totally superficial because he's obviously got a big, stupid heart."

Aidan was overwhelmed with feelings but couldn't put a single one into words.

"I mean, he's not my type," said Gabby. "Obviously. But I totally get why you're into him. I see that reflected in your writing. He seems like someone worth holding on to."

Aidan's breathing became choppy as tears welled up in his eyes.

"Oh!" said Gabby, panicking. "Hey. I didn't say anything wrong, did I?"

Aidan gave a wobbly shake of his head.

Gabby considered this for a moment. "Am I the only person who knows?"

Aidan nodded, and his vision became blurry, and he started to cry.

What a stupid, embarrassing thing to do in front of a ghost who's been dead for the past twenty years. She was living in purgatory in a haunted Witch House with some creepy Backwards Lady, and he had a crush on a boy. What a stupid, *stupid*—

Aidan felt the cool, breeze-like thrum of Gabby's touch. Her arms wrapped around him, and her head settled on top of his.

"Your secret is safe with me," said Gabby. "Sorry for teasing you. I'm just in love with the idea of you two together."

Aidan hugged Gabby back, and he cried harder.

His feelings came like a derecho, passing over the skyline of his heart just as fast. He hiccupped, then sniffed back the last lingering cloud of emotion and mucus, and he was okay. He was fine.

Aidan and Gabby pulled apart but said nothing. What do you say after something like this?

"So what's your type anyway?" Aidan asked. Mostly because he wanted to avoid talking about Kai for the remainder of the evening.

"Oh man," said Gabby. She blew a rogue wisp of blond hair. "You're asking a dead girl who doesn't remember anything."

"You don't remember your type?"

"Maybe I do? Lemme think." Gabby folded one arm over her torso and propped the elbow of her other arm on top as she rubbed her eyes. She glanced at Aidan through her fingers. "Okay, don't take this the wrong way, but I think maybe my type is sort of like you?"

"Oh," said Aidan awkwardly. "Um."

"But obviously *not* you, dum-dum. For starters, my type is older than you. And also the exact opposite of you. But also . . . very similar? Does that make sense?"

No. It did not.

"Like, I think my type has your eyes? Your nose? My type *definitely* has your smile."

"My smile?" Aidan wasn't aware that he had smiled even once in front of Gabby. It hadn't exactly been Happy Fun Times at the Witch House.

"Yeah!" said Gabby. "You don't do it often, but when you do, it's like . . . sunlight. There's warmth, and you can feel it on your skin, and you just want to roll around in it."

"Oh, um . . ." Aidan blushed. "Thanks?"

"Sorry," said Gabby, blushing even harder. "I think I really liked someone when I was alive. I wish I remembered more about them. I guess that's why I'm so obsessed with you and Kai. Your feelings for him are just very . . . familiar. It feels like a long time since I've felt something that real."

Gabby suddenly looked very sad.

"Also . . . this will probably sound strange, but I think there's a connection between the person I liked and the reason I died." Gabby tucked her hands behind her back, and she kicked the floor. "Do you think remembering who that person was could help me get my memories back and free me from this house?"

She seemed to immediately regret that thought.

"Sorry," she said. "That's stupid. I mean, sure, I want to know who that person was, but obviously true love isn't going to break the curse. I've probably watched one too many Disney movies. I'm going to shut up now."

"No!" said Aidan. "Hey! Please don't shut up. We have no idea what'll break the curse. At this point, I think finding out anything and everything could help us—including who you liked." Aidan didn't say it out loud, but obviously learning how Gabby had died would be helpful.

"Okay," said Gabby, nodding hopefully. Her face broke apart, giving way to a smile. "Okay!"

Aidan anticipated a long, lonely, cold bike ride home. It was a brisk fifty-one degrees, according to his phone, which he clutched awkwardly in his hand because his dress lacked pockets. A dress wasn't ideal for bike riding either. One Sunday after church, he made the error of riding his bike before changing out of his slacks. The thin, loose material caught in his bike chain and ripped. A dress would be so much worse.

Still, it beat wearing his puke clothes. Aidan passed the crusty pile of them in a corner in the entrance hall, and they smelled worse than death—no offense to Gabby. He caught a whiff and gagged. He'd return later, collect them in a grocery bag, and tie it shut. Maybe he'd double bag them.

This was where Aidan's thoughts were when he exited the Witch House. There, sitting on the edge of the front porch waiting for him, was Kai.

"What are you still doing here?" said Aidan. He glanced at his phone screen. "It's one in the morning!"

Kai stood upright and shuffled awkwardly. "So don't get mad, but when I threw my bike at the window, it turns out it was actually your bike. And, well, um . . ."

Kai stepped off the porch and lifted Aidan's bicycle. The front wheel was visibly bent. Several spokes were jarred loose. The chain hung off the chainrings because the entire crankset was busted.

"Oh," said Aidan sadly.

"Apparently I threw it really hard," said Kai, kicking the floorboards. "But those windows were harder. In my defense, it's a Huffy, and Huffys suck."

"Oh," Aidan repeated, crestfallen. He liked his Huffy.

"But I'll fix it!" said Kai. "And until then—" He picked up his own bike, an old black-and-blue Trek with a mounted luggage rack and a bungee cord wrapped around it. "Here. You can have my bike."

"Oh, Kai, you don't need to—"

"No, I insist. I'll walk home tonight and then come here tomorrow when it's lighter out, and I'll"—Kai glanced at the disaster that was Aidan's Huffy—"fix it."

"What? No! Kai, you are not *walking* home." Aidan glanced from the bike seat of Kai's Trek to the metal luggage rack over the back seat which was, um . . . *kind of* like a seat? "Maybe we can both fit on your bike?"

"Oh," said Kai, visibly relieved. "I mean, if you're cool with it, I'm totally fine with sitting on the rack. I can walk home from your house. That's closer than here."

Aidan sized up Kai's bike. It was intimidating. Kai's Trek was a large, adult bike, whereas Aidan's Huffy was child size. Kai was longer and ropier than Aidan, with athletic coordination and an adultlike confidence to operate larger machinery. Aidan never witnessed it, but Kai bragged that he drove Kalani's car—a 1970s AMC Gremlin—around the trailer park once.

"Actually," said Aidan, "can you pedal, and I'll ride on back?" Aidan lifted the skirts of his dress as explanation.

"You sure?" said Kai. He glanced at the luggage rack. "It's uncomfortable. When my mom's car broke down, she had to ride my bike once, and I was stuck on back. It sucked."

"I'll be fine!" Aidan offered a smile as evidence.

Kai mounted the Trek first, then patted the rack for Aidan to climb on. Aidan felt his body temperature increase by five degrees as he attempted to do so. He was forced to hike up the dress considerably to get his leg around. Once he was properly seated, there was really no way of pulling it back down.

"You'll wanna hold on tight," said Kai. "Once I start going, it's real easy to lose your balance and fall off."

Aidan was losing his balance just sitting there, so he complied, wrapping his arms around Kai's taut, lean torso. Kai's body radiated such warmth, Aidan accidentally found himself leaning into it.

Kai kicked off with slightly more effort than usual, and as they sailed down the gentle curves of Yeet Street and onto the main road, Aidan found himself giving in, resting his head on Kai's shoulder. As the dark shades of sleepy Curtain Falls swept by like a dream, Aidan thought to himself that nothing had ever felt so right.

Their arrival at Aidan's house came too soon. Aidan had never dreaded anything as much as letting go of Kai and getting off that bike. The Backwards Lady was a dream. *This* was clearly the worst part of the evening.

But even that wasn't terrible. As Aidan attempted to dismount, nearly losing his balance in the process, Kai took Aidan's hand in his to steady him. It was a moment longer than necessary before Kai let go.

Kai walked Aidan to his door.

Aidan's heart didn't race like he thought it might. It fluttered. It soared. The moment was calm and perfect—as if everything in the world was as it should be.

"Tonight doesn't feel real," said Kai.

"No," Aidan agreed, somewhat breathlessly. "It doesn't."

"We're really helping the ghost of Gabby Caldwell."

Oh. That. Aidan nodded, perhaps overenthusiastically. "Yep. We're ghost helpers now. We help ghosts."

Kai seemed less enthusiastic. "What did you see on the back of the Backwards Lady's head?"

Aidan's enthusiasm plunged.

"You saw a face," said Kai. "But it wasn't hers, was it?"

Aidan's stomach twisted at the thought. He had seen *his own face*. The horror of that image left an unholy taste in Aidan's mouth.

Aidan's disturbed thoughts were interrupted as Kai's arms wrapped around him, squeezing him tight.

"I'm glad you're okay," said Kai. "I thought I lost you."

Aidan had no words. Instead, he wrapped his arms around Kai and hugged him back.

Finally, Kai cleared his throat, and the two of them broke away awkwardly.

"Right," said Kai. "I'll see you sometime tomorrow? Probably much later?"

"Yeah!" Aidan beamed. Sleep wasn't a thought in his head.

"Okay. Well. Good night, Aidan."

"Good night, Kai."

Kai mounted his bike swiftly and glided like a kite, out of the cul-de-sac, and into the breaking dawn.

Aidan entered his house in a dreamy haze. Shuffled up the stairs and into his bedroom. He was on a trajectory for his bed when he caught his reflection in the mirrored surface of his sliding closet door. He stopped. Looked at himself.

In the dark, he really did look like a girl. His short hair was pixie-like. This was who Kai took home on the back of his bike. Who he walked to the front door. Who he hugged on the porch and admitted he was afraid he lost them. Aidan had felt awkward and stupid in the dress, but looking at his reflection now, he felt beautiful.

Aidan hugged himself. He could almost feel Kai on that bicycle seat in front of him. He could still smell Kai on his clothes.

Aidan was not ready to let go of this moment. So he crawled into bed, still wearing the dress that *maybe* belonged to Farah Yeet, or *maybe* belonged to a Wet Seal—whatever the heck *that* was—and he replayed that bicycle ride in his mind. He did not remember closing his eyes. He simply drifted like a cloud into a world of exquisite dreams.

CHAPTER 10

Queen Bea vs. Wet Socks

Aidan did not remember what his dreams were about—only that they were wonderful and forgetting them felt like a loss.

When he opened his eyes, his mom was standing in his bedroom doorway, frozen in a sort of stasis. The pieces of last night started to fragment together. He glanced down at himself.

He had slept above his covers, still wearing the white dress.

Aidan yelped, struggling to pull the covers over him, which were tucked into his bed, military-style. Adrenaline prevailed as he gave a mighty tug and yanked the covers free. Inertia and gravity *also* prevailed as he and his bedding toppled to the floor.

Jocelyn Cross snapped out of her stasis and said, "Sorry. I, um . . . sorry!" She hurriedly shut the door.

Aidan remained on the floor in a disheveled heap for a long moment, allowing his rattled nerves to settle. He half-expected his mom to knock on the door, but she didn't.

Aidan crawled out of his heap of bedding and got undressed. He held the bundle of the dress uncertainly. He needed to hide it, but where?

He settled for the deepest, darkest corner of his closet, stuffing it into a nook between boxes of old cosplay for RenFest and LARPing.

Aidan walked on eggshells as he showered and got ready for the day. He never encountered his mom before leaving the house. This was both relieving and unsettling. His mom was a peacemaker. A mediator. She didn't handle uncomfortable things by avoiding them.

Did seeing him in a dress make her *that* uncomfortable?

Aidan tried not to think about it.

He messaged his friends. They decided to meet at the Curtain Falls Public Library to do some research. They needed to learn anything and everything (preferably *facts*, and not just the urban legends everyone and their grandma here in Curtain Falls knew) about three things:

1. Gabby Caldwell
2. Farah Yeet
3. The Backwards Lady

The Curtain Falls Public Library was a small, elevated single story made of red brick, except for about five feet of the visible basement level below, which was made of white stone, with small, separate windows of its own. Concrete steps led to an elevated doorway built in the neoclassical style, with columns on either side and ending in a bold triangular shape on top. Overall, the grandeur of the architecture made its small size appear much bigger.

The same could be said of its library director, Ms. Schleppenbach. She was small but had an overwhelming presence—big, curly bob, rainbow-colored glasses, and a style best described as "library chic."

As Aidan and his friends approached her desk, Ms. Schleppenbach lowered the book she was reading. It looked like some sort of Japanese comic book. She appeared to be reading it backwards, turning pages left to right—meaning the right side was the front cover. It looked unsettling.

"Aren't you too old to be reading picture books?" said Zephyr bluntly.

The others stopped walking and panicked. The thought crossed Aidan's mind that maybe he should pretend not to know Zephyr.

Ms. Schleppenbach pushed her glasses up the bridge of her nose with a neon-green fingernail. "Bruh. First, there are picture books, which are for young children—but can be enjoyed by anyone—and comic books and graphic novels, which are for *all ages*. Once you've wrapped your brain around that, *then* I can tell you about *manga*, which are Japanese comics. This one's from Junji Ito, who *might be* the scariest writer of all time—manga or otherwise."

"How scary can it be if it's got pictures?" said Zephyr.

"Bruh. The pictures are the scariest part."

If Ms. Schleppenbach was looking to hook Zephyr on a new horror addiction, she'd succeeded. Zephyr eyed her manga as if it were Halloween candy.

"This is great and all," said Aidan, "but we actually have some research we need to be doing? After that, I'm sure Zephyr would *love* to check out your manga."

It was up to Kai to rescue this derailed conversation. "So, Ms. Steppenbacher—"

"Schleppenbach," she corrected.

"Schleppenbach," said Kai. "My friends and I are writing a research paper on the Witch House. We need to research Farah Yeet, and also Gabby Caldwell. And while we're at it, could you also help us find information about an urban legend called the Backwards Lady?"

"The *Backwards* Lady?" said Ms. Schleppenbach, scrunching her face.

"Yeah . . . the Backwards Lady," said Kai, nodding stupidly.

"Why are you boys doing a research paper in the summer?" said Ms. Schleppenbach. She narrowed her eyes skeptically.

"Summer school," said Kai.

"It's an extra credit online thing," said Terrance.

"Because learning is power," said Zephyr.

They gave these responses simultaneously. Aidan cringed.

"You know what?" said Ms. Schleppenbach. "It doesn't matter. Four boys at the library? Who am I to argue with that? I'll get each of you on a computer for online research. While you're doing that, I can pull up the microfiche and bring you over individually, and we'll see what we find."

"How are tiny fish supposed to help?" said Zephyr.

"Ha!" Ms. Schleppenbach squawked. "Gen Z. I love you guys. I figure a divide and conquer approach is the best way to tackle this. So if you don't mind, let's say *you're* on the Witch House"—she pointed at Zephyr—"you're on Farah Yeet" (Terrance)—"you're on Gabby Caldwell" (Kai)—"and *you*, Mr. Weasley, are on the Backwards Lady."

Aidan offered a weak smile.

"Sorry, I don't know why I keep making Harry Potter references," said Ms. Schleppenbach. "I don't even like J. K. Rowling anymore."

Aidan offered a more genuine smile at this.

"So," said Ms. Schleppenbach, "how many of you have library cards?"

Terrance alone raised his hand. Not to make excuses, but Aidan's was that he was a bit of a collector and bought all his books from the local Barnes & Noble. He glanced at the others in disbelief. They shuffled their feet awkwardly.

"Seriously?" said Terrance.

Fortunately, Ms. Schleppenbach was a pro at issuing new library cards. She got them situated at their computers one by one. Zephyr, Terrance, and Kai ended up *fairly* close to one another. By Aidan's turn, however, all the main floor computers were occupied. All that was left was basement floor computers. The basement level was the children's library. It felt a bit demeaning to Aidan—being the only one of his friends stuck down here—but he had an important job to do. Aidan resolved to give it his all. The fate of Gabby's literal immortal soul depended on it.

Ms. Schleppenbach helped Aidan log in to his computer and left him to his research.

Aidan typed "backwards lady" into his search bar and turned up nada. A couple of weird songs he'd never heard and that was about it. He searched "backwards lady witch house" and then "backwards lady curtain falls," both of which proved just as fruitless.

Aidan attempted a few more searches, each one straying farther from the mark. When one of his searches accidentally pulled up something naughty—and 100 percent *not* in the demographic of things Aidan was interested in—he yelped, closed his eyes, and blindly fumbled to exit out of the browser.

That was it. Aidan was done.

He retrieved his notebook from his bag, and a pencil that wasn't particularly sharp, but it would have to do.

Aidan promised Gabby pages, and he would deliver them.

He lost himself in his writing. There were things he hadn't figured out, plot-wise, but they always seemed to work themselves out as he wrote. Aidan tended to experience plot twists in the very moments he scribbled them down. Kai Pendragon was an exiled prince? He had legs now? The drama was writing itself!

It was under these circumstances that Aidan heard a girl clear her throat somewhere behind him. This seemed like a fairly normal bodily sound, so Aidan ignored it. She cleared her throat a second time, even louder, which was kind of obnoxious, but what was Aidan going to do? Then someone tapped Aidan on his shoulder. He turned around.

It was the literal "Queen Bea" of Berkshires Middle School—Beatrice McCarthy.

He caught the slightest flash of annoyance on her face before it blossomed into the fakest smile Aidan had ever seen. Bea was beautiful. (Golden hair, flawless complexion, perfectly curated wardrobe.) Bea was popular. (She bafflingly had over ten thousand followers on TikTok.) She was also unfairly smart, with commendable leadership skills, as exhibited in her prestigious position as editor of the school newspaper, the *Berkshires Bulletin*. Bea had only the best things—except for Kai Pendleton, whom she'd been eyeing like some overpriced serum at Sephora since sixth grade.

Technically, she and Kai were friends.

Technically, Kai was friends with *all* the cool kids—although this was more a side effect of Kai's coolness than any real effort exhibited on his part. When you were as cool as Kai, you tended to collect friends like a dog collects fleas.

Bea had shamelessly flirted with Kai for about as long as Aidan could remember, and although Kai flirted back, it never amounted to anything. It was a perplexing back-and-forth tango that brought Aidan endless frustration, but also hope.

Aidan hated this conversation, and it hadn't even started yet.

"You're Kai's friend, right?" she said.

Aidan shared four classes with Bea last year. There was a 100 percent chance she didn't know his name.

"Yeah," said Aidan, offering a smile of equal fakeness. "What brings you here?"

"Oh, you know," she said vaguely.

Aidan did not know. There was a strong chance she had seen Kai and his friends enter the library, and she followed them here. The library was a stone's throw from Zephyr's neighborhood, a.k.a. Where the Rich People Lived. Aidan doubted she lived far.

"It's Adam, right?" said Bea.

"Nope."

Bea waited for him to add something, but he didn't. Her fake smile faltered for a split second.

"Adrien?"

"Closer, but no."

Bea's smile was life-threateningly thin. Aidan wondered if the affluenza in her blood might cause her to murder him, right here and now, in the children's section of the library. "Well, what is it?"

"Aidan." He sounded as exhausted as he felt.

"Aidan!" she exclaimed, the pinnacle of fake excitement. "That was my next guess."

He doubted that.

"Could you do me a favor, Aidan?" said Bea. "I would be so grateful. Like, I would *seriously* owe you one."

Aidan was not committing to jack squat until he knew what it was.

"What is it?" he asked.

Bea pushed her fake smile so far to the brink, it was parody. "Could you find out for me if Kai's planning on coming to my birthday party? It's going to be this Saturday at the roller rink. It's gonna be *totes* amazing."

In the brief period where this invitation gestated—and Aidan had yet to respond—Bea seemed to realize that Aidan *hadn't* received an invitation to her birthday party, and that this might be used against her.

Bea cleared her throat, and awkwardly added, "You're free to come too, of course. Although you'll have to buy your own ticket. I only bought forty-two of them, and they're all claimed."

"Except for Kai's," said Aidan.

Bea's smile faltered. "Yes, well. I would *love* for Kai to make it. You understand."

It was perhaps the *only* thing Aidan understood. He gave a resigned sigh. "You could always ask him yourself. He's upstairs."

"Funny thing," she said. "I've actually already texted him, but I think he forgot to respond? Or maybe it got lost in his texts?"

Aidan said nothing.

Bea also said nothing. It was a deadlock.

"You can still ask him *in person*," Aidan repeated. "Kai's a lazy texter. He forgets to text back all the time. He prefers in-person communication. He didn't even *own* a phone until earlier this year, actually, so . . ."

Aidan trailed off. He wasn't trying to be mean. Quite the opposite, actually. A part of Aidan genuinely sympathized with Bea. She was just another person with a crush on Kai, after all. What was more relatable than that? But if Bea wanted to get to know Kai, she needed to take a big step off her pedestal and *get to know him.*

At least, if Bea was a *character in Aidan's book*, that's how she would do it. Aidan was painfully aware that his only experience with romance was writing it.

However, the look on Bea's face seemed anything but receptive to love advice from Aidan. Instead, she looked like a dingo—Australia's largest, fiercest apex predator—receiving hunting advice from a duck-billed platypus. Her soft jawline was tight as a drum, and her perfectly shaped eyebrows formed a hard, brutal line.

"I'm not *desperate*," said Bea. She said this defensively, but it was laced with danger. "Kai can come if he wants, or he can *not come*. I don't care."

In the wild, this was how you got yourself killed—putting a predator on the defensive. But Aidan was not an animal expert. He wasn't Steve Irwin or Coyote Peterson. He was just a boy in love, and Bea's callousness was making him upset.

"If you *don't care*," said Aidan, "then Kai's never going to like you. Some things—some *people*—are worth being desperate for."

Bea's face was a slow transformation. It went from irritated, to menacing, to lethal in shades.

"You want to know something, Aidan?" said Bea.

Aidan didn't, but he had a feeling she would tell him anyway.

"It's *so obvious* the only reason Kai hangs out with you is because he pities you," she said. "He's just too nice to tell you how boring and pathetic you are."

The line of Aidan's smile flinched. That hurt more than he expected.

"I mean, everyone knows you have a personality like wet socks."

Aidan received that comment like a knee to the stomach. It knocked the wind right out of him.

He needed to get out of here.

He reached for his notebook, but Bea snatched it. "Where do you think you're going?"

Aidan froze. Out of all the terrifying scenarios in the whole universe, the horror of Bea holding his notebook was next level. The Backwards Lady felt like a small blip by comparison. He survived *that*.

"P-p-puh-p-p-please," said Aidan. "G-g-g-guh-g-g-g-geh-g-g-g-gih . . ." "Give it back" was what he was trying to say. He couldn't make it past the *G* sound.

"Oh my God," said Bea, laughing. "You're so pathetic! *Guh-guh-guh*," she mimicked, holding her arms in front of her crookedly.

She held Aidan's notebook loosely enough that he thought he might be able to snatch it back.

He tried. She yanked it just out of his reach.

Bea let out a brief, sharp scream. "Don't you dare touch me, pervert!"

"Please," said Aidan. His voice came out soft and wheezy. He felt dizzy. "Please, I'll d-d-d-do anything."

"You really want this back, huh?" said Bea. She glanced at his notebook with mild interest. "You'll do anything?"

"Anything," said Aidan. He meant it.

Adults were descending the stairs to see what all the commotion was about—Ms. Schleppenbach included.

"Aidan?" she said, looking genuinely concerned.

Bea leaned forwards and whispered into Aidan's ear, "Go back in the dryer, Wet Socks."

She then proceeded to scream at the top of her lungs.

It was a scream that cut like a hot knife through butter. Everything that wasn't her scream melted away.

A crowd formed in the stairwell.

Bea bolted for the stairs. She was just small and swift enough to squeeze through before it clogged like a drain.

Aidan chased after her, but there were too many people in the stairwell. He attempted to push through, but bodies and words ballooned around him, suffocating him.

"Was he harassing that girl?"

"Grab that boy!"

"Isn't there security around here?"

Nobody grabbed him, but it didn't matter. Sensation overload seized Aidan completely. He was halfway up the stairwell when he began seeing little black holes and squiggles eating away at his field of vision. He tried frantically to breathe, but somewhere between his gasps for air, oxygen wasn't making it to where it was supposed to go.

As Aidan collapsed to his knees, the crowd parted and backed away. Only now did they seem to realize maybe *he* was the victim.

At the top of the stairs, Zephyr, Terrance, and Kai appeared wearing looks of alarm.

"Aidan?" said Zephyr.

"What happened?" said Terrance.

Kai rushed down the stairs, catching Aidan before he could hit the floor.

Aidan wanted to look into Kai's eyes—eyes that told him everything would be okay—but instead, his gaze drifted to the woman standing at the top of the stairs. Unlike everyone else in the stairwell, her back was facing Aidan. She wore a long white dress, with a long, black sheet of hair that reached halfway down her back. She was barefoot. Her skin was pale and paper thin, with spidery black veins pulsing underneath. Her nails were painted the color of rot.

Her joints crackled like dry kindling as broken arms with broken fingers parted the hair in the back of her head.

Once again, Aidan was met by his own face. Only now it was smiling.

The most hideous, gut-churning smile Aidan had ever seen—eyes pried all the way open, lips peeled all the way back.

When Kai's head moved back, the Backwards Lady was gone.

A paramedic shone a light in Aidan's eyes. She asked him questions he only vaguely remembered answering. She didn't seem particularly concerned about the state of his health. His chances of living seemed astronomically high.

Meanwhile, Zephyr, Terrance, and Kai existed softly in Aidan's peripheral, fidgeting and anxious.

Aidan never had the chance to talk to them. It was only when Mr. Cross arrived to take Aidan home that the paramedics stopped what they were doing. His dad and one of the paramedics spoke briefly. The consensus was that Aidan should be monitored, but overall, he appeared healthy.

Zephyr, Terrance, and Kai tried to say goodbye to Aidan, but he could only manage a feeble wave. He couldn't even make eye contact.

The drive home was mostly quiet. Aidan leaned against the passenger-side window, observing the passing street in a numb blur. Mr. Cross seemed to want to talk but struggled to find words.

"Did you and your mother have a fight?" Mr. Cross asked finally.

"What?" said Aidan. He snapped rigid and looked at his dad in alarm. "No. Did she *say* we did?"

"No. She's just acting strange."

"Strange how?" Aidan asked. Even though he wasn't sure he wanted to know.

"She asked if I'd pick you up from the library."

That didn't seem so strange, Aidan thought. She could have just been busy.

"It was strange," said Mr. Cross, "because she was the one on the phone with the medics. And when she got off, she asked if I would pick you up instead. I asked if she wanted to come with, but she said no. She didn't give a reason or anything. Just . . . no."

Aidan was drowning in an ocean of sadness. It didn't rain down on top of him. He was just suddenly at the very bottom of it. If the pressure didn't crush him like an aluminum can, suffocation would surely do him in.

"Oh," said Aidan. It was all he could manage.

Mr. Cross immediately seemed to rethink the direction this conversation had taken. "But, uh . . . I wouldn't worry about it. She gets like this sometimes. I'm sure it has nothing to do with you."

"Okay," said Aidan quietly.

Mr. Cross's mouth pulled into a frown. He reached across the passenger seat and ruffled Aidan's bonfire of hair.

"It'll be okay, bud," he said. "Everything will be okay."

Aidan wasn't so sure that it would.

CHAPTER 11

Christopher Cross's Top Secret High School Death Metal Playlist

Aidan didn't recall his dreams that night, but he woke to a nightmare.

He and Kai had been tagged in an online post from Bea McCarthy. It read:

Fact: Aidan spelled backwards is Nadia. And Kai Pendragon bears a striking similarity to ANOTHER Kai we know, doesn't he? So, Aidan, the question we're all dying to ask is, do you want Kai to be your MERMAN?

Attached were scans of every handwritten page of *Fire & Water*. Every. Single. Page.

"No," said Aidan. "No no NO NO NO."

The post went viral. Over a hundred likes and "wow" and "laughing" emojis. There were dozens of comments, which Aidan had no intention—nor the psychological resolve—to read, but the first couple he accidentally absorbed. They read:

WHAT??!?

this is literally the gayest straight romance I've ever read

So are we shipping "Kadia" or "Kaidan"?

Aidan had to step away. He abandoned his phone on his bed, pacing his room in circles and pulling at his hair. It wasn't just that everyone was reading and reacting to the most intimate thing he'd ever written. That was awful, but it was something he could survive.

What he *couldn't* survive was Kai being tagged.

This was what Kai was waking up to. It was being thrust into his face and reacted to by everyone they went to school with.

Aidan didn't know if he would've kept his feelings for Kai a secret forever. Two nights ago, sharing Kai's bicycle, they felt closer than they'd ever felt before. But that night was a distant memory.

This was the worst way for Kai to discover his feelings: as gossip. As cheap entertainment. As an internet joke.

Aidan's Darkness was one thing. What he felt in this moment was stronger, wilder, more chaotic. Like fire. His mind was a house set on fire, and he was burning alive inside it. Aidan didn't know what to do except to get out of that house at all costs.

Aidan changed into black sweats, a black hoodie with the hood up, and running shoes. He pulled the drawstrings on his hood tight, leaving only the smallest part of his face exposed. Aidan was not in a state to be recognized by the general public.

Before leaving his bedroom, he pulled a shoebox out from underneath his bed, removed an ancient, beat-up iPod from a bygone era, and a pair of earbuds.

Aidan marched downstairs on a direct course for the front door, quietly slipped outside, and plugged his dad's death metal playlist into his ears. That's what the playlist was—death metal—but its actual title on the iPod was not so eloquent: merely a string of some of the worst swear words Aidan had ever read. They did not form a coherent sentence, but the gist of their meaning was crystal clear. This was an angry playlist.

Aidan was angry.

Mr. Cross was not aware that Aidan had found his old iPod, and Aidan did not tell him. Bringing it to his attention seemed like a bad idea. Besides, Aidan was fascinated by just how primal, raw, and deranged the playlist was, filled with bands with names like Carcass and Obituary and Cannibal Corpse. It was an odd, one-sided bonding experience with a version of his dad he had never met before. It also made Aidan slightly terrified of his dad. (Like, more than usual.)

Right now, however, the only thing Aidan was afraid of was standing still with his terrible, destructive thoughts. So he cranked the volume up to some ungodly decibel and broke into a full-on sprint. He was not running with a destination in mind.

Aidan ran until his feet hurt.

Aidan ran until his lungs and heart threatened to burst—*Alien*-like— out of his chest.

Aidan ran until he couldn't stop crying—at which point, he forced himself to run even harder.

At one point, Aidan screamed at the top of his lungs. The volume was up so loud, he couldn't hear his own voice. But he did feel his own spittle fling back into his windbitten face.

Aidan ran until he felt dizzy. He felt like he might collapse. Fortunately, he had made a vague loop through his neighborhood. When he was sure he couldn't take one more step, he spotted his house. He now had only one goal, and that was to make it back into his house before he passed out on the street.

When he made it inside his house, his new goal was to make it into his bedroom. There he could die in peace. Well . . . not *peace*, but . . . you know.

Aidan staggered up to his bedroom. Each step felt like trudging through molasses. The bottoms of his feet felt like they were embedded with glass. He was sure he had blisters.

Aidan collapsed face-first onto his bed. He didn't remember hitting the mattress. It was like plunging into water, and from there, he sank.

Deeper and deeper.

Into darkness.

When Aidan woke up, it was in a heavy, sleep-dulled haze. His dad's bloodthirsty death metal playlist was still screaming rabidly into his ears (Death, "Lack of Comprehension"). It was growing dark outside, not quite night yet. Even though Aidan had collapsed onto his covers, he discovered a woven blanket placed gently over him. It seemed like something his mom might have done, until he noticed a sheet of paper with a scribbled note, laid on his pillow beside his head.

I tried waking you for dinner, but you seemed out of it.
I left a plate for you in the fridge. I love you, Aidan.—Dad

Aidan wanted to appreciate the note. He wanted to take it, and put it somewhere special, to remind him that his dad loved him, and here was proof.

Instead, all he could see was that the blanket was his dad's doing. Which meant that his mom was still avoiding him.

That thought alone made Aidan want to cry.

Aidan felt something vibrate beneath him and realized he'd fallen asleep on top of his phone. He rotated like some clumsy beached whale, retrieving the phone from underneath him. It was an incoming call from Zephyr. He almost answered it.

Then he remembered the post—the one that exposed his feelings for his best friend, Kai. Already, this was the worst news ever. But then he realized it wasn't just his friends and everyone at school who knew about those feelings.

He was friends with his parents on social media too.

His dad knew. It put his dad's note in a new light. It was something that *should have* made him happy, but instead, it filled him with shame and dread. It was a conversation with his dad that he wasn't ready to have.

Zephyr was calling because he knew too. All his friends knew. They had probably unanimously agreed that they didn't want to be friends with Aidan anymore. His feelings for Kai made everything awkward and weird. And now here Zephyr was, the proverbial bearer of bad news, calling because delivering this news in person would be too uncomfortable.

Aidan couldn't take it anymore. His thoughts were carnivorous, and they were eating him alive.

He closed his eyes and tried to make everything go away.

And slowly, they did.

Every thought. Every feeling.

Everything.

CHAPTER 12

FARAH, THE GREAT AND TERRIBLE

One of Farah Yeet's earliest memories was on Easter Witches Day, a celebration of her childhood homeland.

Easter Witches Day originated from the first Maundy Thursday when Judas betrayed Jesus. It was believed that on this day, evil was released into the world. It most closely resembled the Halloween tradition of trick-or-treating. (Although Farah would not learn of Halloween until she and Mamma moved to America.) Young children would dress up as witches, wearing pointed hats and old women's and men's clothing, and they would go from door to door offering greetings—sometimes even handmade cards—and they would receive treats in return.

As a young child, Farah was not allowed to participate. She could only watch through the window of her small, crowded living room, nose pressed piggy-like against the cracked glass, fogging it with eager breath.

Not only did Farah not get treats like the other children, but the other children would not even bother to come to her house for treats. This was partly because Farah and Mamma lived in the oldest, ugliest, most dilapidated little shack in the whole village. It was little more than a shed divided into quarters: living room, kitchen, Farah's room, and Mamma's room, each no bigger than a closet. It had no running water. There was a nearby well from which to draw water, and an outhouse. On the outside, it was painted the saddest color of decaying red, like a bloody booger. At least that's what a boy named Karl liked to tell Farah. Farah thought Karl was the bloody booger.

It probably also didn't help that Mamma not only refused to buy treats for the other children, but she shooed them away, saying things like, "Little cretins!" and "Your mothers should be ashamed of you!" All the little costumed children of the village gave Farah's house a wide berth, as if Farah and Mamma were the witches.

The living room was mostly filled with Mamma's loom, which she inherited from her mamma before her, upon which she wove tapestry curtains that she sold for a living. Her handwoven curtains were very ugly. They did not make a lot of money. Hence, the poorness. It also made "living" in their small living room rather unbearable. Farah kneeled on the ottoman in front of the window, while Mamma sat gargoyle-like in their only armchair. Everything else in the living room was yarn, and loom, and ugly, unsold curtains.

"Mamma, why can't I be a witch?" Farah protested sadly.

"It's morbid," Mamma said. "I don't like it."

"Mor-bid?" Farah repeated. "What's that?"

"Two hundred years ago, this town was obsessed with witches," said Mamma. "Everyone thought everyone else was a witch. In a single day, seventy-one people—sixty-five women and six men—were beheaded and then burned. Your great-great-great-grandmamma was one of them."

"What does 'beheaded' mean?" said Farah.

"Their heads were chopped off," said Mamma. She made a slicing gesture across her neck and a macabre sound that went like: *Shiiiiick.*

Farah's eyes doubled in size. That did not sound very nice.

"And then they were set on fire," said Mamma, because she wanted to make sure this traumatic lesson was not soon forgotten. It was not.

"Why would someone do that?" Farah asked.

"Fear makes people do terrible things," said Mamma. "And stupid people are filled with fear. We dress our children up like witches as if it rectifies the past, but such senseless murder cannot be rectified. It can only be remembered."

"Can't it be remembered while I collect treats from the neighbors?" said Farah.

"No," said Mamma.

Farah pouted but resisted the urge to cry. Mamma did not like it when Farah cried.

"Also," said Mamma, "the Devil is real. If he ever comes to you in the middle of the night and invites you to a faraway feast, you will refuse. If I find out that you have gone, I will give you a spanking you will not soon forget. Do I make myself clear?"

This was not the first time Mamma had instructed Farah not to accept midnight trips to feast with the Devil, and it would probably not be the last. Mamma said a lot of strange things, and Farah had learned not to question her.

"Yes, Mamma," said Farah.

Farah awoke to a shadow of a man standing over her bed.

To call him a "shadow" was vague and technically inaccurate. That seemed to imply that he was a man standing in the dark, which was *not* what this man was. Farah did not have words for what he was, and that was the silhouette of a man seemingly cut out of the fabric of existence, leaving behind a nothingness like that of a black hole. This man was a black hole in the shape of a person. Because Farah's bed stretched from one end of her tiny bedroom to the other, the man seemed to fill every last available space with his presence.

"Hello, Farah," he said. "My name is Blåkulla. It is a pleasure to meet you."

He pronounced his name *bloke*-ula, sort of like *Dracula*, which Farah knew nothing about. Bram Stoker had only just written it on the other side of the North Sea. Blåkulla spoke in a silky voice that was both calm and friendly, if not exactly kind. He sounded like someone smiling when they did not mean it. It caused Farah's skin to prickle with fear.

"Are you the Devil?" said Farah. "Because if you are, Mamma told me that I can't go with you. So. Please go away." She pulled her blanket up to her nose to conceal her fear.

"I am not the Devil," said Blåkulla. "Would you believe it if I told you that I'm not a person at all, but rather, a place?"

This was a rather perplexing thing for a person to say, even one who looked like the absence of everything—a person-shaped sheet of pure black—and so no, Farah did not believe him.

"You *look* like a person," said Farah doubtfully. "Sort of. And places can't talk, can they?"

"*Most* places can't talk," said Blåkulla. "But I am not any old place. I am a *magical* place. I am only shaped like a person so that I may commune with you. But if you were to reach your hand out to touch me, you would find *space* instead of *skin*. If you were to step inside of me, you would be transported to what I really am, which is the island of Blåkulla—the Blue Hill—an Earthly court where angels and demons and witches such as yourself can dance and feast in playfulness and peace."

There was an awful lot for Farah to unpack in that last statement, and she tried her best to sound smart and cunning, and not like someone who could be easily duped or distracted by the Devil.

"You just confessed to having devils inside of you," said Farah matter-of-factly.

"I also confessed to having angels inside of me," said Blåkulla. "This is because I am a place of peace. I am a place where angels and demons need not worry about going to war with one another. Because who says angels have to be good, and demons have to be evil?"

"God?" said Farah.

"What if I told you that I *am* God?" said Blåkulla.

Farah squinted her eyes skeptically. "You don't look like God."

"Oh yeah? And what does God look like?"

"He has long hair, and a beard, and, um . . . a halo around his head?" said Farah uncertainly.

"Artists' depictions," Blåkulla scoffed. "Look, I'm not going to convince you that I'm God. I simply am. But did you know that the Devil is an angel?"

"What?" said Farah. "No, he's not."

"He is!" said Blåkulla. "It's in the Bible. You can even ask your Mamma."

Farah would go on to ask Mamma the following morning if the Devil was an angel, and she would confirm Blåkulla's claim—albeit with a myriad of disclaimers.

"This is all beside the point," said Blåkulla. "I just told you that you're a witch, and you haven't said a single thing in response."

"Yeah, well," said Farah, flustered. "That's because Mamma told me that people kill witches. So I don't want to be a witch."

This was not entirely true. Farah was an avid reader of fairy stories, whenever she could get her hands on them, because tales of fairies and magic made her heart sing. Her favorite book in the world was an English-language copy of L. Frank Baum's *The Wonderful Wizard of Oz* that she received for her birthday. It was her favorite birthday present in the world. She all but taught herself English reading that book. Her favorite character was Glinda, the Good Witch of the South. Something about the idea of a "good witch"—especially one as powerful and beautiful as Glinda—rocked Farah's world. Farah would have given any one of her toes to be Glinda. What was one toe anyway?

"She told you that stupid, fearful people kill witches," said Blåkulla. "Not people of quality, such as yourself. Do you know who else is a witch?"

Farah did not, so she shook her head.

"Your mamma," said Blåkulla. "So was your grandmamma. And your great-grandmamma. And your great-great-grandmamma. And your—"

"Great-great-great-grandmamma," said Farah, wide-eyed. "She really was a witch?"

"She really was a witch," said Blåkulla. "Although she wasn't evil. She was an innocent, curious girl, just as yourself! It was the people who killed her who were evil. Stupid, fearful people. Go ask your mamma. Who was evil: your great-great-great-grandmamma or the stupid, fearful people who killed her?"

Farah would go on to ask Mamma who was evil, and once again, Blåkulla's claim would be confirmed. But that was tomorrow, and this was today, and even without Mamma to back up Blåkulla's claims, Farah had to admit that he was awfully persuasive.

"Your mamma is a good person," said Blåkulla. "But you know who else is a good person?"

"Jesus?" said Farah uncertainly.

"You," said Blåkulla. "You are a good person. And I think it is awfully unfair that all those other kids got to go out and be witches tonight, but you, Farah—a real witch—did not. Don't you think that's unfair?"

Farah did think it was unfair. Even though she knew that Mamma would spank her for saying it aloud. And so, she merely gave a slight nod of her head in the mildest display of mutiny.

"What if I told you that you could have all the treats your heart desired tonight? More treats than you could possibly fathom?"

Farah's eyes became like a pair of full moons. She was a stalwart soul, but she had a weakness, and that was treats. She would sell her own soul for treats. In a sense, that is exactly what she did.

"Well, you're in luck, little Farah," said Blåkulla. "Because I am a land of treats."

～

It was all just a dream.

It *had to* have been a dream because the very next thing that happened was that Farah walked through the absence of space that was Blåkulla's body like a portal into a new dimension. The space was a great, cavernous tunnel, walls gleaming and black like obsidian, with a person-shaped opening at the other end. When Farah crossed that space and exited out the opposite side, she stepped barefoot onto the cold, wet grass of a dewy meadow that seemed to stretch on forever in every direction.

At the far end of the meadow was a black iron gate, and on the other side of it was the most beautiful and mysterious house Farah had ever seen.

It was three stories tall, painted white as an angel, and seemed to glow against the night sky. The top floor of the house narrowed, towerlike, to a rounded window in the shape of an all-seeing eye overlooking the meadow with eerie omniscience.

"It's beautiful," Farah marveled. "Is that your house?"

"It is not my house in the sense that you are meaning," said Blåkulla.

"It's not? Then whose is it?"

"It is nobody's house. I *am* the House. The House is my body, and my mind, and my soul. The form you see before you is merely my shadow."

Farah considered this revelation seriously. "This is what you meant when you said that you are a place and not a person?"

"This is what I meant."

"Well," said Farah. "I think that you are beautiful. I would die to live in a House like you."

Farah could sense a smile curling in the vast emptiness of Blåkulla's face. She could feel her insides curling with it. "That is very interesting of you to say, little Farah."

Blåkulla escorted Farah down to the gate, which opened of its own accord, as did the front doors of the House. The more Farah thought about it, the more it made sense. If Blåkulla *was* the House, then of course the doors would open for him! Why wouldn't they?

The entrance hall was as vast as the cavernous space inside Blåkulla's shadow. An all-encompassing balcony surrounded it from the second floor. A crystal chandelier glittered like the reflection of a full moon in a sparkling sea. A multitude of people were crowded in the entrance hall. There was a band in the corner, playing on lutes and flutes, fiddles and pipes, harps and drums. Farther back, past a pair of fluted columns, was a dining hall filled with the richest assortment of food spread across a table nearly three times the length of Farah's own house. Everywhere, people were talking and laughing, singing and dancing, feasting and making merry.

Except not all of them were people.

Some were goats walking on their hind legs. Others were toads the size of small children. The person on the fiddle turned out to be a profoundly large snake, holding their fiddlestick in the winding coils of their tail. There were even angels and demons, fraternizing as if they were the closest of friends. The demons walked on hooves like small tree stumps, with furry legs and tails, and curling horns like twisted, symmetrical tree branches. The angels were scarier than the demons, with as many faces on their bulbous heads as the sides of a die, most of which were hideously ugly, with way too many eyes and noses and mouths.

These were all the things that were *not* people. The things that *were* people were almost weirder. They walked backwards, and they danced with their backs facing each other, and when they ate, they shoveled food into a secret mouth in the backs of their heads, which made Farah wonder if they were even people at all.

It was a good thing this was all just a dream.

As such, Farah was able to follow Blåkulla's shadow with dream-like casualness, past the multitudes in the foyer to the feast in the dining hall. Blåkulla helped Farah assemble a plate, filling it high as she pointed greedily from savory pickled herring to sweet semla buns to striped Polkagris candy. Blåkulla filled her a goblet of icy, lingonberry-flavored saft. They sat together at a pair of tall armchairs around the fireplace, and Farah feasted.

And Blåkulla watched.

There were eyes in that empty face of his, and Farah could feel them. It was a good thing this was a dream, otherwise she might have felt uncomfortable.

"I've been thinking a great deal about what you said, little Farah," said Blåkulla.

Farah had been caught at an inopportune moment, her mouth filled with both herring and sticky caramel. She attempted to nod thoughtfully as she chewed and swallowed.

"About what?" said Farah, finally.

"Why, about you living in a House like me, of course!" said Blåkulla. "What would you be willing to give to live in a House such as this?"

Farah was aware of the wording she had used: *I would die to live in a House like you.* And even though this was a dream, she was beginning to feel uneasy.

"I don't know," said Farah nervously. "I don't have a lot. I don't have anything, really. And, um . . . I don't *actually* want to die to live in this House. Because if I was dead, how would I even *live* in it? No offense."

Blåkulla let out a boisterous crack of laughter that filled the house like thunder. Every single person, animal, and cosmic entity stopped what they were doing to laugh along in unison, like a perfectly synchronized choir.

When Blåkulla stopped laughing, the others stopped as well. The sounds of the party—the chatter, and the feasting, and the music—continued.

"Don't you worry, little Farah," said Blåkulla. "Your life is far too valuable for a House such as this."

"It is?" said Farah. This news came as a great surprise to her. She had always been under the impression that her life was not worth a whole lot.

"Why, of course! You're a witch, are you not? I have great plans in store for you." Blåkulla rubbed the empty space where his chin should have been, musing. "What if what you gave me was your pappa?"

"My pappa?" said Farah.

Farah had never met her pappa. That said, she knew that his name was Yaqeen Yeet, and that he was a sailor and a traveling salesman from a faraway land. Yaqeen was the handsomest, most smooth-talking man who had ever set foot in their coastal village. He swept Mamma off her feet. They kissed, and they held hands, and everyone knows that once you kiss and hold hands long enough, the stork comes along and gives you a little baby. That baby was Farah.

Unfortunately, Yaqeen was also a pirate, and a scam artist, and a no-good, cheating liar. He kissed and held hands with lots of the women in the village, and he also pickpocketed and stole from damn near every single one of them. Also, his products were what Mamma liked to call "dog crap." Everything broke and fell apart within days of use.

Mamma was less upset about the stealing and faulty products than she was about having her heart broken and being taken for a fool. When she found out, she screamed, and she called Yaqeen a dirty, two-faced snake, and she threw a vase at his head, and according to the story as Mamma told it, it connected, and Yaqeen still had the scar to prove it. From that day on, Mamma had a heart of stone, and it served no purpose except to bash Yaqeen's brains in, should he ever show his dirty, rotten face in their village ever again.

It was only when the stork gave Farah to Mamma that she wrote a letter to Yaqeen, directed to the address on his business card in Boston, Massachusetts, United States of America. The address was *obviously* a sham, but she hoped that somehow, it might make its way in front of Yaqeen's weaselly eyes. In that letter, Mamma informed Yaqeen that he had a daughter, and she'd even given her his last name because she thought it sounded nice—it was on her birth certificate and everything—but if he ever wanted to see her, he'd better bring some money, or so help her God, she would smash his face in with every single vase she owned.

Mamma did not own any vases—she'd had to sell them all—but it was the thought that counted. She also included a photograph of Farah because Farah really did look an awful lot like Yaqeen. Farah never knew it then, but it was a source of great pain to Mamma.

Yaqeen never responded to that letter. He probably never even saw it. He'd probably never set foot in Boston, let alone the United States.

"I don't know," said Farah, in response to Blåkulla's proposal. "I've never even met my pappa. And even if I had, I'm not sure he's mine to give away."

"Of course he is," said Blåkulla. "He's *your* blood, isn't he? *Your* pappa? If he's not *yours* to give away, then whose is he?"

Farah did not exactly have a good response to that question.

"And what good has he ever done you and your mamma anyway?" said Blåkulla. "He's only ever broken your poor mamma's heart and stolen what little precious belongings and money you had and left you to wither away in a tiny shack with a mamma who has been so hardened by the world, she won't even let you eat treats on Easter Witches Day."

"How do you know so much?" said Farah.

"I told you that I'm God, didn't I?" said Blåkulla.

After all that Farah had seen and heard this evening, she was beginning to have fewer and fewer arguments on this topic.

"Don't you think it's time that your pappa gave you and your mamma something in return for all the heartache he's caused?" said Blåkulla. "Because I think it's time. God blesses the righteous, and He punishes the wicked, does He not? You are righteous, and your pappa is wicked. Your mamma is a bit on the fence—depriving you of treats and all—but we'll give her the benefit of the doubt for now. Give your pappa to me, and I will give you and your mamma a house that all will admire and adore."

Farah stared into the warm hug of the fireplace, licking and crackling with comfort. She took in the vastness of the dining hall, with all its glittering chandeliers, and steaming food, and respected—if slightly weird—party guests. If Farah had a house like this, her life would be wonderful. Every day would be a party. Every day would be filled with treats.

And yet, something about it all felt wrong.

"What will happen to my pappa?" said Farah.

"Nothing, really," said Blåkulla. "Nothing bad, at least. He will be invited to live on the Island of Blåkulla, in the Meadow of Blåkulla, in the House of Blåkulla as my most esteemed guest! It's actually more of an honor than a punishment if I'm being perfectly honest."

"Your most esteemed guest?"

Blåkulla gestured widely to the party that surrounded them. "All of these people you see before you are the wicked who have been given to me by righteous young witches such as yourself. And in return, I have blessed them with eternal happiness. Nothing has been given or taken that wasn't totally deserved."

Farah glanced around, taking them all in. They all seemed happy, sure. But they were also . . .

"They're all backwards," said Farah.

"Backward, forwards . . . does it really matter which way they are?"

"They're all eating and drinking out of mouths in the back of their heads."

"And just think how quickly you could eat treats if you had a second mouth in the back of *your* head."

Farah pursed her lips skeptically. One mouth was good for her, thank you very much.

"I can see you need time to think this through," said Blåkulla. "That is rightly acceptable because we have over two weeks before our contract needs to be drawn. Until the Black Moon to be exact."

"The Black Moon?" Farah repeated.

"Modern minds like to call it the New Moon—when the moon is closest to the Sun, blocking out its light—but Ancients such as myself know its true name. It is a day of fertile darkness, when the moon acts as a channel to the heavens, and the spirits on the other side. It is a day of the liminal, when the boundaries between our worlds are porous and thin. It is the day when my power is strongest, and when you, little Farah, are most susceptible to my blessings. On the night of the Black Moon, I need you to draw your own blood—a droplet, a pinprick, will suffice. You will then press that drop of blood into the dirt of the earth, and then you must speak these words out loud, clear and concise: 'By my blood, I give you my father, Yaqeen Yeet. In return, give me Blåkulla.'"

"You?" said Farah.

"Ah, you forget," said Blåkulla. "What you see before you is just my shadow. What I truly am is this House."

"So I won't be getting a House *like* you," said Farah. "I will be getting a House that *is* you."

Farah felt Blåkulla's invisible smile curl so deeply, it became a spiral, spinning infinitely.

"Very astute, little Farah. That's how you know the House will be good and not a cheap imitation."

It was at about that moment that Farah began to feel very sleepy, which seemed a very peculiar thing to feel in a dream.

"And you will always have me near, to watch over and protect you," said Blåkulla. Even as the world became wobbly and fuzzy around her, his voice remained as smooth as the finest silk. "And should the day come that you need to ask another favor of me, I will always be there to lend a listening ear and an all-powerful hand."

Farah wondered if there had perhaps been something in her food or drink. She felt herself falling backwards—not down and onto the floor, but she felt like she was falling out of the room. Blåkulla's shadow, and his party, and his dining room—which were all technically a part of the *real* Blåkulla—became distant, like a passing carriage. Like a dream.

"There will be nothing you cannot ask me for," said Blåkulla, "not even to cheat death."

It would be the last thing she heard him say, at least for many, many years. Those last words would be etched in the stone of her mind until the moment she died.

Not even to cheat death, little Farah.

Not even to cheat death.

The Black Moon came and passed.

Farah may have pricked her finger, and pressed it into the earth, and spoke some words that came to her in a dream. But it was only just a dream. It was only for fun. Besides, it wasn't like Farah had better things to do with her time.

Days became weeks, and weeks slipped into months, and Farah all but forgot about the deal that she had made. Sometimes she wondered to herself if she had even done it. Had she dreamed that moment up? What a ridiculous, unsanitary thing, to prick your own finger and then press it into the dirt. Did she want to catch the cholera? She must have daydreamed the whole thing.

But unlike most of Farah's dreams, which faded within moments of waking, her dream of Blåkulla never faded. Quite the opposite, in fact. Her memory of the place—and its shadow—engraved itself upon her soul. It felt very much a part of her. Perhaps because it was one of the few moments of her life, dream or not, which filled her with an unfathomable, unreasonable, unrealistic hope that swelled within her bosom, whispering to her that she was destined for greatness.

And destined for greatness, Farah was.

But like Oz himself, from *The Wonderful Wizard of Oz*, sometimes a person could be both Great and Terrible all at once.

It happened on a perfectly ordinary day in September. The weather was moderate, neither warm nor cool, a perfect balance of sun and clouds filling the sky in peaceful treaty. Farah went to school, learned things that she would soon forget, and then came home. She planned to go straight to her bedroom to reread *The Wonderful Wizard of Oz* for the umpteenth time. It was a perfectly splendid plan when you were poor, and your mother was a literal witch who did not believe in soliciting treats from the neighbors.

Things did not go according to plan.

The first thing Farah noticed as she walked through the front door was Mamma sitting in an armchair in their living room, looking rather discombobulated.

The second thing Farah noticed were colorful stacks of krona (banknotes) on their small ottoman footrest that substituted as their coffee table because they did not have one.

The third thing Farah noticed were multiple pages of a long letter, barely clutched in Mamma's fingers.

Mamma had received a package in the mail from Boston, Massachusetts, United States of America, and enclosed in it was a letter from Farah's biological father, Yaqeen Yeet. The gist of it was that Yaqeen had stumbled upon an incredible sum of money as an inheritance from his late grandfather, Lim Poh Yeet, a business magnate and investor whose business interests (collectively known as the Yeet Group of Companies) ranged from sugar refineries, flour milling, animal feed, oil, mining, finance, hotel, property, trading, freight, and publishing. Considering that Yaqeen and his late grandfather were estranged—and the last thing Lim Poh had called his grandson was "a parasitic leech sucking on the lifeblood of the Yeet name"—the almost obscene amount of inheritance money was eyebrow-raising but not exactly inconceivable. The ultrarich were known to leave ludicrous amounts of money to their least favorite family members as a sort of penance. And so, Yaqeen had accidentally become a millionaire overnight.

This insane amount of money sitting in Yaqeen's lap had caused him to do a bit of soul-searching. Ultimately, it led to the decision that, since he had a daughter—miraculously, the only child he was aware that he had, possibly because Mamma was the only woman who had ever had the gall to reach out to him—they might as well become a proper family.

If they chose to take the money and run, Yaqeen understood. He had, technically, stolen Mamma's life savings—which admittedly was not a lot—but fair was fair. But he hoped they would not, and instead, would use the money to travel to Liverpool in Merseyside, England, and from there, travel on the White Star Line to New York

City. If they could make it there, Yaqeen would have a driver pick them up and take them straight to the beautiful plot of land that he had recently purchased in the Berkshires.

There, Yaqeen was already in the process of building a House for them—a House that he claimed had come to him in his dreams. He claimed to be working intimately with an architect and construction crew to make his literal Dream House a reality.

Mamma carefully explained all of this to Farah. It was possible she was also explaining it to herself, out loud, because the ramifications of this revelation appeared to have shaken her to her very core. Because you see, Yaqeen had also asked Mamma—whose name was Anna Andersson—to marry him and be his wife. He had included a diamond ring in the package. The band was 24-karat gold, and the sparkling rock on top was the size of Farah's thumb.

~

Farah and Mamma traveled to America with naught but the clothes on their backs, Farah's copy of *The Wonderful Wizard of Oz*, and Mamma's loom, which she refused to leave without.

When they set foot in America, a man with a handlebar mustache named Harris, wearing a black trench coat and matching leather gloves, was waiting for them, holding a large paper sign that read: ANNA ANDERSSON AND LITTLE FARAH.

Something about the words "little Farah" caused the tiny hairs on Farah's arms to prick and stand on end.

Harris helped Mamma to clumsily load her loom into the back seat of a Pierce-Arrow Model 66. (The loom was too big and awkwardly shaped for the luggage trunk.) Farah was forced to ride in the back with the loom while Mamma rode up front with Harris. Harris tried his best to make small talk. Mamma, only marginally fluent in English, responded in a rigid yes-or-no fashion, and eventually Harris resigned himself to just driving.

The Berkshires were a pastoral landscape of rolling hills and trees like fire—reds, and yellows, and oranges. It was a land of pure magic, Farah thought.

When they arrived at the House—located at the rather pretentious address of 1 Yeet Street—an invisible thief crept into Farah's lungs and stole the air right out from them.

It was the House from Farah's dreams.

It was Blåkulla.

The House was three stories of pure, brutal geometry, cocooned in an exoskeleton of scaffolding and propped-up ladders. A layer of ethereal white paint was being applied to bare walls by nearly a dozen painters in colorful, paint-spattered coveralls. At its peak was a third-floor window in the shape of an all-seeing eye, unblinking, peering endlessly over treetops and hills.

Harris guided the Model 66 off the dirt road and onto the grassy expanse in front of the House, parking it beside a freshly planted black locust sapling with a slender gray trunk, no more than ten feet tall. Even still, it looked skeletal, and haunted, and had already lost its leaves to the cold before any of the other trees.

Yaqeen must have seen them pulling up because he exited the House before they had even come to a complete stop. He had slick black hair, a neatly trimmed beard, and was wearing a cream-colored suit and no tie. Several buttons of his white button-down were undone, exposing a storm cloud of chest hair.

Farah might have thought him handsome, were it not for the smile on his face. It was too big. Too wide. As if it might come around full circle and continue in an infinite spiral.

Yaqeen approached the car as they exited. To everyone's surprise, he walked right past Mamma and stopped directly in front of Farah.

"Look at you, little Farah!" Yaqeen exclaimed. "You're just as I remembered. Oh, what great things I have in store for you!"

Mamma responded to this awkward situation the way she responded to any situation—by making it even more awkward and uncomfortable for everyone involved.

"Your tree is very ugly," said Mamma. "Why would you plant such an ugly tree in front of such a beautiful house?"

"Oh, Anna," said Yaqeen. "Always the charmer. This is a black locust tree. I'll have you know: this entire House was built from the wood of the black locust. It is strong, rot-resistant, durable wood. It is a symbol of life and death and the thin line we walk in between. But most importantly, it is a magical tree, a bridge to the underworld, with properties sensitive to shadow work and dying, decaying energies. It is the House I intend to die in, so I want to make sure we are able to live comfortably in it *after* we die."

"You are so morbid," said Anna. But even as she said it, there was something adoring in her eyes.

"Of course I'm morbid," said Yaqeen. "Why else would I ask to marry a witch such as yourself?"

Anna slapped Yaqeen in the face.

And then she kissed him. And Yaqeen kissed her back.

They lived comfortably, for a time, like a real-life, happy family. There was something that resembled love in this home.

But there was something else.

It was something invisible, lurking, but always there. Farah felt like she was being watched.

Farah tried to tell herself that it was just the size of the House. It was too big. Farah had been so used to living in a tiny shack with a bedroom that fit like a glove, that now, the wide openness of it all made her feel exposed and vulnerable.

There might have been something to that, psychologically speaking. But Farah knew there was something else. She knew where she had seen this House before, and she knew it was an exact replica.

And she knew what she had given in exchange for it.

There was also the cracking and crunching Farah would sometimes hear downstairs, in the dead of night. She had grown quite proficient at ignoring it. But only because the one time she had gone downstairs to investigate, it had scared her so much, she vowed not only to never do it again, but to pretend it had never happened.

Farah had followed the crunching sound down the stairs, across the foyer, and into the dining hall. Between the fluted columns, the double doors were cracked open. Farah peered between them, breathless.

Yaqeen was standing in front of a crackling fire in the fireplace, staring intensely into its flames. Surely, the crackling of fire and the collapsing of burnt logs was all that sound was.

It was only then that Farah noticed there was something wrong with all of Yaqeen's fingers.

Every single one of them appeared to be broken backwards.

In that exact moment, Yaqeen's right arm broke backwards. Then his left leg.

Farah almost let out a scream, but she slapped her hand over her mouth, and all that escaped was a mouse's squeak. She ran away from that cracked-open door faster than she had ever run from anything in her entire life. Her bare feet slapped quietly against tile and polished hardwood, and then she was up the stairs, diving headfirst into her bed and rolling herself in her covers like a crepe.

Farah heard the gentle clomp of heavy, approaching footsteps.

She heard the creak of her bedroom door opening. She saw the line of fluorescent hallway light stretch and expand across her bedroom in a painted line.

"I told you, little Farah," said a voice that started off as Yaqeen's . . .

. . . and morphed into the silky voice of Blåkulla. "I will always be here to watch over you."

PART II
LIGHT & DARKNESS

CHAPTER 13

The Fictional Aidan and the Real One

Aidan opened his eyes to morning daylight. New day, same hell. He felt sticky, hot, gross, and in a profound mental fog. So when he rolled onto his side and discovered Zephyr sitting on his floor, wide-eyed, reading what looked to be a very scary manga, Aidan was understandably flummoxed. Was this real life?

Zephyr glanced over at Aidan, and his already wide eyes grew wider. "You're awake!"

"What are you doing?" said Aidan. He sounded more confused than anything. He still wasn't convinced Zephyr was real. And if Zephyr *was* real, he *really* needed to get a lock on his door.

Zephyr glanced at the manga in his hand as he stood. "Oh, this? It's called *Uzumaki*. It's literally ruining my life. I love it."

"I mean, what are you doing *here*?"

"Your dad let me in," said Zephyr. "Also, there's something important I need to tell you. I got tired of waiting around for you to answer your phone."

Aidan shrank into his covers. Suddenly, that phone call with Zephyr didn't seem so bad. Having this conversation in person sounded so much worse.

"I don't want to talk right now," said Aidan.

"Oh," said Zephyr, disappointed. "Okay. I get it. I can go." He kicked the floor awkwardly. "Oh, before I forget, your dad told me to tell you he wants to talk to you too. But only when you're ready."

Aidan was flooded with dread. "What if I'm never ready to talk to him?"

Zephyr shrugged. "Then I guess you don't have to talk to him?"

"No," said Aidan. He shook his head, sitting upright. "You don't know my dad. I can't just *not* talk to him. He won't let me."

Zephyr nodded slowly, taking all of this in. And then his head stopped, mid-nod. "Crap. I forgot to tell you the most important part."

Aidan looked defeated. What other ominous and psychologically crushing message could his dad *possibly* give him?

Zephyr wrapped his arms around Aidan and said, "I love you, Aidan."

Zephyr held the hug a moment longer than necessary, then released Aidan and took a step back. "That was from your dad."

"What?" said Aidan. A tear ran down his cheek.

"I mean, technically, he just told me to give you a hug and tell you he loves you, but I wanted to do it too. So I guess that was from me also."

Aidan didn't understand what was happening. And he wasn't sure how to put that into words, except to say, "You still want to be my friend?"

"What?" said Zephyr. "Of course I want to be your friend! When have I *not* wanted to be your friend?"

"B-b-but . . . ," Aidan sputtered. "You had something important to tell me?"

Zephyr blinked slowly.

"I thought Kai and Terrance sent you over here to . . ." Aidan lost his train of thought. It didn't help that Zephyr was squinting at him like he was the most exquisite moron.

"To what?" said Zephyr. "To tell you that we don't want to be friends with you? Are you an idiot?"

Aidan was starting to feel like one.

"Nah, bruh," said Zephyr. "What I wanted to tell you is that Bea McCarthy is the biggest, nastiest buttsnack I know, and I hope she dies in Yankee Stadium, underneath a mountain of Yankee Stadium wieners. Actually, Terrance said the same thing. Not the Yankee Stadium stuff, but he *did* call her a buttsnack. You should have heard it. It was great."

Aidan processed this slowly, like the world's oldest computer. It nearly crashed his brain.

"What about Kai?" said Aidan softly.

Zephyr's smile flattened ever so slightly. Aidan felt a knife inch that much closer to his heart.

"Honestly?" said Zephyr. "I texted him, but he left me on 'read.' I think he's just processing everything. But if he's anything like the Kai *I* know? This doesn't change a thing. Me and Terrance are his friends, but *you're* his best friend. Everyone knows that. Even stupid Bea—may she choke on a Yankee Stadium wiener, in Jesus's name, amen." Zephyr crossed himself.

Aidan gave an emotional laugh, despite being on the verge of tears.

"For what it's worth," said Zephyr, "if, for whatever reason, Kai *doesn't* want to be your friend, and he makes me and Terrance choose between him and you? I'd choose you in a heartbeat. Terrance would too. But that's a multiverse scenario because the Kai in this universe would never do that."

Aidan climbed off his bed and gave Zephyr a hug. "I love you too, Zephyr."

"Bruh," said Zephyr, hugging Aidan back. "I know you do."

When the hug ended, Aidan felt revitalized. Renewed. I mean, he still felt like a dumpster fire filled with garbage juice—obviously—but he also felt like a human being capable of doing things, and that felt like a step in the right direction.

"Now don't take this the wrong way," said Zephyr, "but you need to shower. Badly."

"I know," said Aidan. He could smell himself.

"When was the last time you ate something?"

"Do my fingernails count as something?" Aidan asked.

"Good Lord," said Zephyr. "Shower. Now. I'll whip up something to eat, and that's just the *start* of our day! We've got big plans."

Part of Aidan wanted to protest. He wasn't exactly in a "big plans" mood. He was also hesitant to leave Zephyr unattended in his kitchen.

The other part of him was *so overwhelmingly happy* that he had friends who loved and cared about him, just the way he was, that— sure, fine—he could do "big plans" today. Zephyr could burn down his kitchen, and today wouldn't be a total disaster.

Aidan peeled off his two-day-old clothes. Climbed into the shower and turned the heat to extra piping hot. It felt amazing. The grime, filth, and despair of yesterday melted away.

Aidan put on his favorite pair of skinny jeans and *Skyrim* shirt, which featured an artistic rendition of the opening wagon scene:

"Hey, you. You're finally awake," and his checkered Vans, which he didn't wear often for fear of getting them dirty. He played around with his hair, which he never really did anything with because it always dried into its natural-curl shape. That was okay because his hair looked fine. He looked good. He *felt* great.

Ready to conquer the world, Aidan went downstairs and into the kitchen where he was whacked in the face with a kitchen pan of surprise. The table was filled with a spread of chocolate chip pancakes, bacon, sausage links, scrambled eggs, hash browns, and a tall pitcher of orange juice. Zephyr was already sitting with an overflowing plate, feasting.

"Huwwy, gwab a pwate!" said Zephyr, mouth full. "Da food is getteeg cowd!"

"What?" said Aidan.

Zephyr swallowed. "I said grab a plate, Dapper Dan. The food is getting cold."

"No, I mean . . . how did you make all of this?"

"Your dad helped out before he left for work."

Aidan was speechless.

"I mean, technically, he made all of it except for the bacon, which I made," said Zephyr. "It's a tad crispy. And by that, I mean burnt. Sorry."

"It looks delicious," said Aidan. "And I prefer crispy bacon."

"Bruh. I know you do."

Aidan only said that to preserve Zephyr's feelings. The bacon was burnt to hell.

After breakfast, the plan was to head to Zephyr's house. Zephyr refused to disclose why, only that it was imperative. Aidan relented his curiosity, if only for a moment. There was a slightly bigger problem, which was, he didn't have a bike anymore.

"You have Rollerblades, don't you?" said Zephyr.

Aidan did, in fact, have Rollerblades. He actually loved Rollerblading, although it was a love that was easy to forget. The only setback was that he would have to carry his shoes.

In the garage, Aidan snapped on his Rollerblades and stood up. They still fit snug but comfortable. He was reaching for his Vans when Zephyr said, "Actually, you don't need shoes."

"What do you mean, I don't need shoes?"

"That's classified."

Aidan narrowed his eyes.

"Look, believe me, or don't believe me," said Zephyr. "All I'm saying is, you don't need your shoes for what we have planned. But if you're hoping to get me to spill the beans, you are sorely mistaken. I am an unbreakable bean vault. A vault full of beans. These beans ain't going nowhere."

Aidan sighed, shoved his Vans in the spare backpack he usually carried his Rollerblades in, and pulled it onto his shoulders. Just in case.

When they arrived at Zephyr's house, Aidan was surprised to find Terrance there, sitting on the curb. Aidan was worried their first interaction might be awkward, but Terrance looked relieved to see them. He had several large shopping bags at his side.

"Dude, why didn't you go inside?" said Zephyr.

"Are you kidding me?" said Terrance. "I'm not going in there alone. Yvonne and Adelaide are already texting me, and it's weirding me out."

"Why are Zephyr's sisters texting you?" said Aidan.

"Zephyr, why does your ten-year-old sister have a phone?" said Terrance.

"Zephyr, what's in the shopping bags?" said Aidan.

"These are all excellent questions," said Zephyr. "I think we can find answers to all of them while Yvonne gives Terrance and myself our makeovers."

"While Yvonne gives you your *what*?" said Aidan.

Zephyr reached into one of Terrance's shopping bags. He pulled out a long, mint-green pleated skirt. "Ta-da! We're crashing Bea's stupid birthday party tonight, *and* Terrance and I are cosplaying as characters from your book! I'm Zephanie, and Terrance is Terra. Terrance, this is your skirt, bee-tee-dubs."

He shoved the skirt into Terrance's chest, and Terrance fumbled with it awkwardly, like a hot potato.

"Since this is a fantasy world," said Zephyr, "we decided to take some creative liberty and assigned ourselves colors associated with our elements. Earth is green, and I guess air is purple? The internet told me air is purple."

"Green *is* my favorite color," said Terrance.

Aidan glanced between Zephyr and Terrance like this was some zany Penn & Teller bit. "Why are you doing this?"

"Because you wrote a book!" Zephyr exclaimed. "And it's *good.*"

"It's *really* good," said Terrance. "Speaking as someone who actually reads. And you know I wouldn't lie to you. My dad says I'm chronically honest."

"We know Bea tried to turn your story into a bad thing," said Zephyr, "but it's blowing up in her face because the comments are really supportive. People are asking Bea how she got ahold of your notebook, and now she's trying to pretend like she's *not* an evil clown—which she obviously is."

"Bea is a buttsnack," said Terrance.

Zephyr giggled hysterically at this. "*Literally* the biggest buttsnack ever!"

"But mostly, we just want to be here for you," said Terrance, "in *whatever way* you want us to be."

"I know this probably isn't how you wanted this to happen," said Zephyr, "but we love and support you, and what better way to celebrate Aidan than to cosplay—which you love—as characters from your book? These characters *are* based on us, right?" Zephyr glanced at Aidan for confirmation.

Aidan gave an emotional nod.

Zephyr gave a small pump of his fist. "Yes! I'm a character in a book! Booyah."

"*However*," Terrance interjected loudly, "in the very strong possibility that you *don't* want us to crash Bea's birthday party cosplaying as characters from your book—which I *totally* understand—then we have a backup plan, which is to order a Hawaiian pizza and watch your favorite Studio Ghibli movie—"

Terrance said "*Princess Mononoke*" at the exact same time that Zephyr blurted out, "*Howl's Moving Castle.*" They locked glances, angry and appalled.

"Bruh, do you even *know* Aidan?" said Zephyr. "His favorite Miyazaki is *obviously* the love story with the hot wizard! Plus, *Princess Mononoke*'s way too violent for him. Remember when he covered his eyes throughout our entire *Saw* marathon?"

"*I* covered my eyes throughout your entire *Saw* marathon!" Terrance exclaimed. "And you are *vastly* underestimating Aidan's intellectual ability to appreciate a complex, eco-conscious tale of humans versus nature. Plus, in my *personal opinion*, Ashitaka is hotter than Howl."

Zephyr gave an audible gasp of horror.

So the conversation had sort of moved past Aidan's actual favorite Studio Ghibli movie—which, as it turned out, was *Kiki's Delivery Service*—to Terrance and Zephyr's usual bickering. But that didn't stop what was at the beating heart of it all.

His friends coming together to celebrate *him*.

The *real* Aidan.

"I'm gay," said Aidan.

He said this out loud.

Quietly, but out loud. It was the first time he had said it.

"Heck yeah, you are!" said Zephyr. "And we wouldn't have you any other way. That officially makes this a coming-out party."

Terrance cleared his throat awkwardly, and Aidan looked at him.

"I don't normally hug people," said Terrance. "But I want to make a special exception. Plus, Zephyr told me he cheated and hugged you without me."

Terrance hugged Aidan.

"Also, I probably don't need to say this, but my mom is not homophobic. She's not that sort of Christian. And she told me to tell you she loves you too."

Aidan had never felt as much love as he did in this moment. Terrance was hugging him, and he and Zephyr were throwing a coming-out party for him, and even Aaliyah Adams loved him, and he could feel her hug from a mile away. It was all too much.

Aidan started to cry.

"Gosh dang it, Terry," said Zephyr. "You made Aidan cry."

"It's o-o-okay," Aidan sobbed. "They're happy tears."

"Yeah, they're happy tears, *Zephyr*," said Terrance. "Read the room."

"So which is it?" said Zephyr. "Studio Ghibli night with pizza or crashing Bea's birthday party with cosplay?"

There was an obviously correct answer to this question, and that was *not* to crash the birthday party of the most terrible, hurtful person Aidan had ever met. Why would he ever *willingly* cross paths with Bea McCarthy ever again?

And yet, as Aidan glanced from the mint-green pleated skirt in Terrance's hands to the eager look in Zephyr's eyes, it was becoming increasingly difficult to say no to these two cosplaying as Terra and Zephanie. *That* part of the plan actually sounded too wonderful to be true.

"Maybe we could do the cosplay at Studio Ghibli night *instead* of crashing Bea's party?" Aidan suggested hopefully.

Terrance said, "That is perfectly fine," at the exact same time that Zephyr blurted out, "Kai's gonna be at Bea's party!"

Terrance elbowed Zephyr in the side and said, "Dude!"

"No, I . . . I'm sorry, but I'm not sorry," said Zephyr. "Aidan has a right to know."

Aidan's stomach sank to unfathomable depths. It seemed to settle somewhere far beneath the bottom of his feet.

"Okay, so Kai *might* be at Bea's party," said Terrance. "We actually don't know for sure if he'll be there. We just saw Bea invite him on that post she made, and Kai said he'll think about it. But this isn't about Kai—"

"Like heck it isn't!" said Zephyr. "If I see Kai's punk face at Bea's party, *I'm* gonna have words with him!"

"Yes, but this isn't about *you* and your *penchant for confrontation.* It's about Aidan—"

"You're damn right it is!" Zephyr snapped. "And Aidan deserves to have friends willing to stand up for him! Sure, we can eat pizza and watch anime, but then what? Bea will *still* be a buttsnack. *Unless* we do something about it."

Zephyr took a step towards Aidan, and—to his complete and utter shock—grabbed Aidan's hand and interlocked their fingers. He raised Aidan's hand like damning scientific evidence in one of those "riveting courtroom dramas" his parents liked to watch. "I'm doing this for Aidan! Yes, it will be awkward, and uncomfortable, and it's possible there will be a level of humiliation that we might never recover from, but you know what? I don't care. After what Bea did, I literally do not."

"This is crazy," said Aidan.

"You know what's crazy?" said Zephyr. "The entire time I read your story, I had this strange feeling that Nadia is the real you, and the Aidan I've been friends with this whole time is the fictional character."

That comment caught Aidan off guard. "What?"

"Nadia is brave," said Zephyr. "But you know who else is brave? You! You were the only one of us brave enough to go into the Witch

House when Gabby was freaking out. We just stood there as you went inside. You could have died! I literally thought you were *going to die*. And while on the one hand I think you can be a complete idiot sometimes, the other part of me is reading this character you wrote—Nadia—and I'm like wow. *That* is who went in the Witch House the other day. And I think *that* is the person who needs to talk to Kai today."

Zephyr said this all at once. It came out like a gust of wind.

Aidan glanced at Terrance for his input. He may have the emotional bandwidth of a computer, with feedback that felt like blunt force trauma, but he was rarely wrong. "Is that what you think?"

"I think," said Terrance, "that for once, I don't feel like the smartest person in the room. I'd listen to Zephyr. He sounds right to me."

"Bruh," said Zephyr. "Can I record you saying that? I want to put that on repeat and fall asleep to it every night."

"The moment has passed," said Terrance.

"I want to print those words out as large as possible, frame them, and hang them over the mantelpiece in my super-mansion when I grow up."

"I'm honored that you'd want to hang my words over the mantelpiece in your super-mansion," said Terrance. "But you will never hear those words ever again."

"Bruh," said Zephyr. "What if I give you a dollar?"

"No."

"Five dollars?"

"No."

"Ten dollars. Final offer."

"Show me ten dollars right now, and I'll think about it."

"This is highway robbery!" Zephyr exclaimed. "Why would you charge your best friend *ten dollars* for your words of encouragement? Do you know how many things I can buy off the McDonald's dollar menu for *ten dollars*?"

"Ten?" said Terrance.

Just like that, Aidan's anxiety melted away. Zephyr and Terrance's bickering was like comfort food. They were best friends, and this was what they did. Just like Kai and Aidan were best friends. What exactly was Aidan so afraid of? No one in this world cared for and looked out for Aidan quite the way that Kai did.

And maybe—just maybe—Aidan was feeling brave.

Sk8ers Gonna Sk8

Zephyr tried to walk directly into Yvonne's bedroom—right next door to his own bedroom—but the door was locked. He knocked impatiently.

"Password!" Yvonne barked from the other side.

"Yvonne, I'm not saying that," said Zephyr.

"Password!" Yvonne barked again. "Or you shall be denied entry! And beauty!"

Zephyr groaned as he muttered, "I am but a lowly maiden, homely and unrefined. Please lend me your aid, Queen Yvonne, so I can be super fine."

Yvonne's door flew open, and she struck a crane-like pose with both arms in the air, wrists touching, hands out like wings, her right knee tucked up to her chest.

"Enter, darlings," said Yvonne, "and you shall be fair maidens yet."

Adelaide was also in the room, and she attempted to do the same pose, but with a significant delay. She ended up falling over.

"Forgive my apprentice," said Yvonne. "She's learning."

Yvonne was a taller, gawkier version of the Windon mold. Like most Windon children, she had neat black hair with a ruler-straight part and cat-eye glasses she was legally blind without. Unlike most Windon children—or at least the boys—she had an extra foot of gangliness that she seemed unsure what to do with, so she did weird stuff like this.

Adelaide was a miniature version of Yvonne who worshipped the ground her sister walked on. Also, despite being ten years old, Adelaide was a centimeter taller than Zephyr. For this reason, Zephyr liked her a little bit less than his other siblings.

Adelaide staggered to her feet and adjusted her outfit, which could best be described as ten-year-old-girl chic: unicorn leggings and a pink T-shirt with a heart made of rainbow sequins on the front.

"Hi, Aidan!" said Adelaide. And then her smile increased tenfold, and she waggled her eyebrows at Terrance, and said in a *completely* different tone: "*Hi, Terrance.*"

"Hi, Adelaide," said Aidan.

"Hi, Adelaide," Terrance mumbled, avoiding eye contact.

"Are you boys ready to be girls?" said Yvonne in a deadly serious tone.

"Why are you making this weird, Yvonne?" said Zephyr. "Just make us girls already."

Yvonne gestured dramatically to the door that led to her and Zephyr's shared bathroom, bridging the gap between their rooms. "Change first."

Terrance changed in the shared bathroom, and Zephyr changed in his bedroom, while Aidan waited with Yvonne and Adelaide in Yvonne's bedroom, which had a bit of a theme going on. There were *RuPaul's Drag Race* posters, and a sign that read: BOYS MAKE BETTER GIRLS, and *lots* of anime boys dressed as anime girls—in poster, figurine, and smaller printout style.

"They're called 'traps' because boys fall in love with them, and then when they realize these girls *are* boys, aha!—you've been trapped." Yvonne explained this to Aidan when he couldn't stop staring at all of them.

Aidan nodded in somewhat of a daze.

"I'm pansexual, by the way," said Yvonne. "Always lovely to meet a fellow queer."

"Thanks," said Aidan. He laughed uneasily. "Um. You too."

"I loved your book, by the way. The queer subtext is *sublime*. Actually, *all* of my friends loved it."

Jesus Christ, Aidan thought. How many people had read his book?

At that point, Aidan was hauntingly reminded of his number one fan, Gabby Caldwell, and how she was waiting patiently for pages (to say *nothing* of him solving the twenty-year-old mystery of her death, curse, and lost memories). Now, Aidan didn't even have so much as a notebook to write in! Technically, he *could* still rebuild his story using the pages Bea had scanned for the world to see, but just the *thought* of revisiting that hellish part of the internet settled in Aidan's gut like a cinder block.

Sorry, Gabby. *Fire & Water* was on indefinite hiatus.

The door between the bathroom and Zephyr's bedroom opened. Zephyr's and Terrance's outfits were *mostly* identical (matching white button-down blouses, black flats), except where their color schemes diverted (their skirts and the ribbons tied at their collars were lilac purple and mint green, respectively). Their wigs were quite different as well. Zephyr's was long, straight, and black, like his sisters' hair. Terrance's was a short, curly Afro style. All in all, not quite what Aidan imagined when writing *Fire & Water*—a little too *Sailor Moon* in their color scheme—but surreal to witness with his own eyes. Even without makeup, the two of them legitimately looked like girls.

"Dang, girl," said Zephyr to Terrance. "You look like a girl!"

"You do too," said Terrance.

"I would date myself," said Zephyr. "Terrance, would you date me?"

"I just want to get into MIT," said Terrance. "Then I can worry about dating."

"Hey, I want to go to MIB too!" Adelaide piped in. "We sure have a lot in common, don't we, Terrance?"

"M-I-*T*!" Terrance exclaimed. "Massachusetts Institute of *Technology*. I am not applying to be in the Men in Black!"

"Oh, I *love* technology," said Adelaide adoringly.

"Hey, Terry," said Zephyr. "When you and Addy get married, can I be your best man?"

Terrance rolled his eyes and said, "Can we get these makeovers over with already?"

"Okay, okay, Miss Terra," said Yvonne. "Who would like to go first?"

Zephyr looked at Terrance. "Would *you* like to go first?"

Terrance shook his head vehemently.

"Okay, I'll go first," said Zephyr.

The process was much more involved than Aidan expected. First, Yvonne removed Zephyr's wig, then pulled a wig cap over his head, getting his hair out of the way and compressing it to the shape of his skull. It also served as fiber material to help his wig stick better to his head.

Next was foundation and contouring. Yvonne painted five different shades on Zephyr's face, and the skepticism was evident on both Aidan's and Terrance's expressions—there was no way Yvonne was going to make this work. He looked like a clown. But then, like a Bob Ross painting, all those hues and shades clicked, and suddenly Zephyr had a completely different shape and look to his face. It was fantastic. It was fabulous. It was . . .

"That's so fetch!" said Zephyr, checking himself out in his handheld mirror.

"Babe, we are *just* getting started," said Yvonne.

Lastly were the more traditional steps in the makeup process. Brushes and blush. Lip liner and eyeliner. Lip color and eye makeup, for which Yvonne tapped into Zephyr's elemental theme—lilac.

All the while, Adelaide was on manicure duty. Originally, there had been a plan to use fake nails, but then everyone unanimously agreed that at a fantasy school that practiced battle magic, long nails were impractical. But it would also be a shame not to embrace the color scheme, so Zephyr's nails were painted lilac.

When Zephyr's transformation was complete—the wig reapplied to his head—he looked more like a girl than any girl who ever *girled* before him.

"Are you ready, Terrance?"

"My Terra is going to be the belle of the ball!" said Adelaide. She clasped her hands to the side of her face and swooned.

Terrance sighed.

Once Yvonne finished with Terrance, he truly *was* the belle of the ball. His mint-green eyeshadow was the showstopper. His eyes popped.

"All right, ladies and gents," said Yvonne. "Have fun crashing Beatrice McCarthy's birthday party. But first!"

Yvonne rushed into her closet and returned with a *huge* rainbow-colored, three-foot jumbo greeting card that read: YAY! YOU'RE GAY! She extended it to Aidan.

"We didn't want to give this to you unless you were *officially* out," said Yvonne, "but as of about a half hour ago, Zephyr texted me and said that that *might* be the case? So, here. It's big enough that we were all able to write a little something for you. Zephyr, however, wrote something *really special*."

"Oh my God, Yvonne," said Zephyr. He smacked her on the arm. "Please feel free to shut up forever."

Aidan received the card like a warm hug. He blinked rapidly, and inhaled deeply, so that he didn't break down into tears twice in one day.

"Even if tonight doesn't turn out exactly the way you want it to," said Yvonne, "I want you to know that all my friends and I are your biggest fans. Also, if you ever felt like doing a reading or a Q and A at our book club, we would *seriously* love you forever."

"Yvonne!" Zephyr scolded. "This is Aidan's day, not a hostage negotiation!"

Aidan sniffed back a surge of emotion. "Can you ask me about the book club after tonight? If I'm feeling brave enough, I think that'd be really fun. Thank you so much for everything." He glanced between Zephyr and Terrance, and it was *impossible* not to smile. "You too, Adelaide. Thank you."

"I accept payment in pictures of Terrance," said Adelaide. "Pictures of him sleeping are worth double."

175

Terrance's eyeballs were practically outside his skull.

"I'll, um . . . see what I can do?" said Aidan. He glanced at Zephyr for help, but Zephyr was laughing his butt off.

Sk8ers Gonna Sk8 was a 25,000-square-foot phantasmagoria of lights, music, skating, laser tag, arcade, and karaoke, with enough greasy fried food to kill Guy Fieri.

Yvonne was kind enough to offer the "boys" a ride in her Fiat 500X Crossover. It was beige, but Yvonne referred to the color as "Mohave Sand."

Saturday nights were usually busy at Sk8ers Gonna Sk8, but dang. Yvonne couldn't have parked if she *wanted* to. Several vehicles had already taken the liberty of inventing parking spots where there weren't any.

"You ready for this?" Zephyr asked Aidan.

To be truthful, Aidan was 100 percent *not ready* for this. This was a terrible idea. Whose idea was this, anyway?

"You okay, Aidan?" said Terrance.

"What would Nadia do?" Aidan whispered to himself.

I'd let that blond terror, Buttsnack McCarthy, know that she has no power over me, said the version of Nadia that lived in Aidan's head. *Also, I'd get my friend back.*

"Let's go," said Aidan. He opened the right rear door and hopped out, blazing with the fiery confidence of the strongest, coolest girl in all of Aether.

The closer you were to the building, the more you felt the bass of the music rattling your bones. The moment you stepped inside, you could feel the music in your teeth. It *sounded* like a gaudy pop remix of an older pop song and *felt* like a root canal under dull anesthesia.

"Three tickets for the roller rink, please," said Aidan to the woman at the front desk.

The first thing Aidan noticed were the little white skulls painted on the woman's black nails. Then, the nearly full sleeve of tattoos on her right arm, which Aidan's gaze slowly followed up before settling on the septum piercing in her nose, where he stared in a sort of trance. It took a full three seconds before Aidan remembered that Kai's mom, Kalani, worked at Sk8ers Gonna Sk8, and he realized he was staring at her nose.

Kalani snorted at the sight of them.

Aidan attempted to clear his throat. He needed a drink of water. No. Aidan needed to *say something*.

"Is Kai here?" Aidan croaked in a tiny voice, like the world's thirstiest little frog.

"He's at the birthday party, which is over *that way*."

Kalani pointed a skull-painted fingernail to the far end of Sk8ers Gonna Sk8, where a scene of way too many soon-to-be eighth graders were orbiting around the celestial body known as Beatrice McCarthy. Aidan could have spotted her from a mile away. How could he not? From her golden hair to her glowing complexion, she was as radiant as a star, and just as deadly.

"Hey, Aidan, do me a favor?" said Kalani. "Can you give something to Bea for me?"

Aidan was so unprepared for personal requests from Kalani—let alone ones that entailed interacting with Bea—he could only look at her and gape stupidly.

Kalani raised her left fist, the back of her hand facing him, and with her right hand, she pretended to wind it up like a jack in the box. As she did so, the most inappropriate finger on that particular hand raised up, in increments, until it was fully straight.

"That's for Bea," said Kalani, winking. She pretended to grab her entire left fist with her right hand, and then made a movement like an underhand toss, as if passing the entire offensive gesture to Aidan. Aidan was so poorly equipped to react to this, he reached out to catch it. (Part of him thought she'd actually thrown something at him, and he was trying to catch it before it hit him.) "Your book was rad, by the way. Don't let anyone tell you otherwise. Keep writing."

Aidan's face turned a violent shade of red. He attempted to nod, but it ended up more like the erratic wobbling of a dashboard bobble-head. He veered a sharp one hundred and eighty degrees and power walked towards Bea's birthday party, where certain death surely awaited.

"Gosh dang," said Zephyr. "Kalani sure is cool. Do you think she's into younger guys?"

"I'm gonna stop you right there," said Terrance. "No, Kai's mom is not into *thirteen-year-old boys*."

"Wha—?" Zephyr sputtered. "I wasn't asking for myself! I was asking for . . . um . . ."

He glanced at Aidan, then seemed to realize instantly that that was the wrong answer. Regardless, Aidan turned from red to magenta and shook his head in small, jagged movements.

"Maybe I was asking for *you*, Terry!" Zephyr exclaimed. "Did you ever think about that? I mean, unless you'd rather go to homecoming with Adelaide."

"We can't even go to homecoming until next year! And why are my two romantic options *Kai's mom* and your *ten-year-old sister*?"

"I dunno, man. It'd be a lot easier if you just told us who you liked."

"Told you who I—?" said Terrance incredulously. "Who do *you* like?"

Aidan looked at Zephyr at the exact same moment that Zephyr looked at him.

"Fine, I, uh . . . I like Kalani!" Zephyr exclaimed, about three octaves higher than usual. He sounded like a cartoon character. "Are we gonna crash Bea's birthday party or what?"

Zephyr charged ahead of Aidan and Terrance, full steam ahead. Aidan and Terrance exchanged bewildered glances, then attempted to follow close behind.

The skating rink pulsed and blushed in shades of neon reds, pinks, purples, and even deep, electric blue. Skaters of all ages and sizes moved in a whirlpool of the human condition—from small children shuffling awkwardly like penguins on ice, to elderly couples holding hands, moving with such fluidity and grace, it was obvious they shared regular date nights here.

Bea McCarthy and her forty-two friends, followers, and undoubtedly a few worshippers were not out on the rink, currently. Rather, they occupied a series of chairs and tables that had been pushed haphazardly together. There was a multitiered birthday cake at the center of them, stacked higher than most people's wedding cakes. It was the *Sagrada Família* of cakes—probably aligned with the golden ratio, scientifically perfect. Stacked even higher was a mountain of presents, clustered together like some dragon's glittering hoard of treasure. Bea was in the process of opening them, one by one.

Sitting directly beside Bea was Kai. He was smiling—or at least *trying* to smile.

Aidan's gaze was ripped from Kai's smile to his hand on the table. Bea casually grabbed it. Linked her fingers in his.

It was a gesture that lasted only a second—her hands were occupied with another present the very next—but it gutted Aidan like some old-fashioned torture device. Just ripped him open, allowing his guts to spill out onto the floor for everyone to see.

It took Terrance and Zephyr only a moment longer before they saw what Aidan was seeing.

"Aw, crap," said Terrance.

"That son of a—" Zephyr called Kai something that Aidan thought was pretty unfair to Kalani.

Bea's birthday party apparently overheard him because several heads turned to see what all the hullabaloo was about—Bea included.

The look on Bea's face reminded Aidan of the best villains in fiction—it transformed in shades, from dislike, to cunning, to sickening glee in seconds.

"Oh, Aidan, you came!" Bea exclaimed. She seemed to study him for a moment—a calculated gesture.

"It's okay if you didn't bring a present. You gave me that cute little book of yours, didn't you? I'd say *that's* present enough."

"Oh no, she didn't," Terrance muttered under his breath.

Zephyr said nothing.

His arms were straight lines to his balled-up fists.

Zephyr was *trembling* with rage.

Kai's frail smile turned into a frown. He leaned towards Bea and whispered something that sounded like: *Just leave him alone, Bea.*

Bea did *not* leave Aidan alone. In fact, she now gave herself permission to absorb Zephyr and Terrance in all their fabulous, cosplaying glory.

"I *love* the outfits," said Bea. "Is this what you guys have to do so Aidan doesn't write love stories about you?"

This earned a few giggles. But then, one of the boys beside Bea—a rich little cretin named D'Angelo Prescott—chimed in, "No homo!" And the whole birthday party completely lost it.

Aidan had never heard such laughter. It roared like ocean waves dashing against the rocks. They laughed like what he'd said was comedy gold.

"We're cosplaying as characters in Aidan's book, you d-bags!" Zephyr yelled, but nobody seemed to hear him.

Terrance wilted under the laughter. He didn't say anything, but the look on his face seemed to say that he might never recover from this.

Aidan said nothing.

I'm going to destroy her, said Nadia.

Aidan wasn't here. This wasn't happening.

Aidan, Nadia commanded, with a voice like a fist. *Let me destroy her.*

Aidan handed the reins over to the voice of the destroyer inside his head.

What happened next was, Aidan shouted at the top of his lungs, "HEY, BUTTSNACK MCCARTHY."

If there was a surefire way to get the attention of forty-two little monsters at Beatrice McCarthy's birthday party, it was to replace Beatrice's name with "buttsnack" at the top of your lungs. He snuffed their laughter out like a douter over a candle flame. Just absolutely silenced them.

"I actually do have a birthday present for you," said Aidan. He lifted his left fist, the back of his hand facing them, and proceeded to wind it up with his right hand in a perfect mirror of the gesture Kalani asked him to deliver. Surely, she didn't *actually* mean for Aidan to deliver it, but then again, this wasn't *actually* Aidan. Not completely, anyway. This was someone far more callous and cunning.

"Oh my God," said Terrance. He stared at the person flipping off Bea as if he were a complete stranger.

"Oh my God!" Zephyr exclaimed, far more elated. He looked like a proud parent watching their child win the spelling bee.

What Aidan did next, however, differed wildly from Kalani. He pretended to grab his left fist with his right hand, but instead of an underhand toss, he wound himself up like a top—imitating hours of studying Kai's pitching form—and yeeted that birdie so hard at Bea, it should have broken the sound barrier.

He of course hadn't actually thrown *anything*, but like Aidan with Kalani, Bea didn't know that. All she knew was it *looked* like he'd thrown something, and she tried to dodge it.

Unfortunately for Bea, she was wearing Rollerblades, and so as her traction-less feet slid backwards, her front half went forwards. But her face didn't hit the table.

It was cushioned by all the *many tiers* of her birthday cake.

There was perfect silence as Bea peeled herself out of her cake. Her face was *caked* in frosting. It was impossible to tell what expression she was wearing because she *looked* like the Abominable Snowman.

182

"Buttsnack McCarthy," D'Angelo Prescott chuckled to himself. It was the usual sort of two-timey thing that came out of his little cretin mouth.

Everyone—every single person invited to Bea's birthday party, all forty-two of them—laughed.

Everyone except Kai, that is. Kai was too busy glancing between Aidan and Bea like some impossible multiple-choice question.

CHAPTER 15

Sempai Fighter II

Bea's birthday party scattered and dissipated like leaves off a tree in the changing seasons. Aidan *tried* his best to ignore where Kai went after that, and he failed. He was *acutely aware* that Kai was holed up in the arcade, taking out his frustrations, and game tokens, on their favorite fighting game of all time, *Sempai Fighter II*. Aidan wanted so badly to play it with him. He also wanted to never see Kai's stupid face ever again.

And so Aidan resolved to get his money's worth skating—mostly because he wanted to get the dirty taste of what happened to Bea out of his mouth.

Had she deserved it? Probably. But that didn't mean it tasted good.

Zephyr was *perfectly fine* with this outcome. He looked like he was skating on pure sunshine.

Terrance was less enthusiastic. He left for the arcade after a few minutes, leaving Aidan and Zephyr to skate alone.

Together.

Zephyr was *sort of* acting weird about it. Aidan wondered if it had anything to do with the fact that he was dressed like a girl, and the two of them *looked* like a couple. Aidan might have thought more about it if he didn't feel like hot garbage.

"Are you okay?" asked Zephyr—a very uncharacteristic question coming from him.

Aidan sighed. "Not really," he said in a moment of weakness.

Zephyr frowned. "Why not?"

Aidan shrugged. "I don't feel good making people feel bad."

Zephyr absorbed that quietly. "Even if they deserve it?"

"I don't like thinking about what people deserve or don't deserve. Because then I start thinking about what *I* deserve. Do I deserve *anything* good in my life? Because honestly, I don't feel like I do."

Aidan felt Zephyr take his hand, and it caused his heart to skip a beat—maybe *two beats*—like a double-jump in a video game.

"You deserve every good thing in your life," said Zephyr. "Don't let anyone tell you otherwise."

Aidan glanced down at Zephyr's hand in his. Even though Zephyr's hand was smaller than his, it was weird how perfectly they fit together. Aidan had never thought that about another person's hand before. (Not that Aidan was some connoisseur of hand-holding; he wasn't— no matter *how often* he'd fantasized about holding Kai's hand.)

The moment became awkward for Aidan and Zephyr simultaneously—both clearing their throats and letting go at once.

"Let's go talk to Kai," said Zephyr. "You and me both."

Aidan nearly forgot how to skate. He tripped on absolutely nothing (except the psychological fear of the unknown) and nearly face-planted on the varnished maple hardwood floor.

The thought of initiating a conversation with Kai filled Aidan with such fear and shame, he almost would have rather chased Bea into the girls' bathroom.

"I'll be right there with you," said Zephyr.

Sempai Fighter II was a fighting game that took place in a rough-and-tumble Japanese high school in some alternate-universe take on 1992.

The fighters were a wide range of rowdy delinquents with ridiculous names like Aiko Aikido and Hayate Karate. In single-player mode, you waged war against the League of Evil Teachers at Sempai High— *including* the occasional high-ranking student in cahoots with the League, such as Evil Student Council President Tomo Taekwondo. The endgame was to defeat the evil headmaster of Sempai High, Roboto Righteous, who was—you guessed it—an evil artificial intelligence hell-bent on world domination and creating a techno-dystopia in which teenage dating was outlawed. He would accomplish this by replacing teenage human brains with a hivemind artificial intelligence programmed for the sole purpose of doing homework and getting good grades. The League of Evil Teachers would no longer have to grade homework, because everyone's grades would be perfect! Kids like Aiko and Hayate thought that was "wack."

Anyway, if you succeeded in defeating Headmaster Roboto and his League of Evil Teachers, the player was granted a first date with the character of their choice, which ended in a menagerie of humorous—occasionally steamy—date scenes that played out over the course of the end credits, culminating in an endless wealth of replay value.

In two-player mode, you simply selected your fighter, your battleground of choice—the cafeteria, the library, the parking lot, etc.—and beat the mother-loving crap out of each other. The appeal was simple yet timeless.

Sempai Fighter II was positioned in the dead center of the arcade. Kai and Terrance were hunkered over its control panels, mashing buttons and rattling joysticks like the fate of the world depended on it. (It *sort of* did.) Kai played as his go-to character, Hayate, who, in all seriousness, did look a bit like Kai. Terrance played Evil Student Council President Tomo Taekwondo, mostly because Tomo's catchphrase upon defeating his opponent was "Tomo means 'intelligent,' you know," as he coolly pushed his glasses up the bridge of his nose. Terrance thought that was just *hilarious.*

This was *exactly* what happened as Aidan and Zephyr approached the fight from behind. Kai cursed and groaned, and Terrance laughed and pretended to push a pair of invisible glasses up the bridge of his nose as he parroted Tomo's catchphrase.

"Wow," said Zephyr. "Terrance beat *Kai*? You *know* Kai's having an off day today."

Kai nearly jumped out of his skin.

It seemed possible *he might still* because—as he reluctantly turned to find Zephyr *and* Aidan there—inside his own skin looked like the last place he wanted to be. Aidan wilted.

"Yeah," said Kai, laughing weakly. "Someone else's turn to fight Terrance, I guess."

"Actually, I'm kinda *Sempai Fighter*-ed out," said Terrance. He cast a deliberate glance Aidan's way and said, "You wanna take my place?"

Aidan glanced in horror from Terrance to Kai, whom he fully expected to turn his nose up at this prospect. Maybe invent some imaginary place he needed to be.

Instead, Kai offered Aidan a timid smile and said, "Get over here. Let me kick your butt."

Aidan smiled. A real, genuine—if slightly nervous—smile. "Okay."

Aidan took hold of Terrance's controls, still warm from Terrance's button-mashing.

"You know what sounds good right now?" said Zephyr. "Pizza." He glanced at Terrance. "Doesn't pizza sound good right now, Terry?"

Zephyr's subtlety was on par with a derailed freight train, and Terrance was standing just off the tracks.

"Sure?" said Terrance.

"Can you get me a slice?" said Kai hopefully.

"I guess," said Zephyr. "How about you, Aidan? Hawaiian?"

"Hawaiian sounds amazing, thank you," said Aidan graciously.

"Hey, aren't you gonna ask me what I want?" said Kai.

"I know your boring butt just wants cheese," said Zephyr.

Kai placed a hand over his heart and said, "You know me so well."

Zephyr harrumphed indignantly at this as he turned and left. Terrance matched Zephyr's pace as he said, "Dude, cheese *is* timeless."

Kai reached into the baggy pocket of his cargo shorts, removed a handful of game tokens—he was almost assuredly getting them for free from Kalani—and inserted them one by one into the player one coin slot. Once again, he selected Hayate.

"*You're cruisin' for a bruisin',*" said Hayate.

Aidan selected Aiko—a fiery redhead, not unlike Nadia, with pigtails and a Band-Aid over the bridge of her nose.

"*I'm here to kick butt and chew bubble gum,*" said Aiko. She blew a large pink bubble that popped aggressively in her mouth.

Kai selected "random" for the battleground, and it chose the roof of Sempai High—an accessible part of *every* Japanese high school, at least as far as the world of anime was concerned.

"*Three, two, one—fight!*" a disembodied voice in the game exclaimed.

"Do you like me, Aidan?"

Aidan went rigid at his controls. Hayate landed a flying round-house kick to Aiko's face.

"And I don't mean as a friend," said Kai. "Do you *like me* like me?"

Aidan had been backed into a corner. There was nowhere left for him to go.

He nodded timidly.

Kai nodded slowly in response. Then he rubbed a hand through his hair. "Wow. Okay."

"But I don't want that to stop us from being friends," Aidan blurted out. "Because even though I like you as more than a friend, you're still my best friend. I would do anything in the world for you. Anything. Including setting all my feelings for you aside. I would do that. For you."

Aidan cringed once the words exploded out of his mouth. If he was trying to sound like he wasn't absolutely obsessed with Kai, he was failing.

"I know you would," said Kai. And then he looked sad. "I'm sorry I wasn't there for you yesterday. I'm sure this has been harder for you than it has for me. And . . . I'm sorry for coming to Bea's party. I honestly don't know why I came. I mean . . . I do. But I don't. Does that make sense?"

It 100 percent did not, but Aidan nodded anyway. He thought he understood what Kai meant.

"It's okay," said Aidan.

"No, it's not," said Kai. "You deserve better than me."

"I don't want better than you," said Aidan. "I just want you."

The moment the words came out of his mouth, Aidan nearly went into cardiac arrest.

"As a friend," Aidan quickly amended his statement. "I just want you *as a friend.*"

Kai didn't respond. Instead, he just looked sad. Seeing Kai so sad made Aidan even sadder. This was it. This was the moment when Kai ended their friendship. Could Aidan even blame him? Probably not.

Hayate landed a finishing move on Aiko, kicking her so hard in the head, she flipped backwards a full three hundred and sixty degrees—an arc of blood trailing from her face—and she landed in a broken heap. The game exclaimed, "*KO! Hayate wins.*"

"But I understand if you don't want that anymore—" Aidan started to say.

"Do you know what I've been thinking about this entire time?" Kai cut him off.

This comment caught Aidan off guard. He wasn't sure he understood the question.

"*Round two,*" said the game. "*Three, two, one—fight!*"

"This whole time," said Kai, "while Bea's been opening presents that cost as much as my mom's paycheck, and D'Angelo's been cracking his stupid jokes, and Bea's been trying to hold my hand every other minute, I've been thinking about the moment we became friends." Kai looked at Aidan. "Do you remember?"

"In first grade?"

"That was *when* it happened. But do you remember *how* it happened?"

Aidan thought hard. "We ate lunch together?"

"Yes. And no. I don't know if I ever told you this, but . . . I didn't eat lunch for the first several days of first grade."

"What? Why not?"

"My mom forgot to sign me up for the free lunch program. She *meant* to. She just forgot. And she obviously didn't give me lunch money, and she didn't pack me a lunch. So I just went without lunch. I found a paper bag in the trash, and I filled it with garbage, pretending it was my lunch. I pretended I didn't want to eat it because I said my mom's cooking tasted like—"

"Like garbage," said Aidan. He remembered.

Kai laughed, blinking moisture from his eyes. "But I was lying because I was too embarrassed to admit I didn't have food or money. I just pretended I was too *cool* for my lunch. Do you remember what happened next?"

"I shared my lunch."

"You shared *exactly half* of your lunch," said Kai. "You had a ham and cheese sandwich cut into triangles, and you gave me one of them. And you had a Go-Gurt and string cheese, and you let me choose which one I wanted, and I chose Go-Gurt. And you had a tangerine and baby carrots, and you let me choose between those, and I chose the tangerine, even though neither of us wanted baby carrots, and I felt bad, but you said it was okay because—"

"Because carrots are good for your eyes," said Aidan.

"Because carrots are good for your eyes," said Kai. "And you ate them anyway. *That* was when we became friends. Eventually my mom realized that she hadn't signed me up for free lunch. And when she asked what I'd been eating all that time, I told her you'd been sharing your lunch with me. She was *so* embarrassed. She got it fixed, and I finally started eating cafeteria food. And while I was relieved to be eating my own lunch like a normal kid, all I could think about was how much I missed sharing your lunches with you. That Go-Gurt, and tangerine, and half of a ham and cheese sandwich was the best meal I've ever had. It sounds stupid, but it's the truth."

Aidan's mouth was gaping. How had he not known this?

"I'll be honest," said Aidan. "I wasn't trying to be a good person. I just liked sharing my lunch with you. I just liked . . ."

You.

"I know," said Kai. "That's what I like about you. You weren't pitying me. You were just being my friend." He sniffled and wiped his eyes. "So to answer your question: no, I will not stop being your friend. Not now, not ever."

"Then . . . ," said Aidan. He was having a heck of a time processing everything that'd been said. "Why'd you come here?"

Kai hesitated. "If I'm being completely honest—"

"One slice of Hawaiian pizza," said Zephyr's voice from behind, "for the guy who flipped off Bea at her own birthday party!"

Zephyr dropped a paper plate with a pizza flat on top of Aidan's controls. To say that Aidan and Kai were barely fighting was an understatement. Aidan was playing almost completely on autopilot. However, the plate slapped onto his buttons in such a way that Aiko landed a grappling move, swung Hayate by the necktie of his school uniform, and flung him off the roof of the school.

"*KO!*" the game exclaimed. "*Aiko wins.*"

"Oh snap," said Terrance.

"Hey-o!" Zephyr exclaimed. "You won!"

"If you're being completely honest?" Aidan repeated, uninvested in his own victory. Who was he kidding? Pineapple pizza won that fight.

"Oh, um . . . it's nothing," said Kai. He seemed all too eager to change the subject. "Forget about it."

It certainly didn't *sound* like nothing to Aidan. Then again, who was Aidan to push his luck? He had conquered his fear of Bea and reclaimed Kai's friendship in a single night. Could he really ask for more?

Kai's cryptic disclaimer, "If I'm being completely honest," hovered ominously in the air.

Aidan *wanted* to ask for more. But he wasn't selfish.

He let it slide.

The sun set over Curtain Falls like a reverie, splashing colors and hues across the sleepy horizon. Once again, Yvonne acted as chauffeur, dropping each of the boys off one by one. Because Kalani was working until close, Kai asked if he could "bum a ride" too. Yvonne could barely contain her smile. Never had an older sister been so happy to chauffeur her little brother's friends.

Kai was quiet the entire drive. At first, Aidan was nervous that maybe Kai felt uncomfortable. Then, Kai unceremoniously broke the silence.

"Can we meet at the library tomorrow?" he asked.

Everyone looked at Kai in varying degrees of confusion—including Yvonne from the rearview mirror.

"I may have . . . found something," said Kai. "About Gabby and the Witch House. Maybe. I don't know. I would have told you guys sooner, but . . . well . . . you know."

"Dude, seriously?" said Zephyr. "What did you find?"

"I'll tell you tomorrow," said Kai. "I need to show you something. It's better if we approach this with fresh brains. It's . . . a lot."

Aidan, Terrance, and Zephyr nodded disjointedly, like a collection of bobbleheads. It *had* been a long day.

Yvonne swung by Portière Park first (the trailer park where Kai lived), then Aidan and Terrance's cul-de-sac.

"Don't forget your card!" Zephyr chimed in eagerly.

Aidan waved goodbye to Terrance, crossing to the opposite side of the cul-de-sac, and Zephyr and Yvonne as they flipped a U-ey and drove away.

Aidan opened his front door. The plan had been to sneak into his bedroom and tuck the card somewhere secret—somewhere safe—where he could read what everyone had written in private.

That's when he realized his parents were quietly eating dinner in the dining room—which was in full view of the entryway, and he was holding a rainbow-colored card the size of someone's science fair project that read: YAY! YOU'RE GAY!

There was a long moment when nothing was said. Aidan could only imagine what was going through their heads. So he mumbled, almost indiscernibly, "I'm sorry," and started for his bedroom.

"No, wait—Aidan!" said Mr. Cross. He stood up from his chair. "You don't need to apologize." He gestured a friendly hand at Aidan's usual seat across from him, beside his mom. "Eat dinner with us. Your food's getting cold. We're having chicken alfredo—your favorite!"

Aidan stopped dead in his tracks. Was this a trap? Some sort of intervention? The thought occurred that maybe he should bolt and run away from home, but then what? Where would he live? Perhaps take refuge in an abandoned boxcar? Become a Boxcar Child?

Being an orphan by day and solving mysteries by night didn't sound terrible.

"Who's that from?" Mr. Cross asked. He nodded to the jumbo greeting card.

"The Windons," Aidan mumbled.

"Well, that was very kind of them," said Mr. Cross. "I actually have something for you as well."

Mr. Cross stepped into the kitchen. When he came back out, he was holding Aidan's notebook.

Aidan's heart was in his throat. He was practically choking on it.

"I got ahold of Beatrice McCarthy's dad after I saw that post," he said. "I explained that his daughter was in possession of something that belonged to you. He handed it over, no questions asked. He said his daughter was deeply sorry for taking it. Apparently, she's gotten into a bit of hot water online ever since she made that post."

Aidan stared at his notebook like a mirage. Like it might ripple and disappear the moment he made a move for it.

"I may have introduced myself to Mr. McCarthy as a former FBI employee," said Mr. Cross, and he winked. He extended the notebook. "Here. Take it."

Aidan shuffled over, took the notebook, and held it against his chest.

"You know, I have a coworker who's gay," said Mr. Cross.

Aidan's spine snapped as straight as a streetlamp.

"He's very witty, and funny, and self-aware, and one of my favorite people to work with," said Mr. Cross. He shifted uncomfortably. "What I'm trying to say is, I love you just the way you are. And I hope you never feel like you have to hide a part of yourself from me. That would make me very sad—"

Aidan hugged his dad. He surprised himself with his own boldness.

"Thank you for getting my notebook back," said Aidan.

Mr. Cross hugged Aidan back with one hand, and awkwardly patted his head with the other. He seemed distracted.

Aidan let go of his dad and looked at his mom.

Mrs. Cross smiled pleasantly. But when she met Aidan's gaze, she teared up.

"Sorry, I don't seem to be feeling well," she said. "May I be excused?"

Mrs. Cross pushed her chair back, stood up, and attempted to flee the dining room in as dignified a manner as possible. Aidan tried not to watch as she fled. It was too crushing.

So Aidan was completely blindsided when she turned back around and hugged him from behind. She even kissed the top of his head. Any other day of the week, he might have taken that for granted. Today, he cherished it like the most precious treasure.

"I love you, Aidan," said Mrs. Cross into the top of his head. "Don't mind me. Your ol' mom is just out of sorts lately."

"Are you okay?" Aidan asked.

"I'll *be* okay," said Mrs. Cross. "Just keep being the wonderful kid that you are."

Mrs. Cross retreated to her bedroom, and as she did, Aidan felt an insurmountable weight lift from his shoulders. His mom was back to normal.

Mostly.

CHAPTER 16

Super_Hacker_Kai

The boys convened the next morning in the basement of the library. Kai arrived first. He'd already commandeered a table with a single computer and was in the process of pulling up his research. Aidan, Terrance, and Zephyr grabbed nearby chairs and scooted around him.

Aidan had no idea what Kai's research was, but it was visually loud, and violently pink, and reeked of the ancient days of the internet.

Kai rotated in his swivel chair, blocking Aidan's view of the screen.

"Before I show you what *I* found," said Kai, "did anyone else find anything they want to share?"

For some reason, everyone turned to look at Aidan. Fair enough. Aidan *was* the reason they were even doing this research to begin with.

But Aidan shook his head.

Zephyr raised his hand.

Everyone perked up. The astonishment was palpable.

"I didn't find anything either," Zephyr announced.

Terrance shook his head, unzipping his backpack on his lap and unloading an impressive sheaf of papers stapled together in bunches. "I may have done a little bit of internet research last night."

He leafed through stapled packets and handed them out. They were still warm from the printer.

"Sweet and Sour Jesus," said Zephyr. "A little?"

"I mean, I didn't discover anything profound," said Terrance. "But I did discover *things.*"

Everything Terrance found was almost exclusively from old, digitized Ellis Island records. As Terrance explained it, Ellis Island was home to sixty-five million records of passengers and immigrants arriving to the Port of New York City from 1820 to 1957.

It just so happened that a girl named Farah Yeet—eight years old—arrived in New York from Sweden in 1908 with her mother, Anna Andersson. They moved immediately into the Witch House, which Farah's father, Yaqeen Yeet, had built for them.

She began selling her infamous curtains when she was only eighteen—allegedly still in her last semester of high school.

By 1922, she had skyrocketed to fame. And yet, she was a recluse to all. This was the year she eloped with a young man named Jesse Glass.

Farah died in 1924.

"There's not a lot of information about Farah," said Terrance, "which maybe isn't so weird. It seems she wanted it that way. What *is* weird is how little information there is about Jesse Glass. It's like he's not even a person."

"What do you mean, not even a person?" Aidan asked.

"I mean . . . I realize I've only been looking for a little bit, but I can't find *any information about him*, except as it pertains to Farah Yeet. And then there's *this*—last page."

Everyone flipped to the last page of the packet. It appeared to be some sort of crude legal document.

CURTAIN FALLS, Massachusetts, July 31.

J. Glass was hanged here to-day for obscenity, flirtation with dark forces, and by the majority vote of this here council, possibly being the Devil himself. F. Yeet was forced to witness this execution so that she might be moved to repentance, and the Lord may have mercy on her eternal soul.

"I feel like there's a lot one could interpret from this," said Terrance. "Out of respect for my mother, let's assume that the Devil *is* real. Maybe Jesse Glass *was* the Devil."

"Bruh," Zephyr whispered.

"That would certainly explain why Jesse doesn't seem to exist outside of his relationship with Farah. However, out of respect for science *and* history, let's *also* assume this whole public execution was a kangaroo court. What if they were just an angry mob, and they simply proclaimed Farah a witch like simpleminded, sexist zealots have been doing for centuries, but Farah was too wealthy and powerful for them to do anything about it? So they murdered Jesse instead."

"Yeah, but what do kangaroos gotta do with anything?" Zephyr asked.

"Zephyr," said Terrance, exasperated. "There are no *actual kangaroos* involved in a kangaroo court."

"It's like an unofficial court where a group of people convict someone of a crime without sufficient evidence," Aidan tried to explain.

"It's like the People's Court in Nazi Germany," said Kai. "C'mon, man, we learned about this."

"Well, why not call it an *angry mob court* or a *Nazi court*?" Zephyr protested. "I still don't get what kangaroos have to do with anything!"

"It is *so* not important what kangaroo court means," said Kai, exhausted. "Terrance, is it okay if we move on to what I found?"

"Please," said Terrance.

"Have y'all ever heard of Myspace?"

Between Aidan, Terrance, and Zephyr, there was not one iota of a clue what Myspace was.

"It was basically Facebook before Facebook," Kai explained. "You had your own wallpaper on your page, you could play your own music . . . Millennials like my mom seemed to think it was 'hella rad,'" Kai air-quoted. "But, um . . . well, I'll let you be the judge, but it looks kinda cringe to me."

Kai scooted aside from the computer screen, revealing what appeared to be Kalani's Myspace page. Her backdrop was a black-and-pink, girl-punk design of skulls and crossbones and hearts. Her handle was "Bikini Killani." Appropriately, Bikini Kill's "Rebel Girl" was thrashing on an MP3 player embedded on the page. Her profile picture was at least 90 percent emo bangs swooping over one eye, and 10 percent eyeliner. Emo-ness aside, she definitely *looked* eleven years old, which was weird because her profile read:

Female

14 years old

Curtain Falls, Massachusetts

United States

Mood: cantankerous :{

"Pretty sure she lied about being fourteen," said Kai. "Apparently, you had to be fourteen to have a Myspace."

Kai went on to explain that he only *learned* about Myspace while they were at the library and he was researching Gabby's life in 2004. It wasn't until he came home that night that he hopped onto Kalani's laptop (she was MIA as usual) and hacked into her Myspace. He did so by resetting her password through her email, which she was already logged in to, and then boom—he was in.

Aidan's eyes drifted to Bikini Killani's "Top 8"—which Kai helpfully explained was where one savagely ranked one's eight best friends in order—where she was friends with people like "Vanillangel" and "silent_scream" and some dork named "Scooter" who appeared to have just barely cracked in at #8.

Bikini Killani's #1 was someone named Gabby Patty. It was such a cringey name, Aidan had somehow skipped right past it.

"No," said Aidan, leaning in, scrutinizing her profile picture. The girl in the picture was *literally* posing in front of a computer, presumably checking her Myspace. Her hand was on the mouse and everything. It was so . . . lame.

Kai noticed where Aidan's attention was, and he nodded. "Yeah."

Kai clicked on Gabby Patty's thumbnail. Her profile opened across the entire screen. Gabby's "Top 8" was filled with a menagerie of characters who belonged in drama class, or perhaps a *Clue*-like murder mystery: a boy in a top hat and monocle, a boy in a fez, a red-headed girl in a long white dress. "Living Room" by Tegan and Sara plucked anxiously in the background. Her bio: **Female/16 years old/ Curtain Falls, Massachusetts/United States. Mood: smitten <3**

Her final Myspace post on this mortal plane sent shivers down Aidan's spine:

17 Jul 2004 3:14

Which is harder: a) being in love or b) keeping a secret?

Have you picked yet?

WRONG!!! The correct answer is secret response c) being in love with someone in secret.

I bet you feel real stupid now.

This was, of course, the post that ended up collecting everyone's condolences—106 in total. These included Bikini Killani, who wrote: "You can't see it, but I am crying, and my spirit is hugging you wherever you are."

"I haven't scrolled through everything yet," said Kai. "I figured it'd be better if we all tackled this at once on separate computers."

Aidan, Terrance, and Zephyr nodded disjointedly, like bobble-heads on the dashboard of a vehicle that had come to a complete stop.

"My mom's new password is 'Super_Hacker_Kai,'" said Kai. "Each word is capitalized with underscores in between."

The boys divided and conquered. Fortunately, they were able to log in to computers in each other's general vicinity.

202

There was a liveliness to Gabby's posts. She was witty. Hilarious, even. She always seemed to have a punch line up her sleeve. And she was clearly popular, judging from the sheer volume of people who interacted with her posts. Such as:

15 Jul 2004 2:08

I am just a girl

Standing in front of a boy

Eyes up here, buddy

(This is NOT a haiku)

That one accumulated nearly as much interaction as her final post. However, there was also an underlying pessimism to her posts, such as:

12 Jul 2004 11:31

What if, instead of "rapture," God meant "raptor," and the righteous get eaten by dinosaurs? Food for thought.

And then, while still being jokey, some of her posts were downright sad.

9 Jul 2004 4:29

Do you ever listen to sad love songs on repeat because they didn't do enough damage the first time?

No? Oh. Me neither.

Gabby posted cryptically about being in love quite frequently. Aidan could relate.

That said, Gabby seemed cooler, more popular, more *loved* than Aidan could ever *dream* of being. As Aidan continued to scroll, he couldn't help but wonder if this version of Gabby would have ever become friends with someone like him. The more Aidan scrolled, the worse he spiraled. Was it possible the only reason she liked him was because she hadn't spoken to another human being in twenty years? I mean, make someone lonely enough—desperate enough—and they would befriend *anyone*. When you really got down to it, was it possible Gabby might not even *like* Aidan?

Suddenly, someone slapped Aidan in the face.

Technically, it was Aidan who slapped himself in his own face. But it was so hard, so sudden, it felt like it came from someone else.

Stop asking stupid questions, said Nadia. *That poor girl has been trapped and suffering for twenty years, and you're thinking about yourself?*

"Sorry," Aidan mumbled. His cheek was beginning to sting.

She loved your book! Nadia exclaimed. *And dead or not, she's the first person you came out to. Give the girl some credit!*

Valid points.

Now if you're done feeling sorry for yourself, stop scrolling and read that post a second time.

Aidan stopped scrolling.

A post that he had read on autopilot—and that he nearly scrolled past—stopped as well.

6 Jul 2004 8:05

I've been debating posting this, but I think I'm being followed. But not by a person. Whatever this thing is, I don't think it's human. I don't even dare describe what this thing looked like here—just thinking about it scares me—but I described it in explicit detail to Sheriff Jenkins, and all he did was ask if I'm sleep deprived. (I am, BUT!) I'm being followed! How the eff am I supposed *to sleep if I'm being stalked by a monster? Shouting this*

into the void hoping at least one person will believe me.

Aidan's gut sank as he began reading some of the comments. Comments like:

I mean, how much sleep have you been getting?

And:

i feel ya girl. every time i lay in bed the pile of

clothes on my chair turns into satan

And:

Are you on any meds?

Aidan's gaze drifted back up to "I described it in explicit detail to Sheriff Jenkins," and he stood up in his chair.

"Guys?" said Aidan. And then slightly louder, "Guys! I found something!"

"Shh!" someone violently shushed him. It was Ms. Schleppenbach, rounding the front desk of the children's section of the library. "Aidan? Are you being for real, my dude?"

"Sorry," Aidan whispered, shrinking back into his chair.

Zephyr, Terrance, and Kai, however, were already clambering noisily over to Aidan's computer.

"Bruh!" Zephyr exclaimed. "Did you just read about the freaking *monster* Gabby saw?"

"ZEPHYR OCTAVIUS WINDON," said Ms. Schleppenbach.

"Okay, which of you buttsnacks told her my middle name?" said Zephyr.

Terrance giggled hysterically.

CHAPTER 17

Aidan Rolls a Twenty

Aidan insisted to the others that Sheriff Jenkins be their next sleuthing stop. "Excruciating detail" sounded like an awful lot of detail to him. It seemed highly possible Gabby might have told Sheriff Jenkins something important—something crucial to cracking the mystery.

They arrived by bike (and Rollerblades) at the Curtain Falls Sheriff's Department.

Unfortunately, Sheriff Jenkins was already gone.

"You just missed him," said the secretary at the front desk. Her name was Kimmy, according to the name tag pinned to her sweater vest. She had orange lipstick and a perm. "Can I ask what business you boys have with Sheriff Jenkins?"

"We're solving a twenty-year-old murder mystery," Zephyr announced, with an overly cool tug of his shirt, before anyone could stop him.

Terrance covered his face with his hand in embarrassment. Kai clucked his tongue awkwardly.

"Uh . . . huh," said Kimmy. "Can I leave a message for him?"

"Actually, we were hoping to talk to him in person," said Aidan. "Do you have any idea where he might have gone?"

Kimmy glanced at the time on her phone. "It *is* lunchtime. If you hurry, you might catch him leaving Raising Cane's Chicken—"

The boys darted across the lobby of the Curtain Falls Sheriff's Department. They were out the front door before she could say "Fingers."

Sheriff Jenkins was not at Raising Cane's Chicken Fingers. They circled the Raising Cane's parking lot twice. Not a patrol car in sight.

"You've got to be . . . kidding me," said Kai, in between breaths. He was clearly winded. That was saying something, considering he was the most athletic of the four. Terrance and Zephyr both leaned over their handlebars, out of breath. Aidan couldn't even bother to stand. He sat cross-legged on the hot asphalt of the Raising Cane's parking lot in his Rollerblades.

And then Aidan had an epiphany.

"You know," he said, "I'm pretty positive I've seen Sheriff Jenkins's patrol car at Shipley Do-Nuts *multiple times* during lunch rush."

Aidan said this with such confidence, it resuscitated everyone. They didn't travel *nearly* as fast as they had booked it to Raising Cane's, but there was air in their lungs, they were determined, and they somehow made it to Shipley Do-Nuts in fifteen minutes flat.

Sheriff Jenkins's patrol car was not there. That much was evident before they even pulled into the parking lot, which was a small thing that only existed in front of the building.

Then a car drove past.

Curtain Falls was a small town, with an even *smaller* sheriff's department. Aidan knew that patrol car from a mile away.

Without a single word, he bolted after it in his Rollerblades.

When Zephyr, Terrance, and Kai realized what was going on, they were quick to catch up to him. Miraculously, Zephyr was in the lead. So much so that he passed Aidan. But even Zephyr didn't stand a chance of catching up to Sheriff Jenkins. The gap between them and the patrol car was ever widening.

Zephyr, however, had a different plan. He slid his backpack off one shoulder, repositioning it to his front, unzipped it, and removed something.

"Aidan, catch!" Zephyr exclaimed.

Aidan made a flimsy attempt to blindly catch the thing that Zephyr tossed at him. Somehow, Aidan successfully caught Zephyr's slingshot. This boosted his confidence just enough that he managed to catch the *second* thing Zephyr tossed at him one-handed—a twenty-sided die. Aidan must have accidentally left it at Zephyr's house during their last Dungeons & Dragons session.

"Roll twenty, Aidan!" Zephyr exclaimed.

Still Rollerblading at top speed, Aidan slotted the die in the slingshot, then pulled back.

He then released the tension, and readjusted the D20 so that the number twenty was facing forwards.

Aidan pulled back as far he could, then let go. The D20 cut through the hot summer air like a bullet.

It connected with the center of Sheriff Jenkins's rear windshield—

"Oh yeah!" Zephyr screamed, pumping both fists in the air.

—so hard, in fact, that it caused a spiderweb of cracks to splinter in every direction.

"Oh no," said Zephyr.

Sheriff Jenkins slammed his brakes. His patrol car came to a breathtaking halt, causing his brakes to scream.

Aidan only barely managed to dodge the patrol car, veering to the left.

Zephyr, who was struggling to regain control of his handlebars, hit Sheriff Jenkins's rear bumper with breakneck force, and flipped over the patrol car.

Over the course of the next several minutes, Sheriff Jenkins had flipped his lights on and reparked behind Zephyr's body, lying awkwardly in the middle of the street. He instructed him multiple times, yelling, "Don't move! Why are you moving? I told you not to move!"

"Ugh, but this is boring!" said Zephyr, fidgeting on the asphalt. "I'm not even sleepy."

Sheriff Jenkins reappeared from his patrol car with his cell phone to his ear. He crouched down beside Zephyr and said, "I have a paramedic on the line. Describe your pain level on a scale of one to ten."

"What's a ten?" Zephyr asked.

"Ten is you think you're dying."

"What's a one?"

"One is you got a paper cut on your pinkie finger."

"Owie, those things hurt! What's a five?"

"Number, please!" Sheriff Jenkins grumbled.

"Geez, fine! A one? Maybe an aggressive zero? Paper cuts hurt like the dickens, so this pain scale seems awful extreme to me."

Sheriff Jenkins sighed and stood upright. "I think he's fine. Okay, thanks, Becky. Okay, bye."

He hung up.

Aidan, Terrance, and Kai all sat cross-legged around Zephyr, who finally sat upright as well. It was from this low, vulnerable perspective that they watched Sheriff Jenkins inhale, then exhale, over the longest seconds of their collective lives. He looked like an active volcano on the verge of eruption.

He exploded.

"What in the name of Jesus H. Roosevelt Christ do you boys think you're doing? Why are you chasing my car? Why did you shoot a *rock* into my rear windshield?"

"Technically, it was a D20," said Zephyr.

"What the hell is a D20?"

"It's a twenty-sided die for Dungeons & Dragons."

This explanation only seemed to make Sheriff Jenkins madder. His face turned purple as his nostrils flared like a pair of king cobras, and he threw his hands in the air. "WHY?"

Zephyr looked at Kai, Kai looked at Terrance, and Terrance looked at Aidan.

Aidan did not shrink.

"I lied to you," he said.

"I'm sorry?" said Sheriff Jenkins.

"When we were in your office last week," said Aidan. "I lied to you. I said—"

"Don't worry about it, kid. I get it. When I was your age, I lied about seeing things all the time. Sometimes *we think* we see things, but really—"

"No," said Aidan, so loudly—so firmly—it surprised everyone. "When you showed me that video footage, I lied. I said that my notebook fell out of my backpack, but it didn't. That notebook fell where it did because the ghost of Gabby Caldwell dropped it there."

Sheriff Jenkins's face darkened. "This isn't funny, Aidan."

"I know it's not, but it's the truth," said Aidan. "Just like it was the truth when Gabby Caldwell told you that she was being followed by a something that *wasn't human* days before she died."

Sheriff Jenkins's face morphed, from angry to haunted—truly haunted—like a trick of the light. Aidan had never seen an adult look so scared.

"How do you know about that?" said Sheriff Jenkins.

"I know it," said Aidan, "because I've spoken to Gabby's ghost. We all have. We've also seen the thing that was stalking Gabby."

"We have?" said Zephyr.

"The Backwards Lady," said Aidan, deathly serious. "That's what Gabby told you was following her, wasn't it?"

Terrance and Kai exchanged curious glances.

Sheriff Jenkins's face went pale.

"Do you boys like milkshakes?" he asked.

Milkshakes 'n' More was—you guessed it—a place that sold milk-shakes . . . and more. Aidan ordered strawberry, Zephyr and Kai both got cookies and cream, and Terrance ordered green mint. Sheriff Jenkins ordered a simple vanilla shake, which he slurped nois-ily through a big straw.

"Does your girlfriend know you slurp like that?" Terrance asked.

"Very funny," said Sheriff Jenkins. "I don't have a girlfriend, so joke's on you."

Terrance gave Sheriff Jenkins some bombastic side eye.

"I've never stopped feeling guilty," said Sheriff Jenkins. "I want you to know that."

Everyone stopped drinking their milkshakes.

"It's why I pushed you so bad for a rational explanation about that night." He looked directly at Aidan. "*I* already know I let her down. But to think that there's a version of her, still on this planet, haunting the very place where she died—all because I failed her? I don't think I need to tell you why I wouldn't want to believe that."

"So what *exactly* did she tell you she saw?" said Aidan. "Specifically. Every detail helps."

Sheriff Jenkins gave Aidan a curious look.

"Gabby's memories are fading," said Aidan. "They're almost nonexistent. The longer she's trapped in the Witch House, the more she seems to forget. But we think solving the mystery of her death might free her. We can show her to you if you don't believe us—"

"No, that's"—Sheriff Jenkins raised his meaty hands—"that's okay. I believe you."

He leaned back in his booth seat, deep in thought.

"I mean, it's just like you said. Gabby was being followed by some weird, backwards *lady*. She said she had long black hair, wore a long white dress, and all her joints seemed to be broken backwards—her elbows, her knees . . . even the tiny joints in her fingers. Gabby said it sounded like . . . *twigs breaking*." Sheriff Jenkins shuddered at the thought. "Pretty creepy, huh? Even twenty years later, I still remember that description. You don't forget something like that."

"But this lady was *outside* of the Witch House?" said Kai incredulously.

"Well, yeah."

"Where exactly did Gabby see her?" Terrance asked.

"Pretty much everywhere. At school, at her part-time job—" Sheriff Jenkins glanced around uneasily. "She actually worked *here* after school, believe it or not. It was brand-new back then."

Aidan's skin crawled. He and his friends found themselves glancing around as well. Even though it was small, and lit aggressively bright, the place suddenly felt haunted.

"She even saw the Backwards Lady at home, in her own bedroom," said Sheriff Jenkins. "That's what made me think, you know . . . maybe the whole thing was just a nightmare."

Kai stared at Aidan. Though he said nothing, the question behind his eyes seemed to ask: *How did YOU know the Backwards Lady could leave the Witch House?*

Aidan was doing a spectacular job of pretending he didn't notice.

"Oh—but that's not even the *creepiest part*," said Sheriff Jenkins. The more he talked, the more he seemed relieved to be getting all this out into the open. "You want to know what the creepiest part was? Gabby said there was a *face* on the back of the Backwards Lady's head. Like, a *second face*. Like, she would part the hair on the back of her head, and there would be this second face staring at her."

Now, all of Aidan's friends were staring at him. This rang of déjà vu so loudly, not one of them could avoid it.

"But it wasn't just anyone's face on the back of her head," said Sheriff Jenkins. "Gabby saw *her own face* on the back of the Backwards Lady's head."

"Aidan . . . ," said Kai slowly. Almost angrily. "You said you saw a face on the Backwards Lady's head."

Aidan said nothing. He still refused to meet Kai's gaze.

"Whose face did you see?"

Aidan swallowed hard against a knot like a clenched fist in his throat.

Aidan told them everything.

About the face (his face) on the back of the Backwards Lady's head.

About the Backwards Lady standing at the top of the stairs in the library, his own terrifying face watching him.

Hearing it from his own mouth, Aidan realized it didn't bode well for his future as a living, breathing person.

Sheriff Jenkins kicked things off by saying a swear word. Like, a top-shelf one. A real baddie.

"Sorry," said Sheriff Jenkins. "Don't tell your parents I said that—"

Kai said the same word.

"Okay then," said Sheriff Jenkins.

"Aidan, you're in danger!" Terrance exclaimed.

Aidan shrank in the booth, nodding slowly. He was—unfortunately—quite aware.

"He's in danger!" Terrance exclaimed again, this time directed at Sheriff Jenkins.

"Yeah, I've gathered that much," said Sheriff Jenkins.

"Why didn't you tell us?" said Kai.

Aidan shrugged.

"We're your *friends*, Aidan," said Kai. "If you can't even tell us when you're in danger, what's the point of us?"

Terrance nodded emphatically. "So help me, Aidan, if you die—" His nostrils flared at the thought.

"It's happening again," Sheriff Jenkins mumbled to himself. "My career is over—"

Zephyr slammed the table with both fists, causing all four milkshakes to rattle. "Can we stop talking about Aidan like he's already dead?"

His brazenness silenced everyone.

"It's making me sad," Zephyr continued. He glanced at his milkshake and grimaced. "It's even making my milkshake taste bad."

"Yeah, but . . . ," Kai protested. "We can't just pretend like Aidan's *not* in danger."

"No," said Aidan. "But we *can* do something about it."

Suddenly, Aidan commanded everyone's attention.

"We know *what* killed Gabby," said Aidan. "If we can learn just a little bit more about the circumstances of *why* Gabby died, I think we can not only break Gabby's curse, but we can save me too."

"Yeah, but . . ." Terrance glanced at his watch. "It's getting late."

It *was* getting late. Aidan didn't need a watch to see the purple veil of dusk slipping over the orange horizon.

"We're running out of time," said Kai. "We don't know when this Backwards Lady is going to show up out of nowhere and—"

"She showed up in Gabby's *bedroom*," said Terrance. He shuddered at the thought.

Sheriff Jenkins grimaced. He seemed sorry that he'd mentioned as much.

"We'll have a sleepover," said Aidan, surprising everyone.

"A sleepover?" said Zephyr. He was already interested.

"We need to regroup," Aidan explained. "I feel like we know a lot. Maybe even more than we think we do. We need to go over everything we know—talk everything through—and maybe, just maybe, we'll get to the bottom of this."

Aidan hesitated.

"Unless, of course, you don't feel safe having a sleepover with me," said Aidan, "because the Backwards Lady might show up to kill me—"

"Shut your piehole," said Kai. "We are so having a sleepover tonight. Right, guys?"

"I'm serious," said Aidan. "I don't want to put you guys in danger—"

"Shut your cakehole!" Zephyr exclaimed. "We are for realsies having that sleepover tonight. Right, Terry?"

"I would literally rather die tonight than not have that sleepover," said Terrance. "Although we probably shouldn't have it at my house. My parents don't have fond memories of our last 'sleepover,'" Terrance air-quoted.

"We'll have the sleepover at my house," said Kai.

This announcement sent a jolt of excitement across the booth. They had never had a sleepover at Kai's house.

"My mom won't say no," Kai continued, "and we can grill her about her relationship with Gabby."

Aidan smiled so deep, he felt it in every fiber of his being.

CHAPTER 18

PMS (Paranormal Mystery Sleepover)

The air was electric with excitement and big, dark thunderclouds. A storm was coming. Aidan could feel it in the sharp temperature drop. He could see it in the greenish lens cast over them. The sun dipped behind the horizon, casting shadows across the sky.

It was settled. They were having a sleepover at Kai's place tonight.

After they called their parents, Zephyr pumped his fists in the air and screamed, "It's time to PMS!"

"I'm sorry, what?" said Aidan.

"You know, *PMS*: Paranormal Mystery Sleepover!"

It was unclear if Zephyr was joking or serious, but Aidan couldn't help himself. He also pumped his fists in the air and screamed, "It's PMS time!" At which point, they all pumped their fists in the air and screamed, "PMS time!" and "Paranormal Mystery Sleepover!" and "It's that time of the month!"

"Okay, so," said Kai, "some sleepover rules."

Aidan, Terrance, and Zephyr nodded eagerly. No one had ever been so excited to hear rules.

"My bedroom is small," said Kai. "Literally too small for all four of us to fit into. I'll show it to you, but the sleepover is happening in the living room. And even then, this sleepover is only for *business*.

Aidan's life is on the line, and that's the only reason why I'm inviting you guys over. We can have fun when the Backwards Lady is dead."

"Pretty sure the Backwards Lady already *is* dead," said Terrance.

"You know what I mean!"

The boys nodded sternly. Aidan, personally, was breathless at the thought of a bedroom so small. He was trying hard not to imagine Kai giving him a personal tour of such a claustrophobic space. He imagined them standing so close together, their hands were forced to touch—

STOP IT, Aidan screamed, using a very loud voice inside his head. *HE'S YOUR FRIEND.*

"You okay, Aidan?" said Kai.

"Huh?" said Aidan. He literally had to un-pinch his entire face to respond.

"You were making a weird face just now," said Kai.

Terrance and Zephyr nodded solemnly. Apparently, it hadn't gone unnoticed by *anyone*.

"I just had a . . . bad thought," said Aidan.

All three boys frowned.

"About what?" Kai asked.

"I'd rather not talk about it," said Aidan.

"You know," said Terrance, "that you can talk to us about *anything*."

"I know," said Aidan. Even though he wasn't entirely sure that was true. Not about *everything*.

"Were you thinking about dying?" said Zephyr.

"Jesus," said Kai.

"Do you have a filter?" said Terrance.

"WHAT?" said Zephyr. "Were we not all just thinking that?"

"I wasn't thinking about dying," said Aidan.

"Good," said Kai. "Because you're not dying."

There was a crack of thunder as the sky broke—split open by a bright seam of lightning that illuminated the world with breathtaking, brutal clarity.

It started to rain.

"Just FYI, we're bringing our bikes inside!" Kai shouted over the roar of rainfall as they pulled into Portière Park.

"Seriously?" said Terrance. "They're soaking wet!"

"Yeah, and if we leave them outside, they'll get stolen."

"Whoa," Zephyr mused. "So this is street smarts."

Kai's house was an unspectacular yellow rectangle with brown trim and a rickety wooden staircase leading to the front door. Its single identifying feature was a doormat with a seemingly cute-looking illustration of a frog on it—until you realized the frog was holding a rifle, and you read the greeting: HIPPITY HOPPITY GET OFF MY PROPERTY.

"Ignore that," said Kai when he noticed Aidan staring at it a little too intently. "We don't even own a gun. My mom just likes frogs."

Kai held the screen door open for everyone as they filed inside.

Kai's "living room" more closely resembled a hallway with a couch and a TV. The couch was beat up, with faux-leather upholstery that was peeling like a sunburned lizard. The TV was some giant, ancient cube of olden days, as thick from front to back as it was from side to side. A pair of bunny ear antennas were cocked lackadaisically, grasping for a signal.

Kalani was currently slouched back in the middle of the couch, legs spread, in sweatpants and a black shirt with the words "riot grrrl" printed on the front. She appeared to be watching some generic police procedural / crime drama with a title probably made from random letters. If it was a spinoff, the name of some gaudy city was in the title. In Aidan's head canon, the show was called *ABCIS: Cleveland.* The main character's name was Silver Foxx, an upsettingly handsome man with a young face and sleek gray hair. Mr. Foxx also had a female partner who seemed cool and capable and all, but Aidan was significantly less interested in her.

"*Let's cut to the chase,*" said Silver.

"How did you know Gabby Caldwell?" said Kai, point-blank.

He had only barely put his bike away (leaning it against the hallway) and instructed his friends to do the same when he dropped this bomb. He was still dripping wet from the deluge outside. Personally, Aidan wouldn't have minded changing clothes first. Regardless, he slowly unclamped his Rollerblades from his feet, unable to look away from the exchange. He couldn't even blink.

"Uhh," said Kalani. "Hello, Kai. How was your day?"

"Not great," said Kai. "Now answer the question: How did you know Gabby Caldwell?"

"*If you tell me, I'll tell the judge you cooperated,*" said Silver.

Aidan's, Terrance's, and Zephyr's jaws dropped. Not one of them could get away with talking to their moms like this.

"Nope," said Kalani. "Not until my commercial break. And even then, I'll have to think about it. I don't like your tone."

Kai huffed. "Fine. Then let's talk about the Backwards Lady she saw before she died."

Kalani's head rotated slowly—almost robotically—like a security camera. If there was any humor in the room to begin with, it evaporated instantly. "Where did you hear about that?"

"*Whoa*," said Silver. "*I was not expecting that—*"

Kalani turned the television off.

"Gabby was my babysitter," said Kalani.

Zephyr and Terrance sat on the sofa, on either side of her, while Aidan and Kai sat cross-legged on the floor. They all nodded vaguely. Kalani was pretty young as far as moms go, so that seemed to check out.

"Honestly, I didn't have a clue what was going on in Gabby's life. But she was probably the only real friend I had at the time. I always felt seen by her. What else does an eleven-year-old really need to know about a person? Gabby was great. I loved her."

Aidan could see the "but" quivering on her lips.

"But?" said Aidan.

"But, well . . . something was wrong. She seemed scared. I don't think she was sleeping. I would *ask* her what was wrong, but she would never tell me. She'd say everything was fine. Which was clearly a lie. That's when I started snooping on her phone."

All four boys sat up a little straighter.

"She'd texted someone—probably a boyfriend—about something she was seeing. Something that was *stalking her*. Some ghost woman with broken bones who walked backwards. She said it had *her face*—Gabby's face—on the back of her head."

Aidan's spine snapped perfectly erect. "Boyfriend? Who was she texting?"

Kalani sighed. "I honestly don't remember. I didn't recognize the name."

"Mom," said Kai, disappointed. "Seriously?"

"I'm serious!" Kalani exclaimed. "I was eleven. I was snooping on my babysitter's phone for the *sole purpose* of finding out what was going on with her, and I *sort of* found out what that was. End of story."

"You don't remember *anything* about this person?" said Aidan.

Kalani frowned. Shook her head. "Afraid not, kiddo."

It was a dead end. The boys deflated.

All the boys except for Aidan. He persisted. "Do you remember anything else about Gabby? Anything weird she was doing? Seriously, anything will be helpful."

Kalani resisted the urge to say no so fast. She paused, mulling it over, licking her teeth behind her lips.

A light bulb lit behind her eyes. "She wasn't doing homework."

"I'm sorry?" said Aidan.

"When she babysat me," said Kalani, "she was always reading these big textbooks—like, really digging through them, taking notes, et cetera. I just assumed she was doing homework because she seemed to be studying them so hard. But it *wasn't* homework. She was researching *something* like her life depended on it."

"*What?*" said Aidan, somewhat desperately.

Kalani screwed up her face, trying to remember.

Then her eyes popped open, and she exclaimed, "Sweden! She was studying Sweden."

"Sweden?" Zephyr repeated curiously. "Why does that ring a bell?"

Aidan and Kai both looked at Terrance for confirmation. They remembered. They'd had this conversation just this morning, after all.

"Farah Yeet is from Sweden," said Terrance.

Sweden—population 10.5 million—was a Nordic country, located in the Scandinavian Peninsula of Northern Europe, sandwiched between Norway and Finland, and kissing Denmark on the top of the head. Capital: Stockholm. It had many long lakes and rivers that emptied out into the Baltic Sea. Sweden once even had a Pirate King—Eric XIII—which was a *fascinating* story, but not a particularly important one.

As a matter of fact, all this information was completely useless.

"Sweden" had seemed like an important clue in the heat of the moment, but now that all four boys were desperately scouring the internet—on their phones and Kalani's laptop—for clues, it became evident that they had maybe bitten off more than they could chew. Sweden wasn't a clue. It was a freaking country!

Seeing as none of them had come prepared for a sleepover, and they were all soaking wet, Kai offered them clothes to sleep in.

When it was Aidan's turn, he followed Kai into Kai's bedroom, which elevated his heart rate only slightly. It helped that Kai's bedroom was literally *so small*, it was difficult to feel anything but shocked. The room was a perfect square, with Kai's twin bed stretching from one end to the other. His walls were decorated meagerly in epic athletic moments cut out from old *Sports Illustrated* magazines.

Aidan was so distracted, his hand accidentally brushed up against Kai's hand. They both immediately recoiled. The only thing Aidan hated more than how fast he jerked away was how fast Kai did.

"I hate this," said Kai.

"What?" said Aidan, somewhat breathlessly. He had a feeling he knew what Kai hated.

The bedroom was so small—filled with so little—there wasn't room for Kai to hate anything else but him.

"I'm sorry," Aidan blurted out before Kai could even respond.

"*I know* you like me," said Kai. "*You know* you like me. Is there any way for us to keep being friends like we used to without having to pretend like we don't *both know* that you like me?"

Aidan was 100 percent uncertain how to do that.

"I'm sorry," Aidan repeated. "I'm trying my best. I don't know what else to do."

Kai sighed. "Of course you are. I think we both know what the problem is."

It *sounded* like an exasperated sigh. It *sounded* like a sarcastic "Of course you are." Aidan was so certain that the problem was him, he felt his heart breaking inside of his chest. How could Aidan be cursed to die, and his greatest fear was losing Kai's friendship? Why did death feel like a mercy by comparison?

Kai wrapped his arms around Aidan. Hugged him tightly. "I love you, Aidan."

"What?" said Aidan. It came out as a gasp.

"I said I love you," said Kai. "Just the way you are. The way you've *always* been. I wouldn't change a single thing about you. And I want you to know that."

Aidan didn't dare move. He was afraid to even hug Kai back. So instead, he just stood there, rigidly, like the world's most awkward stop sign.

"I don't have a right to pretend like I'm your best friend," said Kai, "when Zephyr and Terrence were there for you when I wasn't. They hugged you and told you they loved you when everything went down with Bea, and I didn't. *Haven't.* I've been afraid to because I felt like it would be weird coming from me. Honestly, every douchey thing I've done recently was out of fear. I went to Bea's party, and I let her hold my hand, because I was afraid if I *didn't* . . . everyone would think I was gay. And I'm not. Which, I *know* that's a stupid thing to be afraid of, but that's the awful, stupid truth. But, Aidan—I'm not afraid anymore. The only thing I'm afraid of is losing you to some stupid curse and a freaking ghost who walks backwards."

Aidan slowly hugged Kai back.

Squeezed handfuls of Kai's shirt.

Kai said nothing. He didn't need to. He was *there*, and for now, that was all either of them needed.

Finally, they parted.

"How do I make this up to you?" Kai asked.

"Make this up to me?" Aidan repeated.

"Come on," said Kai, rolling his eyes. "I'm not going to pretend like my apology is good enough. Let me do something for you. Something that makes us even again."

Aidan shrugged, genuinely clueless.

"Ask me for anything," Kai insisted. "Go crazy."

Aidan was struck by a shiver of déjà vu rippling down his spine. His mom had said the *exact same thing* to him just last week, hadn't she? It reminded Aidan of a simpler time. Back then, all he'd wanted was his notebook.

Now, Aidan *had* his notebook, but he couldn't find a spare moment to write in it.

No. That wasn't true. He didn't even *want* to write in it anymore. Or maybe it was that he *couldn't* write in it anymore. That part of him seemed to be broken.

It wasn't writer's block. It was deeper than that. At its core, *Fire & Water* had always been about who Aidan *really was*.

Now, Aidan knew that he and Kai would never be together. Not like *that*, anyway. So how was he supposed to finish the story?

Fire & Water was a world he had crafted all on his own. His feelings for Kai were the fuel—the lifeblood—of something very special to him. Could he really throw all that away, just because of a crush that never came to be?

It was in that moment that Aidan realized something.

Kai Pendleton was *not* Kai Pendragon.

Sure, they had an awful lot in common. But they also had a wealth of differences. Biological species was a pretty big one. But Kai Pendragon was also in love with Nadia Cross—just as Nadia loved him—and no creative crisis on Aidan's part could undo such a love.

Aidan's number one fan, Gabby Caldwell, wouldn't hear of it.

Aidan was staring at Kai's T-shirt instead of his eyes when he asked, "Would it bother you if I kept writing *Fire & Water*?" He barely waited for a response when he added, "I can change Kai Pendragon's name if it bothers you—"

"Of course you can keep writing it," said Kai. "And I would actually appreciate it if you kept his name the same."

"Really?"

"You have at least a hundred fans now," said Kai. "My mom included. If you change Kai Pendragon's name, I'm pretty sure I'll never hear the end of it. So please: keep the name."

Aidan nodded slowly. He didn't look it, but he *felt* euphoric.

"That can't be your request, by the way," Kai added. "That's not something I can give you. *Fire & Water* was already yours to begin with."

Aidan was still staring at Kai's shirt when he had a sudden, revelatory thought.

"Can I have one of your shirts?" Aidan asked. "To keep?"

"You want one of my . . . *shirts*?" Kai repeated.

"Sorry if that sounds weird," said Aidan. "I just . . . I know you're straight, and we're only friends. But *Fire & Water* is important to me, and I feel like having one of your shirts would help remind me why I wrote this story to begin with. Why I *really* started writing it. Think of it as a symbolic token. I'm hoping it will help remind *me* of who *I* really am. Does that make sense?"

Of course it didn't. Aidan cringed before he even finished speaking—right around the moment he said "symbolic token." Jesus Christ.

"That makes perfect sense," said Kai. "Although, I'll be honest, that seems like a lowball request. All my shirts are either from Walmart or Goodwill, so—"

"That's okay," said Aidan.

"That's okay?"

"I get a shirt, you get a clean slate? We're even. That sounds like a deal to me."

Kai smiled—such a genuine, heartfelt smile, it gave Aidan a tummy ache that felt like a hernia. Aidan didn't know what a hernia was, but surely it hurt something like this.

Kai opened his dresser and began laying out all his shirts on his bed for Aidan to choose from. However, Aidan found himself distracted by the one shirt that did not appear to be "on the table," so to speak—the shirt Kai was wearing. It was a plain white shirt, completely unremarkable in every way—not to mention, it was still slightly wet and smelled like rain. Then again, it also smelled like Kai. And there was something timeless about cute boys in plain white T-shirts, wasn't there? Aidan was pretty sure Taylor Swift sang something about that, so it had to be true. It also seemed metaphorical of clean slates and new beginnings. Aidan had grown an intense emotional connection to that shirt over the course of the past five minutes, and so it was the only shirt he could focus on.

"What?" said Kai.

"What?" said Aidan, in response to Kai's *what*.

"You keep looking at me."

Aidan blushed. "Can I have *that* shirt?"

Kai glanced down at the shirt he was wearing. "This old thing?"

Aidan nodded.

"It's wet," said Kai.

"It's not that wet," said Aidan, which was a lie.

"It smells."

Aidan shrugged. He'd be lying if he said that wasn't part of the appeal.

Kai shrugged. "If that's what you want . . ." And then he proceeded to pull the shirt off over his head.

Aidan nearly yelped at the amount of skin he was suddenly exposed to. It wasn't anything he hadn't seen before—he'd been to the community pool with Kai a hundred times. It was mostly just the close quarters and the suddenness of it all.

Aidan pretended to be suddenly interested in an image of Gerrit Cole, mid-pitch, arm contorted like Silly Putty. Zephyr would've had a conniption if he'd spotted Yankees paraphernalia in Kai's bedroom.

When Aidan and Kai finally exited—Aidan in Kai's wet, plain white T-shirt and black gym shorts—Terrance did a double take.

"Is Aidan wearing the *wet shirt* you were just wearing?" he asked.

Kai froze up, unable to explain himself.

"It's my Coming Out present," Aidan blurted out. Which was *sort of* the truth. "Kai told me I could have any shirt I wanted. *To keep*. So I picked this one."

There was a moment of breathtaking silence. A fly could have farted and they all would have heard it.

Zephyr started slow-clapping. "Bruh. That's a cool shirt. I love it."

Terrance cringed. As the resident germaphobe of the group, he seemed less than thrilled at this touching moment in LGBTQ+ history.

After the spectacular failure of attempting to "sleuth" the entire country of Sweden, the boys regrouped. They decided to divvy up their research into four topics as they related to Sweden: curses (Zephyr), ghosts (Terrance), haunted houses (Kai), and witchcraft (Aidan).

Meanwhile, Kai pulled out every blanket and pillow in the house that wasn't being used by Kalani, and together, the boys crafted a tangled rat's nest of comfort in the living room. Since all four boys unanimously agreed that they studied better when they had a movie playing in the background, Kai popped a bag of Xtreme Butter popcorn in the microwave, and they voted on a movie. That movie ended up being *Kiki's Delivery Service* because Kai remembered that it was Aidan's favorite.

It was right after Kiki and her talking black cat, Jiji, were caught in a thunderstorm that Jiji offered these helpful instructions: *"All right, first: don't panic! Second: don't panic! And third: Did I mention not to panic?"*

"This feels like a valuable life lesson," said Terrance.

This sent all the boys into a fit of laughter. But it was also an uncomfortable reminder that maybe they *should* all be panicking right now. Their laughter petered out nervously.

Towards the end of the movie, Kiki became depressed because she had inexplicably lost the ability to talk to Jiji. She had also lost the ability to fly. Or maybe these were a side effect of her depression. Either way, she was paid a visit by her friend Ursula, a young painter, who seemed convinced that Kiki's magical crisis was a form of artist's block. And it was here that she imparted wisdom that Aidan felt was the *real* life lesson.

"*Stop trying,*" said Ursula. "*Take long walks. Look at scenery. Doze off at noon. Don't even think about flying. And then, pretty soon, you'll be flying again.*"

Zephyr and Terrance fell asleep before the movie even finished. Aidan was unsure how: it was the best part! Kiki was rescuing a boy named Tombo from a rogue dirigible! Nevertheless, Zephyr's head rested on Terrance's shoulder, and Terrance's head was on top of

Zephyr's. They snored loudly at each other, as if it was a competition. Neither Aidan nor Kai had the heart to wake them up.

They sat in the middle of the couch, between Aidan and Kai, which was probably for the best. Aidan was trying to focus. Still, he would occasionally glance at Kai, beautifully distracted and enraptured by the film, and smile.

Aidan was somewhat mindlessly surfing from hyperlink to hyperlink about Swedish legends when he came across the words "Blue Hill." He was struck by a sudden wave of déjà vu.

When he read the word "Blåkulla" almost immediately after, he stomped the brakes so hard, he nearly gave himself whiplash.

Aidan had read those words before. He could almost *see* the words in his mind's eye, written in some forbidden place. But where?

Aidan suddenly saw himself standing in the weaving room of the Witch House, where an unfinished tapestry curtain hung from the loom against the back wall. On it, a man made of shadow.

Blue Hill.

Blåkulla.

Aidan backpedaled. Reread everything from the beginning.

Blockula (or *Blåkulla* in modern Swedish, meaning "Blue Hill") was a mythological island and home to the Devil's Earthly Court. It was often described as an endless meadow, with a large house atop a hill where the Devil resided during the Witches' Sabbath.

Aidan had woken his friends to show them this, and he was actively gauging their reactions.

"A large house," Aidan repeated, because that part had excited him perhaps a bit more than necessary.

"A large house in *Sweden*," said Terrance, skeptical at best. "On an island that may or may not even exist."

Aidan had already mentioned the tapestry he saw in the weaving room, but he felt the need to mention it again. "That curtain said 'Blue Hill.' It said 'Blåkulla!' I'm not making this up."

"Yeah, but . . . ," said Terrance. "It was just a curtain."

Aidan wanted to argue that perhaps it *wasn't* just a curtain—that maybe none of Farah Yeet's curtains were *just curtains*—but instead, he kept reading aloud.

"'In Blåkulla,'" Aidan read, "'the ordinary world was reversed: witches sat around a table facing outward, old people became young, and women took men's roles.'"

Terrance's mouth became a flat line.

Aidan kept reading.

"'It was believed that the witches would dance so much at Blåkulla that they became dizzy and would say things backwards.'"

"Bruh," said Zephyr. "I'm picking up what you're putting down."

"Are you suggesting Farah Yeet brought the Backwards Lady here from Sweden?" said Kai.

"No way," said Aidan. "Farah Yeet was only eight years old when she immigrated here from Sweden."

Kai seemed relieved.

"I'm suggesting something crazier," said Aidan. "I think Farah Yeet brought something *worse* than the Backwards Lady from Sweden—something pure evil—and that *thing* turned Farah Yeet into the Backwards Lady."

Kai's eyes widened. Zephyr's mouth fell ajar. He had inserted a handful of buttered popcorn into it, so a kernel or two fell right back out.

Terrance was less than impressed.

"I'm being completely honest," he said, "this is all flimsy, circumstantial evidence."

Aidan continued, undeterred. Pressing Ctrl + F, he searched the word "backwards," and, jumping recklessly between excerpts and articles, read aloud.

"'The witches would fly to the Sabbath, generally on a household appliance, such as a broom, or ride *backwards* on a borrowed animal.'

"'They would devour the beautiful food in some cases *backwards* through their necks.'

"'Satan, leading the Witches' Sabbath, would recite the Lord's Prayer *backwards*.'

"'Witches participated in *backwards* dances and walked primarily *backwards*, similar to the dwellers of the world of death.'"

Aidan dared to meet Terrance's gaze again.

Terrance sighed. "So . . . is Blåkulla a house? Or is he the Shadow Man from the curtain?"

"I think," said Aidan, "that Blåkulla is the Shadow Man from the curtain *and* the Witch House—the Devil's house—all rolled into one."

Kai looked genuinely alarmed. "Are you telling me the Witch House is alive?"

Aidan responded bleakly. "I think so."

CHAPTER 19

Titto

It was either hauntingly late at night or deathly early in the morning when the boys decided to pay Gabby Caldwell a visit.

Aidan was excited to see Gabby again. It'd been days since his last visit. He was worried she'd think he'd forgotten about her.

It was only as Aidan turned from the main road onto the loose gravel of Yeet Street that he realized how ill-equipped Rollerblades were for this sort of terrain. He felt every pebble, rattling like a maraca every step of the way.

Kai winced. "I am so sorry, Aidan."

"I-i-i-t-t-t's o-o-o-ka-a-a-ay," said Aidan, vibrating.

When they reached the Witch House, Gabby somehow managed to *fling* the front door open, the way ghosts do only in horror movies. Except Gabby stood in the doorway, fully visible in the sliver of moonlight, hands placed comically on her hips. She did not look happy.

"WHERE HAVE YOU BEEN?" she shouted. "IT HAS BEEN FOUR DAYS!"

"Sorry!" Aidan yelped, struggling to Rollerblade across the unkempt grass. It was possibly even worse than the gravel. Kai cringed.

"'*Sorry*,' he says." Gabby rolled her eyes. "You better at least have some new chap—"

Gabby glanced at Kai. She stomped the brakes so hard on her own sentence, she should have had whiplash.

"Chaps," said Gabby. "Um, leather cowboy chaps. I, uh, sure do love me a man in leather cowboy chaps. Yeehaw." She bowed her legs like a cowboy and slapped her knee.

Aidan sighed. "It's okay. They already know about my book."

Gabby didn't seem to know what to do with this information, so she continued to play dumb. "Book? What book? I don't know no book. Honestly, I'm not even sure I remember how to read. What's a book?"

Aidan was not a good liar, by any definition. But Gabby was *so terrible* at lying, she made him look like Charles Ponzi.

Aidan unstrapped his Rollerblades, abandoned them at the doorway, and escorted her to the living room. Aidan and Gabby took the yellow, chenille-upholstered Victorian love seat, while Zephyr, Terrance, and Kai sat across from them, side by side, on a rose gold sofa. A marble-surfaced, Versailles-style cocktail table separated them. There, Aidan broke down everything that had transpired over the past ninety-six hours: the leaking of his book to the internet. His friends being there for him. The Backwards Lady situation—as it related to both Gabby *and* Aidan, which *seemed* to indicate that he too was cursed to die.

Blåkulla.

Aidan deliberately paid attention to Gabby's reaction during this bit, but her face was blank. Of course it was. She had no recollection of dying! Of course she wouldn't know anything about Blåkulla. She didn't know her own Social Security number!

Her pupils, however, became very, very small.

"I'm assuming you don't know anything about Blåkulla?" Aidan asked.

Gabby shook her head. "Honestly, I forgot about that curtain in the weaving room. It creeped me out so much, I stopped going in there. And then I forgot *why* I stopped."

Gabby looked bleak. Aidan frowned. It was possible this was less *regular forgetfulness* than the *particular brand of forgetfulness* that comes with being a ghost cursed to roam the Witch House for all eternity.

"What about the Backwards Lady?" Aidan asked.

"What *about* the Backwards Lady?" said Gabby.

"Is there maybe anything you know about her that you haven't told us?"

"Like *what*?"

"I dunno. Like . . . do you think it's possible she might be Farah Yeet?"

"Bro. I don't know. You've seen that thing. She's like every horror movie I've ever seen *incarnate*. When she comes crackling down the halls, I hide. And I don't stop hiding for at least an hour after the crackling stops. Sometimes, I just run right out the front door and *disappear*, just so I don't have to deal with her."

"But you're a *ghost*," Zephyr protested. "You're already dead! What's the worst she could do to you?"

Terrance rolled his eyes. Kai put his face in his hands.

"No, I'm serious, though! Have you ever thought of just . . . talking to her? Maybe asking her some questions? Like, maybe how to break the curse or whatever?"

"I'm sorry," said Gabby. "Are we talking about the same Backwards Lady that you *just said* is responsible for killing me and is trying to kill Aidan? You're asking what's the *worst she could do to me*?"

Zephyr shrugged.

"I dunno," said Gabby. "Maybe she'll break all my arms and legs backwards. Maybe she'll grow a second face on the back of my head. Do you think I should go ask her?"

"Oh," said Zephyr. For once in his life, he seemed to realize that maybe he'd said something stupid.

Gabby looked like she was sinking to the bottom of the Atlantic Ocean.

"Hey," said Aidan. He placed a gentle hand on her shoulder. "Let's forget about the Backwards Lady for a second, okay?"

"How can I?" Gabby exclaimed. "You're in danger, Aidan. You're in danger because of me. None of this would have happened if I hadn't asked you for help. It feels like I'm the one who cursed you!"

"That's not true—" Aidan started to say.

"It is true!" Gabby snapped. "What if you die, Aidan? What then?"

"Aidan won't die," said Kai. "Not if I have anything to do with it. I won't let anything happen to him. He's my best friend. You have my word."

"Ditto," said Terrance.

"Titto," said Zephyr. When that earned *immediate* odd looks from everyone, he tried again. "*Tritto*?"

Gabby couldn't help but crack a smile at this. If the protectiveness of Aidan's friends wasn't enough to make her smile, the stupid things that came out of their mouths *surely* were.

"I'm holding you to that," she said. "If Aidan dies on your watch, I'll haunt you. We'll *both* haunt you. We'll do it in shifts. You'll never have a good night's sleep ever again."

"Deal," said Kai, smiling at Gabby.

Terrance glanced at his watch. "Not to sound like a stick in the mud, but if we're going to be smart enough to figure out how to break this curse, we should probably get at least some sleep tonight."

"Bruh," said Zephyr. "You are *such* a stick in the mud. Sleep is for the weak!"

"Actually," said Terrance, "going without sleep for twenty-four hours is equivocal to having a blood alcohol level of point-ten percent."

"Pssh!" Zephyr rolled his eyes. "*Point*-ten? That's not even one percent!"

He then yawned, stretching his arms overdramatically, like a cat bathing in the sun, and rubbed his eyes behind his glasses. "I don't know about you guys, but I'm feeling kind of sleepy. I'm thinking maybe we should get some sleep right about now."

No one bothered arguing. They were too tired.

Aidan, however, hesitated.

"Before we go," said Aidan, returning his attention to Gabby, "there isn't *anything else* you might know? About the curse, about the house . . . anything ghost-related? It's okay if you don't know, but seriously . . . anything helps."

"Ghost-related . . . ," Gabby mumbled to herself. She scrunched her face like a stress ball, mid-squeeze. "Ghost-related . . ."

Aidan felt bad putting so much pressure on her. He was already mentally preparing a speech that it was okay she didn't remember anything when, suddenly, she lit up like a Christmas tree.

"Ghost-related!" Gabby exclaimed. "I remember something!"

"Really?" said Aidan.

"Sometimes—it doesn't happen very often—but *sometimes* I sense another spirit in this house. Just one other spirit. It's not the Backwards Lady, and obviously it's not me, but it's *something else*. I don't know how to describe it, but it's a . . . *gentle* spirit. A *good* spirit. Although—don't ask me how— I can sense that something tragic and terrible happened to it."

Aidan and his friends exchanged epiphanous looks. In that moment, they appeared to be thinking the exact same thing. Who else did they know who had died at the Witch House?

"Assuming the Backwards Lady *is* Farah Yeet," said Kai, "do you suppose this other spirit could be . . . ?"

"Jesse Glass," said Aidan.

CHAPTER 20

FARAH, THE GREAT AND TERRIBLE, PART II

World War I had not even ended yet when a second Horseman of the Apocalypse, Plague, came galloping in the form of the Great Influenza epidemic of 1918. Influenza, the Great and Terrible, swept the world with a ferocity and blind rage not seen since the bubonic plague.

Yaqeen got sick in early October. He died in late October.

His funeral was held on Halloween.

Farah felt very complex feelings over the death of her pappa. On the one hand, he'd given her a life of wealth and comfort of which she never could have possibly dreamed.

On the other hand, she knew that *that thing* was *not* her pappa. Everything that *had been* her pappa had been scooped and hollowed out like a jack-o'-lantern. The carved face that grinned back at her was *not* Yaqeen Yeet.

Farah knew that it was her fault. She had traded her pappa for a house.

And yet, Farah couldn't help herself. As she and Mamma mourned the husk of Yaqeen's body, made pretty with makeup, and as they watched his coffin as it was lowered into its grave, and as the priest said pleasant, hollow words about the indestructible nature of the human soul . . .

. . . Farah was overwhelmed with relief.

~

The money dried up long before Yaqeen died.

Yaqeen wasn't some wealthy businessman or brilliant entrepreneur after all. He was merely a lucky fool who'd inherited a large sum of money. The only thing Yaqeen was really good at was spending money and lying about the truth of their financial situation. And the truth was, they were broke. Only one person was more worried about their finances than Farah, and that was Mamma. Therefore, Mamma fell back on the one and only thing she knew how to do: making and selling the ugliest curtains known to mankind.

Once she'd woven a hideous trove of them, she dragged them out to the road, draped them over random pieces of furniture that she forced Farah to lug out there with her, and peddled them shamelessly to passing automobiles with a poorly handwritten sign that read:

HOMEMADE CURTAINS
VERY GOOD LOOKING
ONE DOLLAR

In the long days that followed, not a soul bought one of Mamma's curtains.

If you could see these curtains for yourself, you wouldn't have bought one either.

Farah was much different than Mamma—and not always in the best ways. Her way of dealing with their financial predicament was to pretend it did not exist. Instead, she did what she'd done for many years now, and that was visit Otto Steinhauser's Corner Store and look at the pictures in fashion magazines like *Harper's Bazaar.*

241

But Farah was not interested in fashion so much as she was in the pretty girls that occupied the magazine's pages. In many ways, Farah's sweet tooth had been replaced entirely by an all-new form of sweetness. She imagined what it would be like to hold hands with one of these glamorous women with their long, manicured nails. To have one hanging off her arm like those fancy (but definitely over-rated) gentlemen with slicked-back, oily hair and goofy, tailored suits.

Farah huffed.

It must be so easy to be a man. They all looked exactly the same to her, and for whatever reason, beautiful women flocked to them. Was it because they had money? *Surely*, it was the money.

Farah imagined what it would be like if she was rich. Not daughter-of-a-man-who-lived-off-his-father's-inheritance *rich*. That wasn't rich at all.

No, Farah imagined being wealthy in the way that respectable, self-made millionaires were wealthy—like America's first million-aire, John Jacob Astor, for example. Investing in real estate in New York City. Having monopolies in the fur trade. Smuggling drugs into China. That sort of thing.

Surely, if she was that wealthy—that powerful—no one would dare call her slurs ever again. She would be free to like whomever she liked. She would be free to be *herself.*

All she needed was, like, a million dollars.

"This isn't the library," said Otto Steinhauser, shattering her day-dream. "You going to buy that magazine or what? You look like you could use some fashion tips."

"I'd rather buy rat poison and eat it than buy your stupid magazine!" Farah retorted rather swiftly, and she stormed out of the Corner Store.

She would be back tomorrow.

Probably.

~

It'd been years since Farah awoke to Blåkulla's shadow standing over her bed. She was much bigger now, and so was her bedroom. And yet Blåkulla appeared to fill every inch of darkness as if it was his own. Was it because she had stepped inside of him and knew what lay within transcended space and time?

"Hello, little Farah," said Blåkulla. The smile in his voice sounded strained.

"I'm not so little anymore," said Farah.

"I know you aren't. It's a term of endearment."

"I don't find it endearing anymore. In fact, I would very much like it if you would go away."

"Go away? I think you forget: I am this very House. If I were to go away, then so would the very roof over your head. Is that what you want?"

Farah hadn't forgotten. The knowledge of *who* and *what* her House was crept across her skin like spiders and breathed down her neck like hunger. She felt it every day she came home from school. She lost herself in the knowledge standing beneath the black locust tree, staring up at that eye-shaped window. The House always stared back. Unblinking.

"Fine," said Farah. "But I was getting along perfectly okay not having these midnight conversations with your shadow."

"Perfectly okay?" said Blåkulla. "With Anna going crazy with her curtains again? With all that fear and dread I see in your heart?"

Farah did not like hearing her mamma's name on Blåkulla's invisible lips. It felt like rot touching an open wound.

"What do you want?" said Farah.

"I only want to help you, little Farah. That's all I've ever wanted."

"Yes, well, I don't want your help."

"I think you do. You may not know it yet, but I think you really do want my help."

"No, I do *not*, because help from you is only going to come at the cost of someone I love. Who will you demand as payment next? Mamma? Forget it. I don't want your help."

"How can you think so little of me? Don't forget, your pappa wanted *nothing to do with you* before I came along. Do you think it was your pappa who brought you to America, and made you this beautiful house, and who took you to the opera in New York City?"

Blåkulla's empty black body filled the room like a storm cloud, bulbous and engorged. His voice rose like the howling wind, with thunder rumbling behind every word.

"NO," said Blåkulla. "IT WAS I, BLÅKULLA. I AM YOUR PAPPA. AND WHEN YOU DISRESPECT ME, THE PERSON YOU ARE DISRESPECTING IS . . . YOUR . . . PAPPA!"

Blåkulla shrank like a deflating balloon. Like a shadow in the presence of light. He crumpled forwards and shook with his invisible face in his hands. It took Farah a moment to realize he was crying.

"Why do you hate me so, Farah? All I ever did was love you. Why do you hate me?"

Farah did feel a bit bad. He was right, after all. He hadn't, technically, done anything bad to *her*. Sure, he possessed her biological cal pappa, to the point that it was possible there was nothing left inside of him but Blåkulla. But was that a bad thing? Was it possible, if anything had been left of Yaqeen Yeet, that he wouldn't have wanted anything to do with her?

"I don't want you possessing any more people," said Farah. "I don't like it. It's wrong."

"Deal," said Blåkulla, switching off his sadness like a light switch. "I don't like possessing people anyway. No offense, but these bags of flesh and bones you call bodies are quite disgusting."

"So how can you help me?"

"I want your curtains."

"I'm sorry? You want Mamma's curtains?"

"Not your mamma's curtains. I want *your* curtains. Every curtain inside of you. Every curtain you will ever make. I will be inside of them. Together, we will craft the most beautiful curtains this world has ever seen. People will travel far and wide to acquire the curtains of Farah Yeet. You will not only be financially stable, and save your mamma from monetary burden, but you will be rich! You will be famous! You will be loved and adored. Worshipped, even!"

"I don't want to be worshipped."

"But you *are* lonely, are you not?"

Farah's mouth crumpled into a defenseless squiggle of a line.

"Imagine how easy it will be to find love when *everyone* loves you in return. It will be as easy as grabbing endless treats off a great long table and stacking them on your plate. You could have any person you wanted. Any *woman* you wanted."

"Women aren't treats," Farah retorted rather sternly. She may have been a social pariah, but she wasn't a barbarian.

"Oh, of course, of course. All I'm saying is, all those pretty girls who treated you so poorly . . . don't you think they might have acted differently if you were the richest, most powerful woman in Shallowgrave County? Maybe they would have been flattered to have been graced by your attention. Maybe—just maybe—they would have adored you the way that you adored them. Isn't that what you want? Isn't it the only thing you *really* want? To have your feelings reciprocated? You have an awful lot of them, I can tell."

Strategically speaking, Blåkulla had gone for Farah's Achilles' heel. But he was right.

All Farah wanted was to be loved. Wasn't that all anyone wanted?

"What do I have to do?" said Farah. Even though she already knew.

"On the day of the Black Moon, you must draw blood from your fingertip. And then you must press that finger into the earth and say these words: 'By my blood, I give you my curtains. Every curtain I will ever create. In return, give me Blåkulla.'"

Farah Yeet did not make just any old curtains. They were tapestry curtains. They were paintings on fabric, with yarn as her brush, and Mamma's loom as her canvas.

Farah knew how to make curtains, sure. But she did not quite know how to make the masterpieces that poured out of her like spirits from the possessed. And yet, her fingers did the work, and her mind instructed her fingers what to do.

The thought occurred to Farah that, if she gave Blåkulla every unmade curtain inside of her, then there was probably a part of Blåkulla that was also inside of her. And that was such an icky thought, it made her want to cry.

But Farah did not cry. She could not. She was a grown lady now—a working woman—and if this was the cost of living, then so be it.

The image on Farah's very first curtain was of that dewy meadow that existed on the other side of Blåkulla's shadow that had seemed to stretch on forever. She called it *The Meadow on the Other Side of Shadow.*

Farah put it out on the road alongside Mamma's curtains, draped over a kitchen chair. She did not tell Mamma about the curtain she'd made, and Mamma wasn't outside to witness it sell in less than ten minutes. Mamma was inside taking a nap. Not one of her curtains had been purchased in the weeks since she'd brought them out there. At this point, Mamma wasn't even worried about her curtains being stolen. In fact, she might have been thrilled if they were.

The first automobile to drive past was Jedediah Lindow's 1919 Rolls-Royce Springfield Silver Ghost. Farah waved meekly at him, and Jedediah vaguely mirrored the gesture, but overall, avoided making eye contact.

He drove about ten yards past Farah and *The Meadow on the Other Side of Shadow.*

And then he slammed on his brakes. The Rolls-Royce screamed like all the banshees of Ireland.

And then it rolled back slowly in reverse.

Jedediah Lindow was a southern gentleman, owner of Lindow's Windows, who hailed originally from Tennessee. He wore three-piece suits in the feverish heat of summer and oiled his slicked-back hair and curling mustache the way he oiled his Rolls.

"I ain't never in all my days seen something like that," said Jedediah. "What *is* it?"

"It's a tapestry curtain," said Farah. When Jedediah failed to have a response to that, she added, "It's like a painting but with yarn. But you still hang it over your window. I call it *The Meadow on the Other Side of Shadow*."

If Jedediah thought this was crazy, then he was infected by the madness. "I'll give you five dollars for that there yarn painting."

Jedediah wasn't being cheap. Five dollars in 1919 would be the equivalent to just under *eighty dollars* a hundred years later. Farah would have accepted the offer, right then and there, if Otto Steinhauser hadn't been driving by in his Dodge Brothers Model 30. He stopped alongside Jedediah's Rolls and leapt out of the driver's seat.

"Whatever Jed is offering for that curtain, I will double it," said Otto.

"You idiot!" said Jedediah. "Farah and I already have a deal. Don't we?"

The moment he and Farah made eye contact, Jedediah seemed to know full well that he and Farah most certainly did not have a deal.

"But in the interest of fairness, I'll match Otto's offer," said Jedediah. "Ten dollars for them curtains."

"Farah, I will give you twenty dollars for the curtains," said Otto. "And a free fashion magazine whenever you come into my store."

"You *idiot*!" said Jedediah. "You can't buy curtains with fashion magazines!"

"They are not curtains, they are *art*," Otto retorted. "Seeing as Farah and I both hail from Europe, we understand that better than a country bumpkin such as yourself."

Jedediah grew red in the face. He was fuming. At any moment, Farah expected steam to come whistling out of his ears like a teapot.

"Fifty dollars!" Jedediah roared. "Fifty dollars for the artsy curtains! And that's my final offer!"

"One hundred dollars," said Otto.

"WHAT?" Jedediah screamed. "You do not have one hundred dollars on you. No way, no how."

Otto reached into his blue jeans pocket, pulled out his wallet, and removed a crisp one-hundred-dollar bill. One hundred years from now, this would be the equivalent of $1,600. Farah's head was spinning. She'd never even *seen* a one-hundred-dollar bill before. Not even Pappa carried Benjamin Franklin around. That was an absurd amount of money to be contained on a single piece of paper.

"This was the first one-hundred-dollar bill I made when I started the Corner Store," said Otto. "I've held on to it as a good luck charm. Looks like today is finally my lucky day!"

Both Farah and Otto glanced at Jedediah in case he had a counteroffer, but Jedediah was gaping like a goldfish.

"It would seem we have a deal," said Otto, grinning.

"I'll give you my car!" Jedediah exclaimed.

Both Farah and Otto stared at Jedediah as if he had offered his firstborn child. To be fair, the Rolls was much prettier to look at than

Jedediah Lindow Jr. That apple had fallen so far from the tree, it might as well have dropped off a cliff.

"It's gently used," said Jedediah, "but that's a sticker price of eleven thousand seven hundred and fifty dollars *for the chassis alone*. I don't have the title on me, but I can give you the car today and get you the title tomorrow. I have Otto here as my witness. Is that fair?"

Jedediah looked like he might start crying if it wasn't.

"That's fair," said Farah.

Together, Farah and Jedediah and even Otto, the most gracious of losers, helped roll up *The Meadow on the Other Side of Shadow* and load it onto Jed's shoulder. Just the sight of it—the feel and texture on Jedediah's fingertips—seemed to reinvigorate him. He'd fought long and hard, and now *The Meadow on the Other Side of Shadow* was his.

Likewise, Otto wilted with loss.

But it wasn't a complete loss. Because as soon as Jedediah hobbled off with the curtain, knees trembling, carrying it with such a weight of destiny like Jesus with his Cross, Otto leaned towards Farah, looking ahead down the road, and said, "I will write you a check for eleven thousand seven hundred and fifty dollars this very moment if you make me another curtain like that one. I don't care how long it takes. I just want one."

Farah looked at Otto, startled. "I can try. But I can't promise it will look exactly like that one."

"What do you mean?"

Even Farah wasn't sure what she meant, but she tried her best to explain. "I feel like it wasn't me who made that curtain. It was like something took control of me, and that *thing that took control*—it made what it *wanted* to make. What I mean to say is, I'm afraid the next curtain might come out looking wildly different than this one. Maybe. Maybe it won't. I just honestly don't know. Does that make sense?"

Otto nodded—even though, from the look on his face, it probably didn't make sense. "You have a gift, Farah. Whatever it was inside of you that made that curtain? I want *that* to make a curtain for me. I don't care what it looks like in the end. All I know is that I want it, and I want to be first in line. Do we have a deal?"

He took out his checkbook, scribbled the absolutely ridiculous amount of money he had promised, and pressed the check into the palm of her hand. He closed her fingers around it.

Otto wasn't taking no for an answer.

About a week later, Farah wove a curtain displaying a scene in the entrance hall of the House of Blåkulla, from that fateful night when she was spirited away in her dreams. She called it *Angels and Demons Sup Together in the House of Madness.*

Even as Farah made it, she felt the blasphemy in each weave. There was no way the good Christian folk of Shallowgrave County would go for pagan sacrilege such as this. It was creepy. Haunting. It made even Farah feel uneasy. She made sure not to cash Otto's check because she was *positive* he'd want his money back. Seeing as Jedediah made good on his promise and delivered the title to his Rolls the very next morning, it was an easy thing not to do. Farah had quietly sold the Rolls, and even though it went for less than the sticker price, it was enough money to carry Farah and Mamma for the rest of the year.

When Farah finished *Angels and Demons Sup Together in the House of Madness*, late Sunday night, she gave Otto a call on her candlestick telephone, and told him it was done.

"If it's to your liking, the curtain is yours to keep," said Farah. Nervously, she added, "Otherwise, you can have your money back. Obviously."

Otto didn't seem worried. "I'll be the judge of that," he said and hung up.

When Otto arrived at the House, Farah led him to Mamma's weaving room, where *Angels and Demons Sup Together in the House of Madness* was on full, breathtaking display.

Otto stood there, staring at it for minutes that stretched like clay. Farah wondered whether the sheer paganism of it all had broken Otto's poor, feeble brain. He was quite old, after all. It was known to happen.

"Mr. Steinhauser?" said Farah. "Are you all right?"

"It's the most incredible thing I've ever seen in my entire life," said Otto, breathless.

"Oh!" said Farah, relieved. "I'm so happy to hear you like it."

"It's like the Voice of God on fabric," said Otto. "You have the fingers of a seer."

"Oh," said Farah again, overwhelmed. That was a bit much. "Not really. They're just regular old fingers."

Otto removed his wallet and proceeded to leaf through crisp, green bills indiscriminately.

"Oh no," said Farah. "You already paid me, remember?"

"Not enough," said Otto. "What you have created is worth far more. I will not cheat an artist out of what they are rightfully owed."

Otto emptied out the entire contents of his wallet—eighty-nine dollars and fifty-seven cents—and dumped it into the palms of Farah's cupped-together hands.

"The next curtain you make," said Otto, "take it to the auction house. Set the starting price at fifteen thousand dollars. Let your next masterpiece be sold for what it is truly worth."

Farah's next tapestry curtain, *A Girl and a God Make a Deal at the Fireplace*, would sell at auction for six hundred and sixty-six thousand dollars.

That would be the lowest price a Farah Yeet curtain was ever sold for.

～

Farah Yeet was more than an artist. She was a sensation.

People traveled far and wide to bid on the next Farah Yeet. Old-money families who sat atop their mountains of fortune, festering. The nouveau riche or "new money"—up-and-coming business owners and philanthropists who shaped the future of the economy. The occasional duchess, earl, countess, viscount, or marquess from overseas. Word of Farah Yeet's curtains spread across the world like the Great Influenza, but it was only contagious among those at the topmost rungs of social ladders. Because to own a Farah Yeet was the ultimate sigil of power and class.

That rural part of Shallowgrave County where Farah lived was elevated on a pedestal with her, and it became known as Curtain Falls. There wasn't a person within a hundred miles whose name held greater power and influence than Farah Yeet's.

But there was one person who had the power to influence Farah.

And that was who came knocking on Farah's door that fateful day, in the bitter, frostbitten corpse of winter, as snow blanketed the ground in a soft, white burial shroud.

It came in the form of three slow, ominous raps—a sort of Grim Reaper's knock, very sure of itself. Farah knew she shouldn't be afraid of answering the door at the ripe old age of her early twenties, but the confidence behind that knock made her just a *little bit* nervous.

Farah answered the door.

Standing on her doorstep was a tall, thin, peculiarly hand-some, and vaguely androgynous-looking young man with red hair combed sharply to one side. (Or so Farah thought.) He was dressed in a raccoon fur coat over a white button-down shirt tucked into tweed slacks. A black bowler hat atop his head acted as yin to the yang of his bright white, suede oxford shoes. He was carrying a briefcase.

"Farah Yeet, I presume?" said the young man.

"This is she," said Farah.

"Splendid," he said, with such a smile, it caused Farah's insides to do a little twist. "Allow me to introduce myself. My name is Jesse Glass, president and owner of Lindow's Windows, Incorporated."

Farah tilted her head ever so slightly and squinted at Jesse.

"Let me cut straight to the chase: my company is the largest, most ambitious, most *lucrative* of its kind in New England. I have numbers and accolades I can show you, if I'm so lucky that you even care so much about my credentials. You, on the other hand: you're Farah Yeet! No introduction necessary. You are to America what da Vinci was to Italy and Van Gogh to France. No offense, Mary Cassatt, but I think *you're better.* I'm biased, of course, because we both have a particular inclination to the window frame as our canvas. Which leads to my point: *a collaboration*"—Jesse gestured grandly—"between you and me. I have ideas on what that collaboration could be, of course, but I'm more interested in your thoughts on a potential collaboration than my own. I'm but a mere businessman. You're the artist."

Farah's head tilted farther, by degrees, and her eyes narrowed to skeptical slits. Ever since moving to this area as a little girl, Farah had known the entire Lindow family in passing, and this man did *not* look like a Lindow. Certainly not Jedediah Lindow Jr., the obvious heir to the Lindow's Windows empire. At least as a child, Jedediah Lindow Jr. had looked like he'd fallen out of the proverbial Ugly Tree, so to speak. *Several* Ugly Trees. He'd climbed and fallen out of an entire Ugly Forest.

As for Jesse, well . . . we won't mince words. He was the most beautiful man she had ever seen. Farah's heart had never skipped for a man before, but it was currently skipping like a little girl through a field of daffodils. He was an excellent salesman, no doubt. For someone pitching to a world-renowned artist, she had difficulty finding a weak moment in his entire spiel.

Unless, of course, the whole thing was a scam.

Jesse read the room like a board book made for babies.

"You're skeptical," said Jesse—a statement, not a question. "Silly me. You're *from* here. Arguably the *original* Curtain Falls native, etymologically speaking. And, as fate would have it, my former boss—and adoptive uncle—Jedediah Lindow Sr., was *also* from here. I'm guessing you must have known the Lindows growing up? You're probably wondering where *I* fit in this elaborate *family business*?"

Farah nodded slowly.

"Have you, by chance, kept in touch with the Lindows in recent years?"

Farah said nothing. Admitting that she *hadn't* seemed like the perfect opportunity to open herself up to be scammed.

"No judgment, of course, if you haven't," said Jesse solemnly. He seemed genuinely sorrowful. "They've gone through some recent— how to put this delicately—*family tragedies.*"

Farah was caught off guard. "What happened?"

"Jedediah Sr. died," said Jesse, frowning. "Of the flu."

"What about Jedediah Jr.?"

Jesse's frown deepened. "He died too. Of the flu. Just like everyone else."

"Just like everyone else" *seemed* like a callous way to address the tragedy and scope of the influenza epidemic. But he wasn't wrong. Mamma had died of influenza just last year. To Farah, that was her entire world. The elderly had it the worst against the Purple Death. They called it that because its victims turned purple as huckleberries.

"What about the rest of the family?" Farah asked.

Jesse frowned so deep, it nearly went full circle.

"Oh," said Farah. She had misunderstood. Jesse didn't mean "Just like everyone else" generally. What he meant to say was: *Just like the entire family.*

Farah felt an unsubtle stabbing in her gut. Mrs. Lindow had been such a gentle soul—the antithesis of Jedediah Sr. In addition to Jedediah Jr., the Lindows had three little girls—ages thirteen to three—at the time that Farah sold her first curtain to them.

"You know," said Jesse, "some say that you selling your first curtain to Jedediah Sr. was the very moment his business took off. Became an empire. Lord knows he bragged about owning your very first curtain to every business partner he encountered. Some say it was a lucky charm. But that's also right about the moment Jedediah Jr. got sick. The kids got sick one by one after that. It's funny how the best of times and the worst of times seem to intertwine so *fiercely*. Dickens must have known what he was talking about, eh?"

At first, Farah nodded, mouth slightly ajar. There was no way selling Jedediah *her curtain* could have done that to the Lindows. Right? That was impossible.

Then, Farah wondered if this was what Jesse was *insinuating*.

A dark shadow fell over Farah's countenance. She didn't *used to* have a temper. Perhaps she had inherited it from Mamma. Perhaps fame and fortune had slowly turned her heart rotten and cold.

Or, perhaps, that little bit of Blåkulla inside of her—the elusive creative genius behind her curtains—was the thing that had the temper.

"Are you suggesting that *my curtain* killed the Lindows?" Farah asked. There wasn't an ounce of friendliness in her tone.

"What?" said Jesse, surprised. "Oh no! Oh, deary me, no. I apologize. I can see how my meaning might have been misconstrued. I am in no position of judgment. One might say that the entire fortune of my career has been built upon the *misfortune* of the Lindows—which I do not revel in the least bit. The Lindows have always been like family to me—loving and caring, forwards and progressive thinkers. They were the family I never had. My own family rejected me when I was quite young. I became Jedediah Sr.'s personal assistant at a very young age—when very few people were willing to take a chance on me—and I have him and his family to thank for that. In fact, one might say that what I'm doing is merely trying to fulfill Jedediah Sr.'s lifelong hopes and ambitions. He'd always *dreamed* of doing a collaboration with you. He was just too afraid to ask. Fortunately for him, I have much less shame. So when I say *the best of times and the worst of times . . .* this is what I mean. I carry an incredible debt upon my shoulders."

Farah stared at Jesse. And not in a bad way. She so desperately wanted to like him. If anything, she felt like maybe she had gotten off on the wrong foot, and she was too awkward and prideful to know how to regain her footing.

"I feel as if I've gotten off on the wrong foot," said Jesse, stealing the words out of Farah's heart. "I believe I need to try harder to regain your trust. What if I told you something that I've never told another soul before? I'm only willing to because I want you to like me, and I want you to know that my admiration for you is genuine and true."

Farah must have looked genuinely intrigued because Jesse lit up with encouragement. "All right. Okay." Jesse took a deep, calming breath.

He then leaned forwards and whispered something into Farah's ear.

Farah's eyes grew three sizes in their sockets.

PART III
FLESH & BLOOD

House of Cats

At 8:00 a.m. sharp, the boys arrived at the Shallowgrave County Clerk's office, a small, orange brick building with tinted black windows and a slanted roof baked ash gray in the sun.

Inside, the walls were painted the palest, blandest shade of beige. Post-and-rope stanchions were set up to organize line formation, except the place was empty as a drum.

A Plexiglas shield separated them from a single woman on the other side of the front desk. She was an older, larger woman with curly hair, a purple blouse, and a smile that seemed desperate for conversation. The name badge pinned to her chest read: MIDGE G.

The closer they drew, the wider her smile became. Aidan wasn't sure if he would describe the smile as sad or unhinged. Either way, it was making all of them slightly anxious.

"Midge *G*?" Zephyr whispered into Aidan's ear. "Do you think there's another Midge that works here? Or does the *G* mean *gangster*?"

Kai accidentally snickered, then slapped his hand over his mouth.

"Oh my God, Zephyr," Terrance muttered under his breath.

Aidan pretended Zephyr didn't exist by matching Midge's unhinged smile.

"Hello," he greeted her.

"Hello to you!" she said cheerfully. "My, you boys are young. To what do I owe this pleasure?"

"We're looking for any information on a person who lived here in the 1920s—a man named Jesse Glass."

"Jesse Glass?" said Midge, lighting up. "You boys researching the Witch House legend?"

"It's for a school project," Terrance explained.

"Ah, I see." Midge looked way more eager than she had any right to be. "What sort of information are you looking for?"

"*Any* information," Aidan repeated. "Birth certificate, marriage license—if it has his name on it, we're interested in it."

If Midge thought this was a strange request, she didn't let it show.

"Okey dokey, artichokey," she said. "I'll see what I can find."

Midge disappeared into the shelves in the back.

"That lady gives me the heebie-jeebies," said Zephyr.

"Don't be mean," said Terrance.

"I'm not being mean!" Zephyr exclaimed. "I'm just saying what we're all thinking! Were we not all thinking that?"

"Just because you think it doesn't mean you have to say it," said Kai.

"Oh my God," said Zephyr. "I'm surrounded by Boy Scouts."

"Technically, they're just called Scouts now," said Terrance, "since the program opened up to girls."

"Oh my *gawd*!" said Zephyr. "See! That is *such* a Boy Scout thing to say."

As Zephyr, Terrance, and Kai continued to bicker, Aidan zoned out. To be fair, he had an awful lot on his mind and was still quite sleep-deprived.

Midge's hands landed loudly on the desktop. Only Aidan jumped at her sudden reappearance.

At first, Aidan was worried she'd overheard Zephyr's comment about her giving him the "heebie-jeebies."

Then he got a good look at her hands, and his skin prickled, from his fingertips to the back of his neck.

She had no fingernails—or so it seemed. This was because her hands were folded backwards, and her rotting, black fingernails were located where the pads of her fingertips should have been, clicking against the countertop. She was longer and thinner now, and wearing a dress the color of rotting bone.

She was standing backwards.

She was *folded* backwards.

Aidan was frozen in terror.

A greasy curtain of black hair nearly touched the countertop. Behind it, the sliver of a face was visible, smiling on the back of her head.

"Jesse Glass is dead," said a whisper that sounded unmistakably like Aidan's voice. "I watched Jesse die. I still remember the way that fool's feet kicked, hanging from the black locust tree."

Aidan trembled as the Backwards Lady leaned forwards across the counter.

"Just like I remember the way Gabby's head split open when I pushed her over the balcony railing."

Greasy black hair, and the face behind it, pressed flat against the shield. Rabid, snarling breath fogged the Plexiglas.

"I can't wait to watch you die. How shall we do it? Shall we peel the skin off your flesh?"

A rotting, broken hand writhed its way between the Backwards

Lady's second face and the Plexiglas. Dug its gnarled fingers into the line of hair and skin where scalp ended and face began.

Aidan began shaking violently.

The Backwards Lady peeled.

The skin of that second face stretched and tore.

The thing behind it was all blood and bone. Muscle and sinew.

Lidless eyes and lipless teeth.

"*Aidan!*" said some distant voice, in a different pocket of reality.

The fluorescent overhead lights flickered, and she was gone.

"Aidan!" Zephyr exclaimed, suddenly in his face. "Are you even listening to me?"

Aidan looked Zephyr straight in the eyes. This was more difficult than it sounded. He had to pry his gaze away from Midge's empty workstation, where the Backwards Lady had been only moments ago.

"I said, what's a greater contribution to society?" said Zephyr. "Eagle Scout projects or Girl Scout cookies?"

"Uh . . ." Aidan attempted to give this silly question more thought than it deserved.

"Aidan, are you okay?" said Kai. "You look pale."

"Are you sweating?" Terrance asked.

Before Aidan had a moment to explain, Midge reappeared, holding a single manila envelope—normal Midge, wearing her normal, overly eager smile. Still, her reappearance caused him to jump.

"So, funny story," said Midge. "Jesse Glass was a married man, and a business owner, but it would seem that he was never actually born."

What Midge found was a marriage certificate—to Farah Yeet, of course—and also the property record of a plot of land owned by

Lindow's Windows. Apparently, Jesse Glass had, for a very brief time, been the owner of Lindow's Windows, which—you guessed it—specialized in making and installing windows.

There was no birth certificate on file.

"You're kidding me," said Terrance. "You're telling me that Jesse Glass was *actually* a window maker?"

Terrance was definitely getting hung up on the wrong information.

"What does that mean then?" said Aidan. "That there's no birth certificate?"

"Is it possible Jesse Glass was Satan?" Zephyr asked.

Midge looked wildly alarmed by this question.

"Please ignore him," said Kai.

"No birth certificate just means he wasn't born here," Midge explained, slightly flustered. She had no reason to even acknowledge Zephyr's question, but she just couldn't seem to let it go. "I don't think Jesse Glass was Satan. I know the stories say he was hanged for unknown reasons, but I think he was probably a good, misunderstood person."

"Why do you think that?" Aidan asked. He didn't doubt her. It just seemed like an odd thing for her to say.

Midge *seemed* like she wanted to say something else. For a moment, Aidan got prematurely excited. Like she might drop a bombshell that could crack the mystery wide open.

"Do you boys mow lawns?" Midge asked.

"I'm sorry?" said Aidan.

"Mow lawns," said Midge. "My lawn has been getting out of hand, and the boy who used to mow my lawn stopped coming by."

"Oh," said Aidan awkwardly.

"I make really good chocolate chip cookies and lemonade," she added hopefully.

Zephyr made sure to give each and every one of his friends his best *I-told-you-so* look. There was nothing subtle about it.

"Oh," said Midge. "I'd pay you, of course! With money. Not chocolate chip cookies. Sorry. I probably should have led with that."

"Actually, we're pretty busy," said Aidan. He was genuinely sorry. She seemed lonely.

"Oh," she said. "All of you are?"

"We've got to go," said Kai. "Thanks for the, um . . ."

All four boys started backing away, like cornered animals.

The bell above the Shallowgrave County Clerk's office entrance chimed. A tall, thin reed of a man—wearing a blue work polo tucked into denim jeans—entered behind them. A noisy ring of keys jangled at his hip, while he pushed an even *noisier* yellow trash can that rumbled as he drove it through the door. He appeared to be collecting trash.

"Hello, Missus Glass," the man greeted.

All four boys returned their attention to Midge.

"Midge *G.*?" said Zephyr incredulously. "The *G* stands for *Glass*? Are you freaking kidding me?"

Midge appeared to melt beneath the heat of their gazes. She broke into a full sweat. Bullets beaded her upper lip.

"Are you related to Jesse Glass?" Aidan asked.

She looked positively guilty.

Margret Glass—a.k.a. Midge—lived in a small bungalow painted pale celery green with an eggshell-colored trim. Both colors were cracked and peeling. There was a garden bed out front full of weeds, thorny and ugly as sin. The stone steps leading to Midge's door were practically submerged, no more than glints of gray in the verdurous abyss.

Rather than give Aidan a straight answer to his question, Midge told him it would be easier if she *showed* him. Aidan wasn't sure what that meant, but fortunately, he had his friends with him in case things got dicey.

She seemed *thrilled* to have so many houseguests at once.

"Don't bother taking off your shoes," said Midge, before opening her front door and plunging them into the pungent smell of thirteen of the fattest, laziest indoor cats Aidan had ever seen.

There were cats lazing in the sun spilling through the bay window.

Stacked on multiple tiers of two separate cat trees.

There were cats on the arms of the sofa, and the back of the sofa, and on every single cushion of the sofa. The sofa itself was more cat hair than sofa.

The largest cat of all—an orange tabby with a head like a pumpkin—met them at the front door. He looked absolutely delighted to see Midge—only to turn his wrath upon the four outsiders who had entered without his express permission. His body compressed like an accordion, and he hissed.

"Mister Whiskers!" said Midge, appalled. "Be nice!"

Every hair on Mister Whiskers' body was an exclamation point. He made a sound that reminded Aidan of the actor Owen Wilson, saying, "Wow." Since the sofa was occupied, Midge guided them to the kitchen, where they gathered around her dining table. There were only three chairs, but she found a barstool that Zephyr claimed because it made him taller than everyone else. Midge opted to stand.

Only now, as she squeezed between them, did Aidan notice the photo album tucked beneath her arm. Its exterior was soft and patchwork, made of a quilt-like material.

"My grandmother's name was Jennifer," said Midge, "but everyone called her Jenny. She was born and raised in Curtain Falls before it was even called Curtain Falls. Her parents, Oscar and Glenda Glass, were cranberry farmers. The way she described her childhood, she was an only child. I honestly never knew she had a sibling. Not until I found this."

Midge opened the photo album to a page with some of the oldest photographs Aidan had ever seen—mostly of a pair of young children. A pair of *sisters*. The photos were yellowish—sometimes overexposed, sometimes with lighting that appeared inverted, like negatives—but the gist of it was an older sister and a younger sister who looked very much alike, maybe only a year or two apart, wearing matching dresses that looked straight out of *The Shining*. Or maybe it was just the serious looks on their faces that reminded Aidan of the horror movie. Aidan had heard they didn't smile in pictures back in the day.

Either way, Aidan fought the shiver crawling up his skin.

"Apparently, her sister died a long time ago," said Midge. "Right around when Grandma Jenny graduated high school. But her parents disowned Grandma Jenny's sister long before then. The way my mom tells it, my Grandma Jenny's sister was some sort of 'sexual deviant,'" she air-quoted. "I always got the impression she was some sort of . . .

well, there's no nice word for what I *thought* she was. But then I saw this photo."

Midge flipped the page. It was a page out of a yearbook.

Midge didn't have to point out her grandaunt. Aidan spotted her like a sunflower in a field of tulips.

Though the photo was black and white, Aidan could feel the red of her hair bleeding through. Freckles speckled across the soft curve of her nose. Aidan couldn't help thinking she looked a bit like an older version of him, with enough confidence for them both. It wasn't the first time he had thought this.

The name beneath the photo read: JESSICA "JESSE" GLASS.

The puzzle pieces clicked into place before Aidan with stirring, picture-perfect clarity. Jesse Glass didn't come from shady roots. Jesse wasn't a Satan worshipper, or hideously ugly, or a kleptomaniac.

Jesse was a woman.

Farah Yeet *married* a woman.

This was the crime that sentenced Jesse to death.

CHAPTER 22

FARAH, THE GREAT AND TERRIBLE, PART III

Farah and Jesse fell in love with each other the way water falls down a waterfall: Breathtakingly. Majestically. Violently.

As for their collaboration, well . . . it had taken a bit of a detour.

"Do you have a particular MO when it comes to making your curtains?" Jesse had once asked, no sooner than that fateful day she told Farah her secret, and Farah invited Jesse into her home.

Farah made tea for them while they discussed ideas.

Farah did, in fact, have an MO (a modus operandi, mode of operation). However, she was slightly shaken after hearing about the Lindow family—to say nothing of the nerves that come from having such a handsome girl in your house, even if she *was* dressed as a beautiful boy—and so she stirred her tea with a small spoon, and asked, "What do you mean?"

"Like, a method to your madness. A secret ingredient or sauce, if you will."

Farah did, indeed, have a secret sauce, and it was her dark contract with Blåkulla. But there wasn't any reasonable means of bringing *him* up in civilized conversation, so she shrugged. "I don't know. I've never really thought about it."

She took a quick sip of tea to hide the lie on her face.

"This is going to sound silly," said Jesse, "but Jedediah Lindow was convinced that you used black magic to make your curtains."

Farah stopped drinking her tea, mid-sip.

"Which, I'm not *accusing you* of witchcraft," said Jesse, "but if, on the off chance, you *do* happen to use black magic to make your curtains, I was wondering if you could maybe *not* use black magic during our collaboration?"

At first, Farah's entire body seized like a clenched jaw. Then, she noticed Jesse smiling playfully, and she realized it was a joke. At least, Farah *thought* it was a joke.

Farah tried to let out of breath of relief without *looking like* that's what she was doing.

When Farah realized she was taking an awful long time to respond to this gag, she continued to stir her tea again, double the speed, and said dryly, "I'll see what I can do."

That was a while ago. In the weeks and months that followed, they had grown breathlessly close. Because Jesse had shared with Farah her deepest, most intimate secret, Farah had no choice but to share hers. They had laid beneath the black locust tree, and when their hands brushed, they lingered, then intertwined.

There, beneath the black locust tree, Farah and Jesse shared their first kiss.

Now, Farah was trying to make Jesse's curtain for her, and Jesse's request lingered—what happened to the *Lindows* lingered—like worms writhing in the dirt before a storm.

Farah would not—*could* not—make a curtain for Jesse using Blåkulla's power.

This was when Farah discovered her baffling inability to weave *anything* without Blåkulla's help, his magic, his *influence.*

Because Farah had become something of an open book around Jesse, she let Jesse know this. And Jesse, ever the empathetic listener, became much more lenient in their collaboration plans. If Farah could make *anything* that didn't feel like it was "dripping in Satan"—Jesse's words, not hers—they could call it a "collaboration" and it would be good.

"Maybe the issue is passion," Jesse suggested.

"Passion?" said Farah.

"Yeah. Forget business. What are you *passionate* about?"

Farah paused and gave this some serious thought, before she came up with, "You?"

Jesse rolled her eyes. She *almost* scoffed.

Then she paused. Mulled it over.

Finally, she nodded. "Very well. Lindow's Windows, Incorporated, will purchase one Farah Yeet curtain—a portrait of its new owner, Jesse Glass, for marketing purposes. I fail to see how that's *not* good publicity. Andersen would *kill* for a Farah Yeet."

"Who's Andersen?" Farah asked.

"Basically Satan. Don't you worry about him. All you need to worry about is making that curtain. How much do you normally charge for a commission such as this?"

Farah stated the range that had become the norm.

Jesse looked pale, as if Farah had foretold the future date and exact time of her death, oracle-like.

"I can give you a discount, though," Farah added timidly.

"No. No! This is *business*, and business requires *marketing*, and marketing costs *money*."

"Okay . . ."

"I wouldn't mind if we rounded *down* in that general ballpark, however, if you would be so generous."

And so, they shifted tracks on the entire trajectory of their collaboration. Farah was to make one curtain of her best friend and lover, Jesse Glass. No restrictions—except for the fairly major, possibly game-breaking restriction of not having Blåkulla's help. For someone who adored Farah's work, it was curious how serious Jesse was about not tapping into Farah's dark muse. Farah imagined it was probably like someone who *admired* grizzly bears but didn't exactly want to walk one on a leash as a pet.

Anyway, all Farah had to do was make a curtain of the one whom she loved more than anything in the world. How hard could it be?

Nearly a week later, Farah determined that it was, in fact, very hard. She simply could not make Jesse's curtain.

Farah was pretty sure she knew why.

"I'm sorry, you're what?" said Jesse.

"I'm not letting you buy a curtain from me," Farah repeated bluntly.

Farah informed Jesse of this over breakfast—scrambled eggs and golden, buttered toast. Jesse had been about to take a bite, but breakfast was suddenly ruined.

"Why not?" said Jesse, on the verge of tears.

"Because I'm going to gift one to you," said Farah. "For free. Because I love you."

Jesse was still on the verge of tears, but the mood behind those tears had changed entirely. "What?"

"I think that's how Blåkulla's magic works," Farah explained. "When I make one of these curtains for money, they're cursed to make people want to throw money at me—as much money as they can. But if there's no money in the equation, there should be no curse, right?"

"Blåkulla?" Jesse repeated blankly.

"He's the demon I made a deal with so I could become rich off my curtains," Farah explained.

This wasn't the first time Farah had mentioned this Dark Deal to Jesse, and it wouldn't be the last. Jesse's reaction was usually to nod politely and not read too much into it. It was possible Jesse assumed Farah's "demon" was more of the metaphorical sort.

"You love me?" said Jesse.

"I what now?" said Farah blankly.

"You said you're going to gift me a curtain because you love me."

"Oh," said Farah.

It was the first time she'd said the L word to Jesse. She hadn't planned to say it so early. Though the urge to walk it back—to pretend it was nothing—was great, it felt wrong. If anything, Farah needed love now more than ever. That was the power with which she intended to make this curtain.

"Is that okay?" said Farah. "That I love you?"

Jesse wiped her tears on her sleeve and smiled gleefully. "Only if it's okay that I love you too."

Farah felt her heart swell like a balloon. It felt like it might float right out of her chest.

"Question," said Farah. "Since this curtain is on me, how terribly opposed would you be to posing for me in a dress? Feel free to say no. But please don't."

Jesse sighed, but her smile was limitless. "Fine. But *I* get to choose the dress."

~

Jesse's curtain was the easiest that Farah had ever made. It was also the greatest—Farah's crowning achievement.

Farah had Jesse pose beneath the black locust tree, wearing the very same white dress that Farah wore when they first met. When Farah asked why Jesse chose that one, Jesse said, "Because it looks and feels like home." Farah swooned privately, in her heart.

Jesse looked transcendent in it—like an angel, or perhaps something *greater than an angel*, and even more difficult to capture on canvas. Like a song, or a poem.

Jesse was the most beautiful poem Farah had ever seen.

When Farah finished Jesse's curtain, she showed it *only* to Jesse. It existed for her eyes only, as a token of Farah's love. And the only payment she received was a kiss on the lips. (Maybe the *greatest* kiss Farah had received up to that point, but still.)

But Jesse's eyes weren't the only ones who saw it.

Blåkulla saw the curtain. And he was very displeased.

It truly was Farah's greatest creation. And Blåkulla had no power over it. Even though he and Farah had drawn up a very specific contract. *Every curtain she would ever make* should have belonged to Blåkulla. And yet, this one did not.

It was a clever loophole Farah had wiggled her way through. She was smart, there was no doubt about it.

But she'd swindled Blåkulla out of what was rightfully his. And every swindler must be punished according to the law.

Jesse's curtain would be his.

~

Jesse proposed to Farah beneath that very same black locust tree.

At least, she tried to. She was just in the process of kneeling—and pulling an expensive ring with a massive rock atop it from her pocket—when a black locust thorn went right into her knee.

"Son of a bigfoot!" Jesse yelped. She fell over sideways, cradling her knee to her chest. "Holy Pukwudgie! Oh, ouchy, that hurts!"

"Pukwudgie?" said Farah, in a state of shock. Mostly she was flustered over the uncertainty of whether she was engaged to be married.

"They're little, wild, humanlike creatures, two to three feet tall, who live in the woods," Jesse explained through her teeth.

"What?" said Farah. "Certainly those can't be real."

"Oh, they're real, all ri—AHHHHH!" Jesse screamed.

Farah had just pulled the thorn out of her knee. Now she was pressing the hem of her dress up against it to stop the bleeding.

"Oh, honey," Jesse moaned. "I'm bleeding all over your dress."

"Forget my dress, silly," said Farah. "Is your knee okay?"

"It actually feels much better now that it isn't being impaled by a small wooden spear. Thank you."

There was a moment of quiet as Farah pretended to nurse Jesse's wound.

"Am I an engaged woman now?" she asked tentatively.

"That's a good question," said Jesse, wincing as she sat upright. "I didn't quite get the question out all the way, so understandably, I haven't quite heard your answer in response—"

"I do," said Farah.

"You do?" said Jesse.

Farah abandoned Jesse's wound, only to tackle her to the ground in a violent hug, kissing her all over her face.

Once the kissing was over, Farah whispered, barely a breath between them, "I do."

~

Blåkulla found a man.

The name of this man is not important. Only that he was a vile creature with a rotten, half-eaten apple core of a heart.

The sort of man who was susceptible to the whisperings of the Devil.

Blåkulla whispered the truth to this man—nothing more, nothing less.

But this man was not the quiet sort. He shared the revelation that he received—that Jesse was a *woman*, not a man—among like-minded townsfolk. And as the truth spread, it grew insidious little lies like appendages. Jesse was pretending to be a man, not only to the residents of Curtain Falls, but to *Farah Yeet herself.* Jesse was a devil, and she had put a spell on Farah not to know the difference. She was a deceitful succubus, milking Farah Yeet for all she was worth (and she was worth a lot).

She had to be stopped.

The lie grew beyond its ability to contain itself.

On July 31, 1924, the night of the New Moon, a mob of three hundred and thirty-three men and women—the whole town, essentially—stormed the Yeet estate. They kicked the front door open. Shattered windows from all corners of the house, climbing through jagged windowsills and crunching broken glass beneath their muddy shoes.

For a brief moment, Jesse held them back with several fierce swings of a baseball bat signed by Ike Boone of the Red Sox. One man was clocked clean unconscious. Another lost a tooth, which he swallowed by accident.

Eventually, Jesse was overpowered. The bat was pried from her grasp.

A monster with six hundred and sixty-six hands—and a single, *hateful* heart beating in its chest—ripped Jesse from Farah's arms. Both women were restrained and brought outside in naught but their nightshirts.

A noose had already been strung from the black locust tree. A dining room chair had been dragged out beneath it.

"No," said Farah softly. And then louder, "No! NO." She kicked and screamed more violently. Four men were required to restrain her. "Blåkulla! Blåkulla, where are you? Save Jesse! Please, I'm begging you. I'll give you anything. Anything you want. Just please, please—"

Farah was gagged with a cloth.

A circle formed around Jesse and the pair of men who restrained each of her arms.

The man who Blåkulla whispered to—who happened to be a man of the cloth—approached her, wearing his finest Sunday robes.

"Would you like to be executed as a witch or a devil?" he asked.

"Go to Hell," said Jesse. She spit in his face.

The Holy Man wiped his face with the sleeve of his robe. "A devil it is."

When everything was said and done, all that was left was the rot of death, the stain of hate, and enough sadness to fill Massachusetts Bay. Jesse Glass continued to hang—lifeless—as Farah Yeet sobbed relentlessly at her feet. The men had left a small lifetime ago, but Farah was unable to get Jesse down. She wasn't strong enough. And even if she was, what was the point? Jesse was dead. She would never come back. Farah would never feel her touch again.

There was nothing left inside of her but the crushing stab of heartbreak.

She felt a hand on her shoulder then—or something that resembled a hand. It thrummed with old, cosmic energy.

"I'm so sorry, little Farah," said Blåkulla.

"Where were you?" Farah growled angrily.

"You were the one who pushed me away. Not the other way around. You expect me to hang on your every word, when you make it so clear that you hate me and all I've given you? I'm truly sorry for your loss, little Farah, but Jesse's death is *your* fault—not mine."

Farah dropped her hands into her lap and sobbed. He was right. This *was* her fault. Farah had always known marrying Jesse was a bad idea. Why was Jesse dead, and Farah still alive? Because Farah was too wealthy, too powerful, to ever be in real danger. She had the aid of a God—a Devil—on her side. Jesse had nothing but Farah.

And now Jesse was dead. And it was all Farah's fault.

"What would you be willing to give me?" said Blåkulla. "In exchange for Jesse's immortal soul?"

Farah wiped her face with her sleeve. Gazed upon the black hole of Blåkulla's face with bleary, bloodshot eyes.

"I could give her back to you," said Blåkulla. "The two of you could live forever in this house. But I require payment. Perhaps . . . the blood of any children from this wretched town that *you* created who dare to disturb you?"

Hate contorted Farah's face into a mask. There was barely a person behind it. She nodded.

"Very good. Although . . . I needn't have to tell you this, but resurrecting an immortal soul, especially one so dear to you, and binding it to this house, will require just a little bit *more* from you. Tell me, little Farah: What *else* are you willing to give me?"

"Everything," said Farah.

"Even that curtain you made *just* for Jesse? That you so greedily kept from me, despite our contract?"

Farah nodded again.

"Even your immortal soul?"

"*Everything*," Farah snarled venomously.

Blåkulla leaned back. Folded the silhouette of his arms. Farah was too distraught to see it, but there came a smile, swirling endlessly behind his infinite pool of darkness. "Very well, little Farah. You know what to do."

Farah lifted her thumb to her mouth. She bit it so hard, she nearly crushed it before drawing blood.

But draw blood, she did. And she pressed her mangled, bleeding thumb into the shadow of the soil beneath Jesse's hanging body.

"By my blood, I give you everything," said Farah. "In return, give me Blåkulla."

CHAPTER 23

Gabby Caldwell's Number One

Aidan marveled that they had seemingly blown the mystery of Farah Yeet wide open. And yet . . .

Victory had never felt so hollow.

If Farah Yeet *was* the Backwards Lady, and this was her revenge on the town that betrayed her, could he really blame her?

They left Midge's house slowly, walking their bikes, with no destination in mind. Aidan rolled slowly in his Rollerblades. He hadn't spoken it aloud to anyone, but he realized something. He'd realized it as soon as he saw Jesse's unmistakable face on that old yearbook page.

"I touched that curtain," said Aidan. "The one of Jesse Glass, above the mantelpiece in Farah Yeet's bedroom."

"Okay . . . ," said Terrance. "And?"

"And something happened when I did. I don't know how to describe it, but . . . I think I was drawn to it. Like, drawn in the supernatural sense."

Aidan took a deep breath before saying what he said next.

"I think touching that curtain is the reason I'm cursed." He hesitated a moment before adding, "In fact, I'm certain of it."

Aidan let this announcement settle like a cloud of dust. It felt more like radioactive fallout.

"Bruh," said Zephyr. "What are we waiting for? If that's what cursed you, let's set that freaking curtain on fire!"

"Whoa," said Terrance. He raised both palms up in a *hold-your-horses* motion. "Whoa, whoa, whoa. Let's think about this for a second. Supposing that curtain *is* the reason Aidan is cursed: What proof do we have that burning it will break the curse?"

"Proof?" said Zephyr. "How about every movie where the villain's immortal soul is tied to an evil inanimate object? Have you seen *Harry Potter*? Bruh, have you seen *The Lord of the Rings*? We should toss that freaking curtain in a volcano!"

The others couldn't really counter this logic.

In his mind's eye, Aidan stared at the tapestry curtain of Jesse Glass. Something about it seemed familiar . . . the way she posed, the dress, the intense redness of her hair. It wasn't Jesse's yearbook photo that was giving Aidan déjà vu.

The imagery of red hair—juxtaposed against a white dress—ate away at him in some forgotten compartment of his mind.

The dress she wore was *almost* identical to the dress Aidan woke up in, after puking in his clothes—and *he* had red hair. But that wasn't it. Where else had he seen that image?

And then it clicked. Aidan knew exactly where he had seen it before. The realization caused him to shudder.

"I have to go home," said Aidan.

"You have to *what*?" said Zephyr incredulously.

"This is an emergency."

"Not to be dismissive," said Terrance, "but *keeping you alive* is an emergency."

"I know. I don't expect you to understand, but this is more important."

All three boys looked enormously skeptical.

"I need you guys to trust me on this," said Aidan. "I'll explain later. I promise."

Kai was the first to relent. "I trust you."

Zephyr, not to be beat by Kai, caved immediately after. "Me too."

Terrance rolled his eyes with visible aggravation. He clearly wasn't happy about it, but he sighed, and said, "Titto."

Aidan had seen it on Myspace.

At the time, he'd thought nothing of it. He'd been so totally distracted by "Gabby Patty" having a social media presence—being an alive human person and all—that there had been little room for him to process anything else. But this thing he'd seen had wormed its way into his subconscious.

Aidan hadn't even made it home when he removed his phone from his pocket and logged into Myspace. He signed into Bikini Killani's account and immediately clicked on the number one friend of her "Top 8": Gabby Patty.

But it wasn't Gabby herself who Aidan was interested in. It was *Gabby's* number one: a girl with red hair, wearing a long white dress.

Aidan hadn't paid attention to her before. Perhaps it hadn't quite sunk in yet that the top-left account was the coveted number one spot. Or that being Gabby's number one might have held an extra special meaning. But the longer he stared at her thumbnail, the more he realized she was *definitely* wearing the same dress *he* had worn—a lookalike of the dress that Jesse Glass was wearing in the tapestry—with the mock neck, gathered sleeves, and layered ruffles, all the way down to her shoes.

Her handle was an entire sentence: "your smile is like sunlight"—quotation marks and all. Why did that sound . . . familiar?

"I think my type has your eyes? Your nose? My type definitely *has your smile."*

"My smile?"

"Yeah! You don't do it often, but when you do, it's like . . . sunlight."

"No," said Aidan. There was *no way* the secret person Gabby liked was her number one on Myspace. No way it could be so simple.

He clicked on the profile.

There was something familiar about her surroundings too. She posed in front of the gnarled, shadowy husk of a dark, ancient tree—the black locust tree in front of the Witch House. The picture mimicked the tapestry curtain in Farah Yeet's bedroom.

The most hauntingly familiar thing, however, was the girl's face. It was alien, but also as familiar as the back of his hand. Perhaps because she was twenty years younger than the person Aidan knew today.

It was his mom.

Aidan could have slipped into his house undetected if he wanted to. But he didn't want to. Or rather, he couldn't.

Mrs. Cross was on the phone, pacing circles in the kitchen. With whom, Aidan did not know. It wasn't important. Nothing was as important as this.

Aidan was about to have the most important, grown-up conversation of his life. "I know Gabby Caldwell liked you," said Aidan.

Mrs. Cross stopped talking.

She stopped breathing.

She stopped everything.

"I was on Gabby's Myspace page," said Aidan. "You were her number one friend. And in your profile pic, you're wearing the exact same white dress I was wearing when you walked in on me the other day. But you weren't upset because I was wearing a dress. You were upset because it was the same dress you wore when you visited the Yeet house with Gabby Caldwell. I'm assuming Gabby was the one who took the picture? Tell me I'm wrong."

Mrs. Cross did not tell Aidan he was wrong. Instead, her phone fell out of her limp grasp and hit the kitchen tile, screen first, with a soul-shattering *thwack*. If she didn't have a giant crack across her screen, it would be a miracle.

"That's why you've been so distant lately," said Aidan. "Not because I came out. It's because you . . ."

Aidan hadn't quite figured out how to finish that sentence because he *didn't* know the nature of the relationship between Gabby and his mom. Not completely, anyway.

Fortunately, he didn't have to.

Mrs. Cross's bottom lip trembled. Her eyes welled up with tears that spilled freely down her cheeks. She rushed forwards, wrapping her arms fiercely around Aidan.

And she completely fell apart.

"Oh, Aidan," she sobbed. "Oh my God, Aidan, I'm so sorry. I

don't know what's wrong with me. Please forgive me, Aidan. I'm so sorry."

The conversation that followed was perhaps the most unusual one Aidan had ever had. Even more unusual than his conversations with a ghost. He told Mrs. Cross the facts as he knew them:

1. He was friends with the ghost of Gabby Caldwell.
2. He had been cursed by the same thing that had cursed Gabby Caldwell—the Backwards Lady.
3. Tonight, he was going to d—

"The Broken Bones Woman?" Mrs. Cross interrupted.

"I'm sorry, what?" said Aidan.

"The Broken Bones Woman," Mrs. Cross repeated. "The woman that walked around with all her bones broken. That's who you're talking about, right?"

Aidan had never heard of a "Broken Bones Woman" before, but technically, she fit the description of the Backwards Lady, and so he nodded slowly. "Is that what you and Gabby called her?"

"That's what *Gabby* called her. Honestly, Gabby told me a lot of things that were just . . . a *little bit crazy*. She was like that ever since she touched that curtain in Farah Yeet's bedroom."

Aidan's entire body went rigid with excitement and fear.

"She touched that curtain?" Aidan repeated.

"She said it shocked her—like, a literal electric shock—but honestly, it was more like it *possessed* her. Suddenly, her entire life revolved around Farah Yeet. Her grades plummeted because, suddenly, the only thing she would study was Sweden. Can you believe that?"

The way Mrs. Cross said all this—with such dismissal—it sounded like she *truly believed* Gabby was crazy.

"Okay, well . . . ," said Aidan. "She *wasn't* crazy."

"Oh, Aidan," said Mrs. Cross, frowning. "It doesn't matter if she was or wasn't. She's not with us anymore."

Aidan's entire body tensed. "No. She's dead, sure, but her *ghost* is still with us."

The corners of Mrs. Cross's mouth sank farther, and Aidan's heart sank with them.

"Do you not believe I'm friends with Gabby?" he asked, dumbfounded.

"Oh, baby," said Mrs. Cross sadly. "I believe *you believe* you're friends with Gabby.

"You've gone through something very traumatic recently. Believe me, I know. Trauma makes us see, and hear, and *think* things that aren't necessarily real. There was a while—after Gabby died—when she really had me convinced the Broken Bones Woman is what killed her. I had to talk to a lot of therapists to get that delusion out of my head—"

"Mom," said Aidan, deadly serious. "The Backwards Lady is going to kill me tonight."

Mrs. Cross's mouth became small, and her eyes turned angry.

"But . . . ," said Aidan, unable to pull away from her glare, "we have a plan. I'm *convinced* that that curtain hanging in Farah Yeet's bedroom is what cursed me. What cursed *both of us*—me *and* Gabby. If we burn it, my friends and I think it might break the—"

"No," said Mrs. Cross.

"No?" said Aidan, confused.

"You are not to go anywhere near that house. Not now, not ever. But *especially* not tonight."

"But I'm going to *die*, just like Gab—"

"Enough!" snapped Mrs. Cross. "That house is what killed Gabby. She wasn't in her right mind, and she tripped over the balcony, and she broke her neck—"

"She didn't break her neck," said Aidan.

"—and you are *grounded* until I say otherwise," said Mrs. Cross, talking over him. "And I am setting up an appointment with Doctor Jozwiak, and she's going to talk to you, and she's going to clear your head, and everything is going to be—"

"I can't believe Gabby liked you," said Aidan.

Even as Aidan said it, he knew it was too much. He knew it was unfair. But one thing was for sure: it slapped the words right out of Mrs. Cross's mouth, which was exactly what he'd *wanted* to do. Her eyes quivered, and her mouth opened and closed like a goldfish, but nothing came out.

Aidan stormed up to his bedroom, before she could realize he regretted what he said.

Already, Aidan was cooling down. So much so that he managed to shut his bedroom door softly rather than slam it, which he *surely* would have done if it had been fifteen seconds earlier. He needed to be calm and collected if he was going to survive this. His actual life was at stake.

Aidan belly flopped onto his bed. He was already group texting his friends before he landed.

Aidan: **Meet me at the Witch House tonight.**

Aidan: **Don't tell anyone.**

Aidan: **We're setting that curtain on fire.**

CHAPTER 24

Tapestry of a Woman on Fire

Kai was on pyrotechnics duty. He had access to the most lighters and lighter fluid, thanks to Kalani.

Terrance was on extinguishing duty—fire extinguisher, blankets, wet towels, et cetera. The boys were covering their bases.

Zephyr was on transportation duty with his brother's bike cargo wagon. He'd swing by Terrance's house first, then Kai's, helping to load up their respective gear.

Aidan's job was simple: get Gabby on board with the plan. Remove the curtain from the mantelpiece.

Prepare it for burning.

After dinner—and before going upstairs to his bedroom—he made the briefest detour into the garage. There, he grabbed one of his dad's road flares—Mr. Cross had a whole case of them; the box advertised thirty-six total—and shoved it down the leg of his pants. Sure, Kai was on pyrotechnic duty, but it seemed foolish not to have a backup plan.

In his bedroom, Aidan waited for a very specific window of time—when *he* was usually in bed, asleep, but Mr. Cross was still awake, keeping Mrs. Cross preoccupied. To kill time, he stuffed an assortment of pillows and clothes beneath his bedding, molding it into the vague shape of his body.

When the allotted time arrived, Aidan slid open his bedroom window, dangled his legs out the windowsill, and dropped.

He landed in a roll, easing the impact on his shins. He wasn't sure how he'd learned to do that.

It just seemed like something Nadia would do.

The Witch House looked hungry.

The eye of its attic window gleamed waywardly in the twilight. Its cracked, ashen paint looked positively famished. The front door hung open, maw-like. The door—creaking in the prevailing westerly winds—reminded Aidan of a lolling tongue, hanging off to one side.

His friends would be here soon. When they had made their plan, Aidan had felt braver. But now, standing before the Witch House, he felt like a small field mouse standing before a great, leering cat.

Aidan swapped out his Rollerblades for the checkered Vans he'd stowed in his backpack. He stepped up the patio stairs, stopping just in front of the open doorway. A sudden gust of fear swelled in his chest.

"Gabby?" Aidan called out. All he needed was to hear her voice. *Then* he would have the courage to do what must be done.

"Aidan!" Gabby's voice exclaimed. "You came!"

Aidan's heart lifted. He almost rushed inside.

And then he hesitated.

"Where are you?" he asked.

"I'm right here, silly. Are you even looking?"

Aidan leaned closer to the doorway. He removed the pen flashlight from his pocket. From left to right, he searched the shadows of the foyer, the darkness thick as soup. There was not much to see but detritus on the floor and cobwebs in the corners.

And then there was Gabby, standing dead center, at the back end of the foyer, in front of the double doors. A fluted column flanked her on either side. She was smiling.

"Why are you all the way back there?" Aidan asked.

"I could ask you the same thing," said Gabby.

The longer he stared at her smile, the more it unnerved him. Nothing existed behind it.

Nothing but hunger.

"Tell me something only Gabby would know," said Aidan.

Her smile grew wider.

"When I died," said Gabby, "I learned something about the Backwards Lady. I learned that she couldn't *actually* leave the Witch House. She was a prisoner here, just like I am now."

Aidan's skin crawled. Something wasn't right.

"Which means," said Gabby, "that all those times I *thought* I saw the Backwards Lady outside the Witch House—they were, in fact, hallucinations she'd planted in my head."

This was a trap. Aidan knew it in every prickling hair of his skin. And yet, he couldn't bring himself to move.

"Which begs the question," said Gabby. "If *I'm* a hallucination— where do you think the Backwards Lady is right now?"

Aidan heard a crackle to his right—somewhere deep in the vacuum of darkness. Somewhere he had yet to shine his flashlight.

He heard it a mere breath away.

He *felt* it a mere breath away.

Breath like rot.

For the briefest moment, the Backwards Lady was illuminated in the high-powered beam of his penlight—contorted, broken, backwards—laced in spidery black veins and a muck of greasy black hair. She stood just inside the doorway, off to the right, flattened against the wall like a very disgusting pancake.

With powerful, arachnid-like hands, she grabbed him by his shirt collar and whisked him effortlessly—violently—into the mouth of the Witch House.

The door slammed shut behind him.

Mr. Cross was a snorer.

Mrs. Cross was normally not so thrilled about this. Today was an exception. Because as Mr. Cross slipped into dreamland, and a sound came from the back of his throat like a crack of thunder, it was Mrs. Cross's alarm, telling her it was time to check on Aidan.

She nearly leapt out of bed to do so.

He's fine, thought Mrs. Cross. *He's just upset. What's the worst that could happen?*

She pried Aidan's door slowly open, peeking inside. The light was out, but the window was open, allowing starlight to spill across the shape of Aidan's body beneath the blanket.

Mrs. Cross was almost content.

She *almost* shut the door.

Then she did a double take. That's when Mrs. Cross noticed that Aidan looked unusually bloated—like a small Michelin Man. Not to mention, he always slept on his side and the thing in his bed laid flat on its back, arms and legs sprawled awkwardly, like a chalk line at a crime scene.

Mrs. Cross shoved the door wide open, marched right into Aidan's bedroom, and flung the blanket off his body.

Except it *wasn't* his body. It was a carefully shaped pile of pillows and clothes.

Mrs. Cross glanced up at the open window. She felt the breeze and the carefully calculated deception.

She said a swear word.

In a moment of stunned silence, Mrs. Cross leaned over Aidan's bed and peered out the window, observing the distance he would have had to fall to jump out.

Something crackled beneath her bare right foot.

She took a step back and removed a slightly crumpled sheet of paper from the floor—a ripped-out leaf from a notebook. She might have tossed it aside, had she not noticed what was smeared across its surface.

As a criminal defense attorney, Mrs. Cross had seen *more* than her fair share of blood—usually as photographic evidence. The words finger-written on this page were *unmistakably* blood.

I only appear at night.

I'm trapped here.

Help me.

The pupils of Mrs. Cross's eyes constricted, becoming the tiniest black specks in the entire known universe.

The Backwards Lady's strength was superhuman. She held Aidan by his shirt collar with one hand, and by the very ginger hair of his head with the other. Even though the face that stared back at Aidan was his own—peering between curtains of black hair—not a muscle in her pale, broken body appeared strained.

"Any . . . last . . . words?" the Backwards Lady croaked through her second mouth—Aidan's mouth—on the back of her head.

In that moment, a strange calmness washed over Aidan. A moment of clarity trickled over him like water. He *knew* what he had to do.

And he had the confidence to do it.

Aidan leaned forwards.

"Yeah," said Aidan. "Eat a Yankee Stadium wiener, you backwards buttsnack."

The Backwards Lady seemed momentarily stunned by this response, which was to Aidan's advantage. He was able to reach into the leg of his pants, remove the road flare, and break the cap atop the stick. There was a violent hiss, a flood of red light beneath their faces, and a sudden gust of warmth.

He shoved the fiery end into the Backwards Lady's mouth. He forced it all the way into the back of her throat.

She attempted to scream, but it came out as a violent gurgle.

She dropped Aidan.

Aidan landed on his feet, *nearly* fell from lack of balance, but gyrated his arms and found his equilibrium lithely, like a cat. He scanned his surroundings.

The Witch House was whole again—every window unbroken. Aidan didn't have time to waste on a front door he knew was a dead end.

Then he felt a hand intertwine in his own. It thrummed with gentle energy.

It was the *real* Gabby. Aidan just knew. Had she been invisible this entire time?

She appeared beside him, her eyes defiant, her mouth a determined line.

"We need to get to Farah Yeet's bedroom," said Aidan.

If Gabby needed further explanation, she didn't let it show. She simply nodded.

"Run," she said.

Hand in hand, Aidan and Gabby broke into a sprint for the western corridor that led to the library, the weaving room, and eventually, Farah Yeet's bedroom.

The Backwards Lady leapt—defying gravity—blocking the path between them and the western corridor. With broken joints, she filled the space like a spider, gripping the edges of each wall.

Her face—Aidan's face—was burnt, blistered, and bubbling from the nose down. Pus oozed like syrup from her scalded mouth. She let out a terrible scream.

Gabby let go of Aidan's hand and pushed him towards the double doors in the back of the foyer.

"Take the long way around!" Gabby shouted. She stepped between the Backwards Lady and Aidan. "I'll hold her back."

What else could Aidan do?

He ran.

Night was painting its first brushstrokes across the sky as Mrs. Cross stomped on the gas. She pushed the CX-5 to its conceivable limit. Real Vin Diesel stuff. Mrs. Cross wasn't quite sure what a "Tokyo drift" was, but she had a feeling she might have done one.

She was halfway to Yeet Street when she passed three boys on bikes. The boy in the lead wore a Yankees cap, with a clip-on bike headlamp illuminating the path forwards. The boy bringing up the rear towed a cargo wagon, filled with—among other things—not one but *two* fire extinguishers.

Mrs. Cross stomped her brakes. Reversed until she was parallel to the bikes and rolled her window down. All three boys stopped beside her. She must have looked slightly upset because Zephyr, Terrance, and Kai looked *mortified*.

"Where is Aidan?" said Mrs. Cross.

Zephyr opened his mouth.

"Don't lie to me," said Mrs. Cross.

Zephyr closed his mouth.

"He's at the Witch House," said Kai quietly.

Mrs. Cross's nostrils flared. She refastened her grip on the steering wheel. "Get in the car."

All three boys hesitated.

"Do you want to save Aidan?" she asked impatiently. "This is faster."

Not one of the boys had an argument for that, so they dismounted their bikes, dropped them to the side of the road, and climbed in with all their equipment.

Mrs. Cross floored it.

Aidan bolted north out of the foyer, straight back through the elegant double doors, into the dining room. Past a rustic kitchen with twin cast iron stoves at its ancient heart.

He burst out the doors of the pantry leading to the back of the house where several large glass windows were made whole again, overlooking a vast stone patio overtaken by ragged weeds, and probably an acre of tall grass that had been growing and seeding for generations.

Something scurried down the west wing corridor to Aidan's left—the path back to Farah Yeet's bedroom.

The Backwards Lady rounded the corner on all fours—belly up, black hair sweeping the floor.

She was faster than Aidan had ever seen her.

And she was coming in hot.

Mrs. Cross throttled the steering wheel, only barely tapping the brake as she made a tire-screeching turn onto Yeet Street. Gravel and a cloud of dust spewed madly behind them.

As they drove headlong into the open field that surrounded the Witch House, something was visibly wrong. The entire aura of the place felt different—alive in a way that writhed under the skin, a feeling of death and decay.

"Oh no," said Terrance.

Every single window of the Witch House was whole and intact.

"No," said Kai, breathless, shaking his head. "No no no no NO NO NO."

"What's going on?" said Mrs. Cross. She pressed her eyes shut and then opened them again—a soft reset—hoping that the horrific sight before her would somehow make sense. It did not. "Why are the windows not broken? What is happening?"

"It's the Backwards Lady," said Terrance, bleak and full of dread.

"Who?" said Mrs. Cross.

"Farah Yeet," said Zephyr. He sniffled loudly. "She has Aidan."

Mrs. Cross lost herself behind the wheel. The sound of the boys' voices faded, replaced by a high-pitched frequency, a flatline inside her head. Her foot slowly let off the gas, and the distance between herself and the steering wheel seemed to stretch into infinity. She had lost Gabby, and now she was going to lose Aidan. The feeling of helplessness was too great. She felt the strength drain from every muscle in her body.

Go around back, Joss, said a voice inside Mrs. Cross's head. Although it felt like it had been whispered into her ear.

Mrs. Cross turned around in the driver's seat. There was no one there.

It sounded like . . .

No. That was impossible.

Go!

Mrs. Cross reapplied her foot to the gas. The black CX-5 revved high, a banshee's scream, and momentum flattened everyone against their seats. She veered right, narrowly missing the front corner of the house. They skewed so close to the right wall, Mrs. Cross could see inside the windows as they sped past. No sign of Aidan.

Sheer velocity flattened the boys to their seats. If they were concerned, they sure didn't voice those concerns to the woman behind the wheel. She seemed to know what she was doing.

The grass grew thicker in the back, a jungle of weeds that had been seeding for decades, brushing against the windows of the SUV. They rounded the corner into the courtyard, wide stairs leading up to a flat plane of stone bricks, great stone pots filled with scraggly bouquets of weeds taller than Mr. Cross. A panorama of tall, wide windows lined the back of the house, exposing the north hall liberally.

Two figures were standing inside that hall, visible as day. One of them was Aidan.

The other was a woman in a tattered white dress with slimy black hair who appeared to be spider-crawling across the floor. Her body was twisted like some sort of nightmare.

Mrs. Cross stopped the car. Her fingers refastened themselves on the steering wheel, gripping it deathly tight.

"Boys," said Mrs. Cross. "I'm going to need you to get out of the car right now."

"What?" said Kai.

"But, Mrs. Cross—!" Zephyr protested.

"NOW!" Mrs. Cross barked.

"Yes, ma'am," said Terrance obediently.

All three boys filed out of the CX-5 and into the tall, weedy grass that tickled their noses.

At the sound of the last door closing, Mrs. Cross stomped the gas so hard, it touched the floor.

Two things happened at once.

1. The Backwards Lady rushed Aidan. She moved in jagged steps, leading with the heels of her hands and feet, like some clay figure brought to life through the power of stop-motion animation. It was unnatural. Just the

sight of it twisted Aidan's insides like spaghetti around a fork.

2. A 2.5-liter, 4-cylinder engine roared like some ancient horror of cosmic origins. A black compact SUV caught some serious airtime—not a single tire touching the ground—then landed with such jarring force, the entire bottom of the car made a sonic boom against the stone bricks of the courtyard, steel scraping against stone, sending a flurry of sparks. But even if the engine was wrecked, sheer momentum carried the SUV forwards like a meteor hell-bent on mass extinction.

The windows of the Witch House may have been supernaturally strong, but even they were no match for the laws of physics: four thousand pounds careening at eighty miles per hour. The entire back entrance of the house exploded as a shadow manufactured by Mazda ripped through like paper, coming in at a sharp, swerving angle. It wiped the Backwards Lady clean out of existence. Figuratively. The SUV smashed her into the wall.

Aidan felt the wind of the car slice past him like a bullet. It missed him by feet that felt like inches.

There was now a hole the size of a CX-5 in the back of the house, and on the other side of it, freedom. But Aidan couldn't bring himself to make the easy escape. For starters, his mom was in that car. But that wasn't the only reason.

Aidan didn't come here to run away. And he didn't come *just* to save himself.

"Aidan!" Kai shouted.

Aidan glanced into the cool, open mouth of night, across the dark courtyard. Rustling through the tall grass, coming in at a full sprint, were all three of his friends.

"We're coming, Aidan!" Zephyr screamed, farthest behind, through no fault of his own. He had the shortest legs and the smallest lungs.

In that very instant, the broken hole of the house began to crystallize and reseal itself.

"You've gotta be kidding me," Terrance huffed, exasperated. He ran faster.

Kai was in the lead—he was the fastest of the three of them—and even *he knew* he wouldn't make it. Instead, he reached into his pocket and pulled out a cherry-red Zippo lighter.

"Aidan, go long!" he yelled.

Kai rechanneled his momentum into a winding pitch—tucking his left knee to his chest, rearing his right arm back, hopping to a halt on his right leg. When he released, his right arm moved like rubber. It was a true Gerrit Cole of a pitch. That Zippo lighter stopped just short of the sound barrier.

The hole in the Witch House had resealed to roughly the size of a softball when Kalani's Zippo lighter passed through. Aidan caught it in his right hand—the most miraculous catch he had ever performed.

"Holy crap, did you see that catch!" Zephyr marveled. "I mean, your throw wasn't terrible either, but *that catch*—!"

It was the last thing Aidan heard before the glassy, north side of the Witch House sealed impenetrably shut.

The air bag had deployed, and Mrs. Cross was conscious, groaning in the driver's seat. Aidan hurried to her side, opening the driver's-side door and unbuckling her seat belt.

"Mom! Are you okay?"

"Never better," Mrs. Cross mumbled, staggering out of the car.

"That was really cool."

"What can I say?" said Mrs. Cross with a disoriented look on her face. "Moms are cool." Aidan had a feeling she was slightly concussed.

Aidan wrapped one of her arms around his shoulders, and together, they hobbled towards the west wing corridor. He dared to cast a glance at the Backwards Lady–shaped hole in the wall, and the CX-5 wedged halfway into it. The creature deep within appeared to be immobilized. At least for now.

Together, they rounded the corner left, then turned right into the very first door—Farah Yeet's bedroom.

Aidan shut the door behind them. He was relieved to see an antique, key-shaped lock above the doorknob. The old, rusted metal resisted, but finally, the lock gave way.

There was a quiet sound, like the ripple of fabric, behind them.

When Aidan and Mrs. Cross turned, there Gabby was, standing directly in front of them. She was looking straight at Mrs. Cross.

Mrs. Cross gave a high, sharp gasp. Her arm was no longer around Aidan's shoulders because she needed it to cover her mouth with both hands.

"It's okay, Mom," said Aidan.

Mrs. Cross nodded, eyes wide, but did not remove her hands from her mouth.

"Do I know you?" said Gabby. She didn't look like she outright *didn't know* Mrs. Cross. More like the knowledge was lost somewhere in her head.

Mrs. Cross nodded, hands still over her mouth.

She shot a pleading glance at Aidan.

"Do you not recognize her?" said Aidan.

Gabby stared at Mrs. Cross like the last autumn leaf on a high-up branch. Like something just out of reach.

At that moment, something came crunching down the west wing corridor. Aidan heard the bare slap of flesh against tile, drawing ever nearer.

Maybe this *wasn't* the best time to take a stroll down memory lane.

"Crap," said Aidan.

"What do we do?" said Gabby.

Aidan removed the Zippo lighter from his pocket and tossed it to his mom; she only barely caught it. He pointed to the fireplace. "You two, get that started."

Bam. The Backwards Lady smashed against the door. She continued, slow and rhythmic but growing in intensity, rattling the door in its frame: *Bam! BAM. BAM!*

Gabby and Mrs. Cross got to work. Meanwhile, Aidan scoured the room for things to step on. He started with a chair. Then a side table. Then a second chair, which he stacked on top of the table.

"What exactly"—*THWACK!*—"are we doing again?" Gabby asked. She was in the process of breaking and tearing apart various wooden and flammable things—baskets, picture frames, a chair that she smashed like a rock star smashing their electric guitar onstage, casting them into the fire.

"You've touched that curtain before," said Aidan. "Haven't you?"

At first, Gabby looked confused. Then her eyes widened, her jaw slackened, and her mouth opened incrementally, like a drawbridge.

"I know *I* have," said Aidan. "And I'm positive that's what cursed me. And I'm pretty sure that's what cursed you too."

"So, what?" Mrs. Cross asked. "We're burning a curtain?"

From the bottom chair to the table to the top chair, Aidan made it onto the mantelpiece in four wibbly-wobbly steps. From there, he stared at the tapestry, nose and belly up against it.

"Yeah," said Aidan. "We're burning a curtain."

He took a deep breath as he gripped the fabric of the curtain firmly, then jumped up and slightly backwards.

Aidan came down, and inertia did the rest.

Farah's curtain was tough. Rather than tear, the wooden curtain rod snapped in half. Aidan landed with a bundle of cloth on top of him.

"Oof," he croaked.

He heard something crackle, followed by a sound like someone blowing out birthday candles, and then a *whoosh*. The crackle increased tenfold as the flames took hold.

The door to Farah Yeet's bedroom exploded open, taking a chunk of the doorframe with it. Splinters and wooden shrapnel rained down like confetti.

Standing upright, the Backwards Lady staggered through the broken doorway in sloppy, unsteady strides. For a ghost, the creature looked exhausted—from the heaviness of its eyelids to the droop of its gaping mouth. The task of killing Aidan had evidently become a bit of a chore.

"Sorry, Farah," said Gabby, folding the curtain into a sloppy bundle, "but this is for your own good."

She tossed the curtain into the fire.

The Backwards Lady continued to approach Aidan.

"Um," said Mrs. Cross, low-key panicking. "Should something be happening now?"

"Crap," said Aidan.

Both Gabby and Mrs. Cross closed ranks in front of him.

In that moment, a noxious-looking black smoke—the color of the deepest, darkest depths of the ocean—gathered tempest-like in the fireplace. Something more than mere cloth was burning in that fire. It seeped and spilled out of the curtain like oil into the ocean. Plumes of smoke reached out, tentacle-like, grasping at nothing.

And then the smoke faded.

A single white light emerged from the smoke. It floated like an ember but shone like starlight.

The light moved with elegant, *deliberate* grace until it filled the space between the Backwards Lady and Aidan, Gabby, and Mrs. Cross. As it did, it took shape. Sprouted strong, ropy arms and long legs. A slender, sturdy torso.

And the most beautiful face the Backwards Lady had ever seen. It halted her in her backwards tracks.

The light faded. In its place was a person with clean-cut red hair and a jawline that could've sliced your finger. She wore a button-down shirt, tweed slacks, and a pair of white suede oxford shoes.

"Farah," said Jesse. There were tears in her eyes. "Please, stop this."

She then did the unthinkable: she grabbed the Backwards Lady by her shoulders.

Something about this physical contact caused the creature to shudder. The Backwards Lady *tried* to recoil, but Jesse did not—would not—let go.

"Where are you?" Jesse demanded angrily. She shook the Backwards Lady. "Where is Farah Yeet? Where is *my wife*? Give her back to me!"

Once the shaking had ceased, a single tear streamed down the Backwards Lady's second face. She managed to croak out a single word. "*Jehhh-sseee?*"

"Yes!" Jesse exclaimed. She sniffed and wiped her eyes fiercely. "It's me! Where are you?"

"Where . . . are . . . ?" said the Backwards Lady, confused.

"Where . . . *am* . . . ?" she tried again.

Her eyes grew wide—in the slowest of increments—until they were filled with both horror and perfect clarity.

The Backwards Lady shrieked and then crumpled to the floor. The surface of her skin rippled, softly at first. Then it began to bubble like boiling water. Aidan's likeness melted away from the back of her head. Her bones cracked beneath her flesh.

And then, her form became still.

When the Backwards Lady stood, she was no longer backwards. Her spine was straight, and she filled her tattered dress with an awkward elegance that had been preserved over the course of a hundred years. She had eyes like almonds and a thin mouth pressed into a quivering line.

"Farah?" said Jesse.

Farah gave a feeble nod. She couldn't speak. She was overwhelmed.

"Say something for me," said Jesse. "Please. Just so I know you're you."

"You're alive," said Farah in the smallest voice.

Jesse gave an emotional chuckle at this. Sniffed and wiped her eyes again. "Not quite."

"I m-m-mean . . . ," Farah stammered. "You know what I mean. You're *here*. With *me*!"

"I've always been here," said Jesse.

Farah did not seem so happy to hear this. She shook her head, distraught. Her lost gaze wandered from Gabby—whom she *had killed*—to Aidan—whom she had been *about to kill*.

Farah looked physically ill. "What have I done?"

Jesse responded with a frown. *Terrible things*, her frown seemed to say. *Terrible things*.

"What can I do?" said Farah. She turned in a vague circle, looking at everyone and no one at once. "How do I make this right?"

"Blåkulla is the House," said Aidan. "Isn't he?"

This response garnered *everyone's* attention—Farah's most of all.

"How do *you* know about . . . ?" Farah started to say. She realized it didn't matter, then nodded. "Yes."

She noticed Aidan glancing at the fire. Fire that had successfully burned a *part* of Blåkulla.

In that moment, they both knew what needed to be done.

Jesse turned her attention to Aidan, Gabby, and Mrs. Cross. "You three need to get out of here. The sealing spell on the house is gone now. You're free to leave."

She looked specifically at Gabby.

"All of you."

Gabby nodded blankly.

Slowly, Aidan grabbed Gabby's hand—a gentle thrum of cosmic energy. He squeezed it.

Gabby looked at him. A single tear streamed down her cheek. A *real* tear.

No blood.

With that, Farah reached her right hand into the fire. Whatever ghosts were made of—ectoplasm?—was apparently flammable. The fire took to her hand, and it spread up her arm.

"What do you say, my love?" Farah asked Jesse, extending her fiery right arm, palm open. "Shall we burn this wretched house to the ground?"

"Yes," said Jesse. "Let's."

Together, the couple went up in flames.

And so, as Aidan and Gabby assisted Mrs. Cross—who was still a little wobbly from the car wreck—out of Farah Yeet's bedroom, Farah Yeet and Jesse Glass, burning brighter than the noonday sun, strolled leisurely through the House on Yeet Street, weaving their fingers across walls, picture frames, and furniture, sending it all up in serpentine tongues of flame. The image they wove across the corridors of the Witch House was maybe the greatest Farah Yeet tapestry of all.

And she couldn't have woven it without Jesse.

Aidan, Gabby, and Mrs. Cross exited the front door, coughing, as smoke swelled out behind them. They were greeted hysterically by Zephyr, Terrance, and Kai, who lifted Aidan off the ground and swung him around in circles, whooping and screaming.

"That catch, man!" Kai exclaimed. "Where'd you learn to catch like that?"

Gabby hadn't said anything until now, but as they'd staggered through the smoke-filled house, she couldn't help stealing glances Mrs. Cross's way.

Only now did she give herself permission to look at Mrs. Cross freely.

"Hey, Joss."

Mrs. Cross's eyes grew wide and her mouth grew small. Her voice was a whisper. "You remember me?"

"I remember," said Gabby. The dam of her feelings broke, and they flooded freely down her face. "I remember everything."

"I'm sorry," said Mrs. Cross.

"Don't be sorry," said Gabby, smiling despite her tears. "All my favorite memories are you."

Aidan watched his mom's lower lip tremble. She was on the precipice of disaster. "I never forgot about you. I never—"

"I know," said Gabby, placing a hand on Mrs. Cross's chest. "But it's okay. You can let go now."

Mrs. Cross shook her head fiercely. "I can't do that."

"I'm free," said Gabby softly.

Aidan felt her grab his hand.

She seemed . . . lighter. No. Fainter. Like her presence was slowly fading. Aidan could see Zephyr, a few steps away, right through her.

"Will I ever see you again?" said Aidan, tears streaming down his face.

"Tell you what: Whatever comes after this, when your time comes? I'll find you. I promise."

"I'm going to miss you."

"I'm going to miss you too." Gabby leaned forwards, and softly, delicately—so as not to go through him—wrapped her arms around Aidan. He felt the gentle thrum of her energy.

Then Gabby faded like the New Moon into the purple fabric of dawn. The orange of morning spilled over the Berkshires, brisk and bright. The disk of the sun peeked out over the mountaintops.

Gabby was gone. Aidan was still holding his hand out, but there was no one there to hold it.

But only for a moment.

The very next instant, Zephyr took his hand. Interlocked his fingers with Aidan's.

"It's okay," said Zephyr. "We're still here for you."

"Ditto," said Kai, wrapping an arm around each of their shoulders.

"Titto!" Terrance exclaimed, wrapping his arms around their shoulders from the other side.

Mrs. Cross smiled warmly at the four friends. She had no idea what a "titto" was, but she refrained from commenting.

There was a soft thud as something landed on the grass between them all—a small, ancient-looking, leather-bound book.

"Someone tell me I'm hallucinating," said Zephyr, "and that book didn't just fall out of nowhere."

Terrance broke their circle to stoop down and pick it up. He casually flipped through aged, yellow pages.

"Dudes," he said, "I think this is a . . . diary?"

"It didn't come out of *nowhere*," said Aidan.

Outside the circle of Aidan's friends stood Farah Yeet and Jesse Glass. They were no longer on fire. They still held hands.

Aidan and Farah exchanged a look. *Write our story* is what the look in her eyes seemed to say. *The true story of Farah Yeet and Jesse Glass.*

Aidan nodded.

Farah smiled.

And then Farah and Jesse faded into the fabric of dawn.

Holy Fork

Life was strange that summer after the Witch House burned down.

The four friends still spent every waking moment in each other's company. But when they *finished* hanging out, Aidan and Zephyr always lingered longer. Whenever this happened, Zephyr somehow inexplicably lost his ability to talk. Aidan was forced to lead conversations, and they ended up making dumb small talk, like about the weather. But it was very difficult for either of them to end the conversation and go home.

Then, one day, Zephyr blurted out: "How old do *you* have to be to be able to date?"

Aidan might as well have gazed upon Medusa's slithering hairdo. He fossilized.

"Because *I* have to be sixteen," said Zephyr glumly.

Aidan hadn't answered Zephyr's question, and yet, Zephyr seemed quite eager to move on. It was possible he felt embarrassed for asking—and Aidan didn't *want* him to feel embarrassed—so he blurted out: "I'm not exactly sure when I'm allowed to date. I've never asked."

"Oh," said Zephyr. For an ambiguous nonanswer, he seemed awfully riveted by it.

"I could always ask," said Aidan, "if you *wanted* me to ask."

"I mean, I wouldn't be terribly offended if you asked," said Zephyr, shrugging nonchalantly. "Not that there's a hurry. But asking sometime in the next three years would be nice."

"Okay," said Aidan.

"Cool," said Zephyr.

The conversation almost ended with that. But Aidan didn't *want* it to end with that. He was a much braver person than he'd been in June, and so he said, "Do you know what I think about a lot?"

Zephyr looked at him.

"I think about how girls get to hold hands with each other all the time," Aidan continued, "and no one bats an eye. It's cute. Girls are cute, and holding hands is cute, and so girls get to show all this platonic affection towards their friends, and it's the most normal thing in the world. But if two boys do the exact same thing, it's weird. And I think that is stupid."

Zephyr stared at Aidan.

"What I'm trying to say is," said Aidan, "if you wanted to hold hands, as friends, until you're old enough to date, I would be okay with that. Actually, I would like it a lot—"

Zephyr grabbed Aidan's hand before he could finish that sentence. He squeezed it tightly.

They remained that way—holding hands—until the sun began to set, and curfew threatened to get them both in trouble.

They held hands often after that.

This development with Zephyr was surprising, sure, but not as much as the new friend Aidan had obtained. It was maybe the strangest friendship he'd ever had, and that was saying something. Up until a few weeks ago, he had been friends with a ghost.

It all started with a simple text from Aidan: I'm sorry about what happened at your birthday party.

Bea McCarthy texted back: Not one of my friends has apologized to me about what happened. Some of them even said I deserved it. Why would YOU, of all people, say sorry?

Aidan replied: Because I don't believe anyone deserves to be humiliated like that.

He added: I especially don't want to be the one doing the humiliating. That's not me.

Bea: I'm sorry too.

Bea: Not just because of all the internet backlash I've gotten . . . which has been AWFUL by the way.

Bea: Let me start over. I can already tell this isn't a very good apology.

Bea: You are a very good person, Aidan. EVERYONE can see that. Even me. And what I did to you was truly awful, and I wish I could take it back, but I can't. All I can do is say I'm sorry and hope that you can eventually find it in yourself to forgive me.

Bea: In the meantime, if there's anything I can ever do for you to make it up to you, consider this your free, limitless IOU coupon. Whatever you need, I've got it. Or . . . I will get it. Whatever. It doesn't expire until you forgive me.

Aidan: I forgive you.

Bea: Damn you, Aidan!

Bea: You can't see it, but I'm crying. I'm not lying.

Aidan: I believe you.

Bea: I guess I was just jealous because I like Kai.

Aidan: Understandable. He's very likeable.

Bea: Isn't he, though??

Bea: I THOUGHT you liked Kai too. But I just saw you holding hands with ZEPHYR WINDON AT THE LIBRARY THE OTHER DAY WHATTTTTTT

Bea: ???

Aidan: I did like Kai. I still do. But Kai loves me as a friend, and I would never change the way he feels about me.

Aidan: Zephyr is great, though.

Aidan: I like holding hands with him.

Bea: It sure LOOKS LIKE YOU DO.

Bea: It looks like he likes holding hands with you too ♥

Aidan: Can I ask you a favor?

Aidan: It's okay if you say no.

Bea: Yes.

Bea: I'm saying yes to the favor, not yes to you asking if you can ask me a favor.

Bea: So this favor better be doable, or I'm going to look like a damn fool.

Aidan: You're editor of the school newspaper, right? The Berkshires Bulletin?

Bea: Yeeeeessss?

Aidan: I was hoping to write something for it.

Aidan: It's about the true story of Farah Yeet.

Bea: What is it, like a ghost story?

Aidan: **It's actually more of a love story.**
Bea: **I love it already. Tell me more.**

In the first week of September—the first week of school—Aidan became the newest member of the school newspaper. He also wrote the headline story of their first issue of the school year: THE ABSOLUTELY TRUE STORY OF FARAH YEET. To be fair, he'd spent all summer writing it.

Was it a feel-good article? Well, no. Then again, Aidan didn't think history was *meant* to make you feel good. It was meant to make you wiser. More tolerant. History was only doomed to repeat itself if you didn't understand it in the first place. That was Aidan's one and only goal when writing this piece: to make people *understand* Farah Yeet and what happened to her and Jesse Glass.

The article released to such universal praise around school— among the student body and faculty alike—Bea was beside herself. She was actually physically incapable of leaving Aidan alone. Which, Bea was great and all, but Aidan ate lunch with *his friends*, and she ate lunch with *her friends*, and after making it through the lunch line, Bea had somehow accidentally followed Aidan all the way to his table with Zephyr, Terrance, and Kai.

"Oh," said Bea, mostly when she realized she was standing five feet from Kai.

Kai opened his mouth to say something. But then he looked at Aidan, and he closed it immediately. Bea and Kai both seemed to be making a strenuous effort not to acknowledge each other's existence. And though it certainly wasn't Aidan's fault, he felt like *maybe* he was slightly responsible for the tension.

"Right," said Bea. "Well, sorry for talking your ear off, Aidan. The article was amazing, in case I haven't made that explicitly clear already. Um. Okay, bye."

"Would you like to eat with us?" Aidan asked.

He said this to Bea, but he also glanced at Kai, just to make sure he wasn't giving out unwanted invitations.

"Oh," said Bea. "Um."

"I mean," said Kai, "if you *want* to."

"Sure, like, if you're all cool with it."

"I'm cool," said Kai, then added, haphazardly, "*with it.*"

Terrance rolled his eyes fiercely, like a pair of trick yo-yos. Zephyr, on the other hand, was uncharacteristically quiet. But not for lack of something to say. He seemed to want to say something so badly, he looked like a balloon resting on a bed of needles.

Bea sat down with her lunch tray, next to Aidan, across from Kai. She accidentally made eye contact with Zephyr, looked away, then looked at him again. "Are you okay, Zephyr? You look . . . ?"

He *looked* like someone holding in the world's most ancient fart. And Aidan thought this as someone who slightly adored him.

"I can go on dates now," Zephyr blurted out.

Aidan, himself, nearly farted from the shock.

"I can't date anyone," Zephyr continued to explain. "Like, I can't have a boyfriend"—He glanced nervously at Aidan—"or a girlfriend, or whatever! But I can go on dates, under two conditions. One: it has to be a double date. Two: we have to have a chaperone. Fortunately, Yvonne has agreed to be my permanent double-date chaperone, so long as I'm going out with Aidan, so . . ."

Aidan nearly choked on his rectangular lunch cafeteria pizza. Bea patted his back but couldn't stop herself from grinning gleefully the entire time. Aidan was *pretty sure* she was grinning about his future double dates, and not about him choking to death on pizza.

Zephyr turned his attention ferociously to Kai and Bea and said, "Will you two *puh-leeeeease* go on a double date with Aidan and me?"

Kai *actually* choked on his rectangle pizza. Bea continued to slap Aidan on the back, even though he had stopped coughing, as she stared off into space in a trance.

"Are you kidding me with this right now?" said Terrance, glancing between the four of them jealously. "What am I, chopped liver? Y'all are *seriously* gonna do a cute little double date without me? Am I being punished?" He stared up at the distant cafeteria ceiling, which had a metal fork sticking out of it. The fork had been there since 2018. Kids had jokingly taken to calling it the Holy Fork. "Holy Fork, are you punishing me for pursuing academics instead of girls? I've even been going to church with my mom! Is this the thanks I get?"

It was at that exact moment that the heavens parted. And by "the heavens," that is to say, the double cafeteria doors opened. One of Berkshires Middle School's newest sixth graders—Adelaide Windon—had finally arrived for lunch. (A.k.a., she'd figured out how to operate the lock on her locker.)

First, Adelaide spotted Zephyr, and her eyes filled with relief.

Then she spotted Terrance, and her eyes filled with all the love and prayers of a pair of blue moons.

Terrance returned his attention to the Holy Fork. "On second thought, Holy Fork, please disregard everything I just said? I am doing just fine. In fact, I think a life of abstinence is right for me. I'll dedicate my life to the priesthood of science."

"What, like a Scientologist?" Zephyr asked curiously.

"Zephyr," said Terrance, with a slightly deranged grin, "what is your ten-year-old sister doing at *our middle school?*"

"Funny you should ask," said Adelaide. She'd suddenly appeared behind Terrance, like a wraith. Terrance stiffened like papier-mâché. "I actually turned eleven years old on September first—the cut-off for sixth grade!" She walked her index and middle finger across Terrance's shoulder like a pair of legs. His entire body went tight like a fist. "One might say I'm a *woman* now."

"Literally no one is saying that," said Zephyr.

"Okay, but . . . !" Adelaide pouted, dropping her fists at her sides. "Can Terrance and I go on the double date with you guys?"

"No, because then it would be a *triple date,*" said Zephyr. "Mom and Dad didn't say *anything* about triple dates." Zephyr winked at Terrance, and Terrance mouthed: *Thank you.*

"Do you think I'm an idiot!" Adelaide exclaimed. "Obviously triple dates are okay! The more people there are, the less likely you are to get frisky with your boy toy!"

The entire table erupted into a fit of gasps, shrieks, and laughter. Aidan specifically reacted by turning the exact same color as the hair on his head.

"I actually just remembered that I have *so much homework,*" said Terrance. "So, unfortunately—"

"Ooh, what kind of homework?" asked Adelaide. "Can I help?"

And so, as Adelaide and Terrance bickered about his homework, and Kai and Bea giggled and exchanged flirtatious glances at the spectacle of it all, a comfortable sense of normalcy fell over Aidan, like a warm blanket.

But that didn't mean there weren't moments of surreal strangeness. Such as when Zephyr, sitting on Aidan's other side, touched the top of Aidan's hand with his index finger and drew the shape of a heart.

Aidan had nearly returned to a normal human flesh color, but that caused him to turn the color of the red planet, Mars, all over again. He drew a quick heart on Zephyr's hand, then gave it a squeeze to let Zephyr know that he meant it.

Seeing the smile on Zephyr's face caused Aidan to smile as well—a smile Aidan felt in every muscle of his body.

Then again, maybe sometimes strange could be good.

Sometimes, it could be great even.

ACKNOWLEDGMENTS

What is a book without an agent and/or editor? Jenny Bent (my agent) and Laura Schreiber (my editor) are the Yin and Yang of keeping my writing career moving forwards. Without them, I imagine I would be nothing more than a mad person in their bathrobe, scribbling unintelligible ciphers on the wall with a big purple crayon.

Alas, as is the way with Laura, she has (once again) left me for a different publisher, HarperCollins, to focus on *adult* books—the audacity of her to try to grow up without me! Historically, I tend to follow her wherever she goes, but also historically, our publishers have had a tragic tendency of collapsing (folding/restructuring) beneath our feet, and as far as I can tell, Union Square Kids seems to be standing on a sturdy pair of legs, so hopefully I get to stay and settle in for once.

In Laura's place, I have been blessed with the lovely Stefanie Chin as my editorial contact, and editorial director Tracey Keevan, who I have fewer interactions with and think of more as the all-seeing Eye of Sauron (but in a benevolent, less ominous and evil way). Stefanie, meanwhile, is endlessly helpful, friendly, and kind, *and* she's a fellow *Kiki's Delivery Service* fan, so you *know* she's a real one.

As with all books, it takes a village, and mine is populated with the best of them: Grace House and Renee Yewdaev (managing editorial), Melissa Farris and Marcie Lawrence (design—Marcie had the delightful honor of giving Kai a mouth at the very last minute), Jenny Lu (publicity), Daniel Denning (marketing), and a very luxurious shout-out to the artist, Jensine Eckwall, for dreaming up such a luscious cover that is equal parts spooky and fun. Eat your heart out, artificial intelligence!

Last but absolutely not least, the most heartfelt of appreciation to my partner, Erin Rene, for loving me, and teaching me daily to love myself. <3

ABOUT THE AUTHOR

Preston Norton teaches environmental science to fifth graders. He is the author of *Neanderthal Opens the Door to the Universe*, *Where I End & You Begin*, and *Hopepunk*. He is married with three cats.